across the HORIZON

Geni,
Take your shirt off!

USA TODAY BESTSELLING AUTHOR

ALY MARTINEZ

Across the Horizon

Cover Designer: Jay Aheer
Photography: Wander Aguiar
Editing: Mickey Reed
Proofreader: Julie Deaton
Formatting: Stacey Blake

Amie Knight, Miranda Arnold, Megan Cooke,
Bianca Smith, and Kelly Markham

I honestly don't know what I'd do without you. Never leave me. It would be really awkward if I stalked you down, stood outside your window, and read my books out loud. Though, it might be easier to pick out typos.

I love you!

across the HORIZON

ONE

Rita

"GET OUT!" I SCREAMED, HURLING MY WINE GLASS across the room. It shattered into a million pieces at his feet.

Just like my heart.

"Rita, baby. You have to let me explain." He took two steps toward me, his long legs devouring the distance between us. If only he had done that sooner. Like maybe if he had closed the distance six months earlier rather than walking into another woman's arms.

I stepped away.

If only I had done *that* sooner.

Like maybe before I'd given up my entire life for him.

Though, for seven years, I'd had no regrets.

I'd thought he was my dream man.

No, we weren't perfect together. Far from it. We fought and bickered. And over the years, there had been plenty of problems and bumps along the way. But didn't every marriage have those? I'd assumed that was how it went when you were with someone for almost a decade.

"Please!" He reached out and the tips of his fingers grazed a burning path across my skin.

"Don't you dare touch me," I seethed, tears trailing black mascara down my cheeks.

"Just listen… I love you." He blew out a ragged breath and raked a hand through his hair.

His words evaporated before they ever breezed past my ears.

He didn't love me.

I couldn't be sure he ever had.

For some strange reason, I focused on his hand. It was the hand he had used to slide my wedding ring on my finger while vowing until death do us part. The hand that had held mine the day my mother was lowered into the ground. The hand that had rested on my stomach as the doctor told us that I'd miscarried. And the same damn hand he'd used to touch her naked body day after day for the last six months.

A sob tore from my throat as I clutched my chest. "I hate you so fucking much."

He shook his head ruefully. "Honey, please."

Narrowing my eyes, I tilted my head and stared at him. He'd aged since we'd first met in college. I had plans to follow him to medical school—medical school I'd never started because he'd asked me to marry him when he'd accepted an out-of-state residency. His brown hair was now thinning, and slight wrinkles lined the corners of his eyes. He was a far cry from that twenty-four-year-old kid who'd smiled at me from across the bar. But, if possible, he'd only gotten better with age. I was well aware that women noticed him. He was a handsome, successful doctor with a wide smile and a gentle demeanor. I'd never concerned myself with jealousy though. I'd naïvely assumed he was mine.

I sure as hell had been his.

Now, she was his too.

The few jagged shards that hung in my chest ached, and my chin quivered as I glanced around the room. We'd bought that house two years earlier, days after we'd decided to start a family. I'd spent countless hours decorating that three-thousand-square-foot shell. Love hung in photographs on the walls, and the furniture had been chosen specifically to fill the space with warmth. As far as I had been concerned, those walls and windows represented forever. We were going to raise our children in that house. Two rough and tumble boys with his dark hair and a blond princess who loved manicures and heels as much as I did. It was where we were going to celebrate anniversaries and holidays, host birthday parties and barbeques, and spend quiet nights curled up on the couch, basking in the life we had made for ourselves.

But right then, as I stared into his brown eyes, his lies and deceit tainted the beauty of that room.

My whole life was imploding inside that brick two-story.

And I had no way to escape.

Stupidly, so much of my identity was wrapped up in Greg Laughlin. Everything I had was tied to him in one way or another. The bank accounts, credit cards, the house—hell, even my car was in his name.

And with one choice, and countless lies, I was losing it all.

He shuffled forward. "Baby, it didn't mean anything. I swear."

He was so cliché. We'd been together for nine years, married for seven, and the fact that he wasn't in love with her was supposed to somehow make an affair acceptable? Forget that I was dying inside. Forget that, since I'd first laid eyes on him, I had never considered being with another man. Forget that I'd given him my entire life. Every hope. Every dream. Every want. Every desire. And he'd thrown them all away for a piece of ass.

But I shouldn't have worried. Because it meant *nothing* to him.

Squaring my shoulders, I willed my tears to stop. "I'm sorry to hear that. Because it meant *everything* to me." I aimed a pointed finger over his shoulder at the door and allowed my anger to override my devastation. "Get. Out."

His tall body swayed, looming over me as his hand cupped the back of my neck and pulled me close.

I knew what would follow next:

He'd dip low until our mouths were almost touching. His breath would mingle with mine and he'd breathe in as though he could inhale me. His other hand would go to my hip before sliding around to splay across my lower back, forcing me against his front. And then he'd sigh, long and content, as if holding me were the cure for his every ailment.

Before that moment, I'd always loved when he held me like that. It had made me feel cherished.

Now, it felt like a fraud—just like him.

And, as I'd found out only minutes earlier, just like our marriage.

I shoved his chest hard. "You're not allowed to touch me anymore."

"Rita, stop," he pleaded.

"Stop?" I yelled, throwing my hands up and then slapping them against my thighs. "Yes. Please. Fucking *stop*, Greg!" I closed my eyes and pinched the bridge of my nose, my stomach churning. "How many times did you come home to *me*, sleep in *our* bed, after you left *her*?"

"Rita," he whispered, and then I heard his knees hit the wood floor.

I kept my eyes closed, unable to bear the sight of him anymore. "How many times did you bring her into that bed with us, Greg?"

"Never. I swear."

More lies. Lies that, only hours ago, I didn't know he was capable of.

And then I said the words I never thought *I'd* be capable of. "I want a divorce."

He sucked in sharply. "Don't say that. We just need to talk."

"Is that what you did before you ruined us? Did *you* talk to *me*? Or what about *after* you slept with her the first time? Did you drop to your knees then, begging for my forgiveness? No. Talking hasn't been real high on your agenda recently. So I need you to listen up, because this is the last conversation we will *ever* have. I want a divorce. I want you out. And I want the seven fucking years of my life that you stole from me back."

"I made a mistake, sweetheart. But that was all she ever was. *A mistake*. I love you and I know you love me." His arms wrapped around my hips and he pressed his head to my stomach. "We can get through this. I know we can."

I squeezed my eyes tighter and a tear leaked out the side.

This was going to be one of the hardest things I'd ever done.

Greg had been sewn into the fabric of my life. He had been my first love.

And, now, he was my first heartbreak.

"There is no 'we' anymore," I stated in a shaky voice. "And there is no getting through this."

He hugged me tighter. "There will *always* be an us. I'm not giving up on you."

I pried his arms from around my hips and finally opened my eyes.

Staring down at the only man I'd ever loved, I felt a stab from the cold blade of reality. "But you did give up on me." I stepped out of his reach. "And it happened six months ago."

Steeling myself for agony, I took one last glance at the two rings he'd given me all those years ago. I'd been on cloud nine the first time he'd dropped to his knees and asked me to be his wife.

And then I took them off. Every part of my body screamed at me to put them back on. Well, every part except my heart.

He'd made it more than clear that the promises he'd made with those rings had never been more than a figment of my imagination.

"No," he gasped as his eyes flared wide.

"You can have these back," I whispered, dropping both rings to the floor in front of him. "I don't need them anymore."

And then, with my heart in my throat and tears streaming down my face, I walked away.

TWO

Tanner

"GET OUT!" I SHOUTED AS THE DOOR TO MY BEDROOM swung open.

Andrea stopped short and curled her lip. "Seriously?"

Beads of water dripped from the ends of my straight, blond hair as I snatched my pants over my ass and yanked the zipper up. "Yeah. I'm fucking serious."

She smirked and raked her eyes down my bare chest to the button on my jeans. "Trust me, there is nothing you have that I haven't already seen." She crossed her arms over her chest and leaned toward me. "*Multiple* times."

Thrusting a hand into the top of my hair, I combed it out of my eyes. "Three drunken nights, one of which I'm almost positive you roofied me, hardly give you an all-access pass to my bedroom. Besides, don't you have a girlfriend now?"

She pouted her lips. "Awww, Tanner. Are you jealous?"

"Absolutely. Nicole was a beast in the sack." I winked.

Her smile fell and her eyes bulged. "You did not have sex with my girlfriend."

I barked a laugh. "No. I was kidding. I have a yearly crazy quota, and between you and Shana, I'm maxed out for the next decade. Nicole's virtue is safe." Barefoot, I padded across the dark mahogany floors to my dresser and dragged out a T-shirt.

"Oh, how is Shana?" she asked, prodding me with a fiery branding iron.

"Crazy. Delusional. Obsessed. Now that you mention it, a lot like you, actually."

She shot me an icy glare. Before I had the chance to slip the shirt over my head, she walked over and snatched it from my hand. "Not so fast. You'll need a tank. Your mic was distorted on the final cut. We need to do it again."

We'd been filming all day—for the third week in a row—with at least two more weeks of the same schedule in our future. It was safe to say we were all exhausted.

As the number-one rated cooking show on television, *Simmer* was in high demand. The Food Channel had ordered triple the amount of episodes for season seven. It seemed America couldn't get enough of Chef Tanner Reese. Or at least they couldn't get enough of my chest as I tore my shirt off in the middle of every episode. There was something to be said about understanding your target audience. And, for me, it was women.

Old women.

Young women.

Tall women.

Short women.

Married women.

Single women.

A white smile, two dimples, and a six-pack seemed to be the universal language. Thanks to good genetics, I'd become fluent at a very young age. But I'd always assumed that those skills were limited to my personal life. However, the pretty face definitely hadn't hurt when my agent had pitched me for my own show, and during episode two, when I'd spilled marinara on my shirt and jokingly taken it off, my producers had decided that the six-pack wouldn't hurt, either.

They weren't wrong.

Within a matter of weeks, my ratings had spiked to unfathomable highs, my face—and abs—had been plastered on magazine covers, and my show had been renewed for the foreseeable future.

I was a classically trained chef who'd graduated from New York's Institute of Culinary Education before studying under the finest chefs in France for three years. My place was in the kitchen. But when my paycheck from *Simmer* had jumped from "hey, this is something fun to do while I'm not working at the restaurant" to "welcome to the millionaire club," it had become clear that my place was actually in the kitchen while in front of a camera.

And I'll be honest, having thousands of adoring fans and becoming *People Magazine*'s sexiest chef in America definitely had a few perks too. Mainly for my ego. But that didn't mean any of it was easy. Sure, I wasn't exactly digging ditches, but smiling and filming for hours on end was grueling.

"Oh, come on! I just took a shower," I argued.

There wasn't a hint of apology in her voice as she said, "Sorry."

Andrea Garnis was the borderline-crazy—that border being only about a millimeter thick—director of *Simmer*. She'd been with me through every shirtless episode—and even a few shirtless nights that we both agreed never should have happened. Then we'd agreed that they would never happen again each and every time it happened. She was rude and crass, quite possibly the biggest bitch I had ever met, but she was loyal to a fault and had defended me more times than I could count.

I shouldn't have been complaining to her about reshooting a few simple scenes.

And yet, I was.

Because, deep down, I hated that job with the fire of a thousand suns.

Would I admit that? Never. I didn't even allow myself to *think* it most of the time.

But it was always there, festering beneath the surface, infecting me from the inside out. I could have quit. Broken my contract. Paid the network back a boatload of money.

But quitting meant admitting that the haters were right.

And, God, were they fucking right.

While the women of America loved me, the early rumblings from foodies and other professionals in the industry were not as warm. I'd quickly become the butt of all jokes in the culinary world, labeled as a talentless sellout who cared more about getting naked than the food I sent to plate.

What I'd learned from this was that there are assholes everywhere, ready to take shits all over a person's success.

What did I do about it? I smoked a cigarette as I laughed my way to the bank.

Fuck 'em. All of 'em. The haters and the cheats. The liars and the… Well, that's a Taylor Swift song for another day.

For five years, I'd worked my ass off to prove everyone wrong about me. And, for the most part, it had worked. Seven years later, I was once again at the top of the culinary world, respected from coast to coast. Admitting defeat now wasn't an option.

But even though I hated my name being synonymous with my abs, I still loved that I had made a career for myself in food. I'd been cooking since the day I was born. Not literally—I doubt I garnished my baby bottles. But, for as long as I could remember, I'd been in the kitchen. What had first started as me whipping up random concoctions of condiments from the pantry when my mom wasn't looking quickly became my passion. As a kid, while everyone else was out riding their bikes or playing video games, I was at home, nursing my obsession for public broadcast cooking shows, *Mr. Food*, and *Southern Living Magazine*. I was eight the first time my parents let me cook a full meal by myself. I prepared duck confit, mashed parsnips, and roasted peaches with a red wine sauce and a shallot ring garnish.

My father sat me down the same day and told me that it was okay that I was gay.

Years later, when he caught me in a clench with the girl from next door, I'd never seen him more surprised—or relieved. That relief faded after the second pregnancy scare from my high school girlfriend. (See aforementioned part about the smile, dimples, and six-pack.)

"Can't we finish tomorrow?" I complained.

Andrea shook her head. "Nope. Tomorrow, we have three more episodes to film."

I dropped my head back to stare at the ceiling. "I need a vacation."

"We all d—shit!"

My gaze jumped to her in time to see Porter barging into the room, nearly plowing her over.

"We need to talk!" he declared.

My brother was the biggest pain in my ass I had ever experienced. We looked alike—all sandy-blond hair and blue eyes. But, being two years older, he had been graced with the original smile-and-ab package, while I'd gotten the 2.0 version, which included the dimples. Looks aside, we couldn't have been more different.

I was the creative mind. He was all numbers and practicality.

I was the dreamer. He was the planner.

I was the wild child. He was the family man.

We gave each other immense shit and agreed on virtually nothing, but at the end of the day, we couldn't have been closer. And if I was being completely honest, I gave Porter the most shit because I was jealous of him—not that I'd ever admit it. It was just that the free-spirited-bachelor bit was only fun for so long. When I'd hit it big, I'd embraced that life harder than anyone in the world. It was what I'd thought I'd always want. Beautiful women. Impromptu vacations to exotic locations. Nothing tying me down. I was in the prime of my life. Who needed kids and a wife complicating it all?

I can tell you who. My brother.

God, I'd thought he was such a moron for getting married in his twenties. Joke was on me though. By the time I'd realized how right he was, I was thirty-two with no idea how to escape. My first and only attempt had gone up in flames like a dumpster fire. I was still paying the price for that one.

Though, as jealous as I was, Porter's life was no walk in the park.

Three years earlier, my brother's wife had unexpectedly passed away, leaving him a widower with two young kids. Along with our mom and dad, I rallied around him. His son, Travis, was eight and Hannah was only six months old when Catherine died. The kids struggled, but it was Porter who took it the hardest. Watching him fall apart under the grief and agony of his loss was one of the most painful things I'd ever experienced.

So one fated Friday, after he'd punched his boss and lost his job, I'd done the only thing I could think of to ease his shattered life.

I'd proposed that we start a restaurant together.

Did I have time? Fuck. No.

Simmer was soaring and I was slammed with a filming schedule I could barely keep up with. But Porter desperately needed the distraction.

And I desperately needed him to be happy again.

Given how much we fought, going into business together probably wasn't our brightest idea. But when push came to shove, we were the Reese brothers. We made shit happen.

Porter had a fancy-ass college degree in business, but he was an investment banker with absolutely no experience as a restaurateur. I assured him I knew what I was doing. It might have been a slight exaggeration. I could run a kitchen like a beast. But after the food hit the plate, my expertise was limited.

Whatever. We could figure out the rest as we went along.

Porter disagreed.

He presented me with a Trapper Keeper of graphs and charts. Yes. A fucking Trapper Keeper like he was eight again. I hadn't known you could still buy those damn things.

I presented him with an unimpressed glare and a few choice words.

I threw the first punch.

He threw the last, which led to me getting six stitches above one of my baby-blue moneymakers and a threatening letter from my producer.

After that, we were forced to get creative on how we solved our copious amounts of arguments. Building a Ninja Warrior course in my backyard seemed like the logical answer. That course served as our own personal judge. Winner took all and decisions were final.

Six months later, The Porterhouse was born. Despite the stupid name, we garnered rave reviews from critics and patrons alike. And within a matter of days, we were fully booked for the rest of the year. It wasn't long before we were making plans to open a second restaurant, The Tannerhouse. Yeah. I'd won the course the day we'd named that one. Truthfully, I had only been joking when I'd suggested the nonsensical name, but it pissed my brother off to no end, so I decided to keep it.

With only a few weeks before the soft opening of The Tannerhouse, Porter had been bombarding me with shit that was his job to stress about.

Shit that I did not have time to stress about too.

Shit that ultimately we'd both stress about until it was done.

And there he was, ready to dump more of it at my feet.

"Of course we do," I groaned.

"I need some advice," he stated, fisting his hands on his hips.

My eyebrows nearly touched my hairline, and a slow, arrogant smile curled my lips. "I'm sorry. Did you say you need *advice*?"

"Don't be an asshole."

"No. I'm serious. Could you repeat that?" I grinned like the smug bastard I pretended to be with him.

He glared and it made me laugh.

Opening my bottom drawer to grab one of my signature white tanks, I said, "You have asked me for advice exactly three times in our lives. The first was when you wanted to know the best way to scramble an egg without burning it. Second was when you needed to know how much water went in Rice-a-Roni after you accidentally threw out the directions. And last was when you asked for my advice on the best way to salvage a frying pan after you scraped the Teflon off while trying to scrub away a layer of the aforementioned scrambled egg." I arched an eyebrow. "Notice a pattern?"

"Cry me a river. You aren't exactly known for your sage wisdom. Crème de la fru fru or whatever the hell that shit is that you cook? Absolutely. But real-life advice that's applicable to anyone with even the most sluggish moral compass? Not a chance."

I blinked and a satisfied smile grew on my lips. Nothing Porter could say could hurt me, but knowing that I'd gotten under his skin was more satisfying than any insult I could have hurled back at him. Slinging shit at each other was what we did.

"And yet here you are, asking for advice."

He blew out a hard breath and raked a hand through his hair. With desperation in his eyes, he opened his mouth, but Andrea got there first.

"Later." She grabbed my arm and pulled me toward the door. "Let's go, pretty boy. You and your brother can hold hands and cry over whatever boy band tragically broke up while I'm at home."

Porter turned his scowl on her.

I grinned, remembering all over again why I gave Andrea a yearly Christmas bonus.

THREE

Rita

"JUST DO IT. RIP THE BAND-AID OFF." I STOPPED PACING and gave her my eyes.

Charlotte was staring at me, her face emotionless. This wasn't unusual. Some people had resting bitch face. Charlotte had resting *blank* face. She'd been my best friend for nine years and I still couldn't read her sometimes. But if I knew anything about her, it was that a snarky comment was headed my way.

"It'd probably be more satisfying to rip his balls off instead," she said as she got busy scanning the papers I'd handed her shortly after dragging her into her office and locking the door behind us.

The contents of that envelope were too ugly and embarrassing to be unleashed in public.

I smiled, and it was genuine, but it did nothing to quell the nerves ricocheting inside me. I'd been losing my mind about this moment since I'd found Tammy's texts on Greg's iPad. Poor dumbass, graduated from medical school at the top of his class, but he couldn't figure out how to unlink Messenger from his phone and iPad.

Or maybe I was the dumbass because it had taken me six months of suspicions to finally check up on him.

My heart sank and a herd of angry barn moths armed with daggers and spears fluttered in my stomach.

"That would definitely be better," I replied. "But he's not mine to castrate anymore."

Her dark-brown eyes grew soft and she avoided my gaze. Charlotte wasn't the nurturing, pep-talk kind of best friend. But that was probably why we got along so well. I was the busybody, meddle-in-everyone's-personal-life type in our relationship. And God knew I'd been trying to puppet-master some happiness into her life since the drunken night when she'd told Greg and me about her hollow existence.

To say Charlotte's life had been tough would be the understatement of the century. I couldn't even fathom how she'd survived after losing her only son ten years earlier. But, somehow, she'd used the tragedy to fuel her success—at least professionally. She'd not only graduated med school, even closer to the top than Greg, but she'd become one of the leading pulmonologists in the state, if not the country. Her dedication to her patients and her career made Greg look like a monkey in a lab coat.

I was going to miss seeing her every day when Greg finally canned me.

I'd been the office manager at North Point Pulmonology since Charlotte and Greg had gone into private practice together years earlier. Until ten days ago, I had loved my job. Sure, it wasn't nearly as glamorous as having an M.D. after my name. But I'd gotten to work with the man I loved, stealing kisses in his office and sharing lunches in the breakroom. Now, all of that was out the window, and the only perk I had was knowing that the woman he had chosen to abandon our marriage for was no longer stealing those same kisses or sharing those same lunches. Charlotte had fired Tammy approximately ten minutes after she'd found out about the affair. She'd lied and told the rest of the office that she'd quit. But I knew.

So yeah, Charlotte wasn't the girlfriend you called if you wanted someone to commiserate with. She was, however, the one you called if you wanted clear and concise action taken without question.

I swallowed hard and sat down in the chair across from her desk. "Okay. I'm ready. Give it to me straight."

I hadn't slept in days, partly because my entire life had been flipped upside down and partly because… Yeah, okay—that was all of it. But that horrifying envelope was one less thing I had to obsess about.

Her face remained stoic as she announced, "You don't have any STDs."

Tears welled in my eyes. "HIV, chlamydia, gonorrhea, anything?"

She offered me a weak smile. "*Nothing*. You're completely clean."

Christ. How was this my life?

Short bursts of the breath I had been holding escaped as my shoulders shook with silent sobs. I'd been with one man my entire life. I'd married him. I'd loved him. And there I was, celebrating that he hadn't given me an STD when he'd cheated on me.

"You okay?" Charlotte asked.

I shook my head, unable to formulate a response.

"This is good news, Rita."

I shifted in my chair. "I know. But the fact that I'm even sitting here is asinine. This was not supposed to be my life. This kind of stuff happens to other people." I smoothed down the top of my short, blond hair.

Greg liked it when I kept it styled in a short, angled bob. He said that it made me look young and smart—the perfect doctor's wife, as though I were an accessory and not a person. I did daily yoga and Pilates to keep in shape and wore expensive dresses and heels because he always commented on how much he liked them. I'd just turned thirty, but I spent hundreds of dollars on weekly facials to keep my skin bright and wrinkle-free for no other reason than I adored the way his face would light with pride when his friends and colleagues checked me out. My nails were always freshly manicured. My toes polished to match. Legs shaved. Skin lotioned. Makeup done. Jewelry on.

Because *Greg* liked me that way.

But then he'd cheated on me with Tammy Grigs. A woman so different from me that the only thing we had in common was the fact that we both had a vagina. She had long, brown hair that was constantly pulled back in a messy bun. She wore ill-fitting scrubs to work every day, and if her attire at the office get-togethers was any indication, tattered jeans and dingy T-shirts made up the majority of her wardrobe. She had large breasts and a similarly sized ass. She was a thirty-three-year-old single mother of two with a few rogue gray hairs and crow's feet to show for it.

Sure, she was cute. But she was no sex kitten. Definitely not the kind of woman a wife—jealous or not—would worry about her husband stepping out with.

No. I'd been bested by a regular woman who hadn't even been on my radar as competition.

"You do realize he slept with Tammy Grigs, right?" I whispered. "Tammy fucking Grigs, of all damn people."

Charlotte leaned back in her chair and folded her hands before resting them on the desk between us. "He slept with," she stated matter-of-factly.

"What?" I snapped.

"He slept with. Those are the only words in that sentence that matter. He could have slept with a Victoria's Secret model or an eighty-year-old nun and it wouldn't matter. It's the fact that he did it."

I stabbed my finger down on the desk. "But I was better than her. I worked my ass off to be the wife he wanted me to be. And he chose *her*?"

She shook her head and leaned forward, propping herself up on her elbows. "Stop worrying about whether you're better than Tammy and focus on the fact that you *are* better than Greg. He slept with another woman. *He* did it. And he did it to *you*."

My chest caved in like she had punched me. "I don't know what the hell to do with that," I admitted.

She looked down at the papers and whispered, "There's nothing to do with it, Rita. Life isn't fair. It's cruel and calculating. But it is real. Accept it. Or don't. It won't change anything."

Charlotte had a way with words. She was blunt and honest, which was nice for the age-old does-this-dress-make-my-ass-look-fat debate, but not so much for the I'm-dying-inside-please-make-me-feel-better discussion.

I crossed my arms and rested them on her desk. Then I folded over to rest my head on them. "I need a new best friend. One who will bring over cupcakes and wine and then help me build a dummy and burn it in effigy."

She laughed softly and then went silent.

I peeked my head up and her face was once again blank.

"What?" I asked.

"We didn't get to the results of your pregnancy test."

My back shot ramrod straight as chills pebbled over my skin. I'd gone off birth control almost two years earlier. We'd gotten pregnant right away only for it to end in an early first trimester miscarriage. Greg and I were devastated, but we remained hopeful for the future. From the start, we decided not to *try* to have babies. No charting or plotting my cycle. I didn't want the pressure or stress of trying to conceive to create problems in our marriage. Though, over the last year, our sex life had become strained at best.

I didn't think much of it at first. Our lives were busy. He was at work, spending several nights a week at the hospital with his patients. I was planning the Spring Fling, hitting speed bumps at every turn. But that was how it went in marriages; there were ebbs and flows. Greg and I had definitely been in an ebb, our only physical connection being the occasional obligatory quickie when he'd get home late and crawl into bed with me.

Little had I known then, he'd just crawled out of someone else's bed.

So, while it was highly unlikely that we'd created a child, it wasn't impossible.

I covered my mouth with my hand and then asked around it. "Am I pregnant?"

"Do you want to be?"

My stomach knotted, and I toyed with the strand of pearls at my neck. Pearls *he* had given me. "No. I mean… maybe. I don't know. It's not exactly a choice I get to make at this point."

"I know you and Greg were trying there for a while."

I laughed, but it held no humor. "Well, that's not saying much. Technically, he was *trying* with Tammy too. Maybe not to have a baby, but same deed."

"Let me rephrase. I know *you* wanted a baby."

"I did." The admission burned on the tip of my tongue.

"And now you don't?"

"Again, it's not up to me at this point. Am I pregnant?"

"Would you stay with him if you were?" she asked, dragging her long, raven hair up into a ponytail before releasing it back down to her shoulders.

My heart raced, and I stood from my chair as a blast of adrenaline hit my system. "I don't know. Maybe."

She frowned. "Kids fix everything, huh?"

"I didn't say that."

Staying was the easy route—the cop-out. I wasn't too proud to admit that I'd considered taking that route a few times since I'd first read those text messages. We could have gone to counseling, figured out the root cause of why he had done it. I would have pretended to forgive him. He would have pretended that he would never do it again. And then, in a few years, after the monotony of marriage had settled back in, one of us would stop pretending. I'd forget I wasn't allowed to be bitter. He'd forget he wasn't allowed to sleep with every woman who opened her legs. And then we'd be right here all over again. Only this time with a kid or two and a few more years of our short lives faded into the past.

Staying in a marriage where only one person was committed wasn't an option. I'd given up too much of my life already. I'd be damned if I gave more.

"I lied," I mumbled.

I felt like a rubber band was winding inside me. The mounting pressures of the future were wrenching it tighter with every tick of the second hand.

She arched a knowing eyebrow. "So you wouldn't stay with him?"

"No. But that's not what I lied about." I chewed on my bottom lip. "The truth is, I never wanted a baby." I lifted my eyes to hers. "I wanted a family, Charlotte. You know Jon and I didn't have much when we were growing up. Our parents… Well, they just sucked. I'd vowed to myself to get out of that life. I wanted the husband, the house, the dog, the picket fence, the two-point-five kids. I wanted the full package." I swept invisible tears from under my eyes. "But Greg isn't that husband. And I'm going to have to sell our house because I can't afford to keep it on my own. And let's be honest here. Even if I found another man, I don't want to be that woman who has two-point-five kids with two-point-five different men." I shot her a shaky smile. "Honestly, I'm not even sure if I like dogs. Some of them—"

"You're not pregnant," she blurted.

"What!" I yelled, shooting to my feet as the most amazing—and telling—blast of relief filled my veins.

"You're not pregnant," she repeated.

"Then why the hell did you act like I was!"

She rose from her chair and walked around her desk. "Because I was scared that, when shit got hard and the darkness closed in on you, you'd run back to Greg. I had a speech planned and everything. I went so far as to price out a plane ticket and private cabana in Barbados to get you away from him until you got your head straight."

I blinked at her, my emotions even more scattered than they had been when I'd walked into her office.

I had no STDs.

And I wasn't pregnant.

There was absolutely nothing tying me to the man I had committed my life to seven years earlier.

I should have been relieved. It was exactly what I'd wanted when I'd asked her to read me the results.

Yet it was the emptiest feeling in my life.

I swallowed hard. "First of all, you are fired as my best friend for making me believe I was pregnant."

Her lips curled up into a small smile.

My heels clipped on the floor as I closed the distance between us. Pulling her into a hug, I whispered, "But I officially rehire you, seeing as how you were contemplating sending me to Barbados in order to keep me away from my no-good piece-of-shit soon-to-be ex-husband."

She returned the embrace for only a second before setting me away. Touching wasn't her thing. But it was my thing, so she put up with it in small doses.

"Are you sure you don't need a place to stay?" she asked, moving back behind her desk.

"Nah. He hasn't tried to come home. I may or may not have programmed our address into his GPS as a location called I Will Neuter You."

She chuckled. "Okay. Well, if you need anything, you know where I am."

"At the hospital with a patient?" I teased.

"More than likely."

I turned my attention to her office door. I'd walked in and out of that door countless times, but right then, it felt like a portal to a different universe. One that divided the past from the future.

Greg was out there, moving on with his life.

Now, it was my turn.

It was time.

Time to move on.

Time to let go.

Time to start over.

But, as I stared at that door, it seemed impossible.

Charlotte followed my gaze. "One step at a time, Rita."

I nodded absently, wondering how many of those steps it would take until I stopped hurting.

How many until he was a distant memory?

How many until I felt like myself again? And not Rita, Greg Laughlin's perfect little wife. But rather Rita Hartley, the girl with more dreams than stars in the sky.

It might have taken me a lifetime, but that woman was somewhere on the other side of that door, and I'd be damned if I wasn't going to find her.

Rolling my shoulders back and standing tall, I took the very first step toward the rest of my life.

FOUR

Tanner

THE HAMMOCK SWAYED AS I STARED OUT AT THE POND rippling in my backyard. Two years earlier, I'd bought that house specifically for that view. Well, the view *and* the five-thousand-square-foot plantation house on two acres. The kitchen had needed a serious overhaul, but finding a place that big so close to the city was a rarity. And the price tag proved that the sellers knew it.

But I had the money.

I traveled a good bit back and forth between LA and New York for work. And while I loved the hustle and bustle of city life, Atlanta had always been my home. It was a different kind of big city. We had multiple professional sports teams, and traffic was a nightmare, but we also had a quaint farmers market where I randomly ran into people I went to high school with. Plus, Porter and the kids lived about fifteen minutes away and my parents were only twenty minutes in the other direction.

So I'd bought the overpriced house.

After lifting the cigarette to my lips, I inhaled deeply, filling my lungs with the sweet burn of tobacco. I'd been trying to quit smoking for three months, and for the most part, I'd been successful. But I couldn't seem to give up that first-thing-in-the-morning smoke. It was like the strongest cup of coffee for my lungs. It woke me from the inside out, invigorating me in ways nothing other a woman moaning my name ever had.

But with women came responsibility. My cigarette never stalked me, sliced the tires on my car, or sold a selfie of us lying in bed together to the tabloids. And considering all of that had happened to me in the last two months, I was swearing off women and sticking with my early morning smoke.

My phone started ringing on the small table beside my hammock. I swayed, reaching for it, then grinned huge when I lifted it to my ear. "Well, hello there, pretty lady."

"Don't give me that 'pretty lady' crap. I'm sixty, and when I'm not wearing a bra, my nipples make a break to find my belly button."

I gagged. "Jesus, Mom."

"Good morning, sweetie."

"I'm not sure if I'd call it *good*. That horrific mental image is going to stick with me the rest of the day."

"Your father doesn't think it's all that horrific. Actually, just last night—"

"Ahhhh!" I yelled to drown out the rest of her sentence. "What the hell is wrong with you this morning?"

"I don't have any daughters," she stated matter-of-factly. "So, it's your job as my favorite child to listen to me talk about my marriage and all that comes with it."

My mom always told me I was her favorite even in front of Porter. We all knew it was bullshit. She loved my asshole big brother something fierce. As teens, Porter had been far more compliant. He followed the rules, made good grades, and always came home by curfew. I, on the other hand… Well, I did none of those things. But favorites and love aside, there was no denying that my mom was my best friend.

Yeah. Yeah. Yeah. Muck it up. I was a big ole mama's boy. I could give a negative amount of fucks about what anyone thought about our relationship.

My mom was an incredible woman. She volunteered with elderly patients at various nursing homes across the city, and she acted as the neighborhood grandma, babysitting, tutoring, and dishing out secret sweets to all the kids who stopped by to say hello.

But above and beyond all of that, she was just fucking cool. When I was growing up, my dad and Porter were tight. They'd sneak away almost every weekend to go fishing or whatever manly activity my father was trying to force on my brother that week. Meanwhile, Mom carted me to cooking classes and the occasional competition.

I'll never forget the way she used to sit in the kitchen for hours on end, talking and tasting, as I prepped dinner. She could have gone on about her day. Used that time to do something for herself. But no, she sat with me. And it wasn't just about teaching me the fine art of using a ricer to smooth out a sweet potato casserole. We talked about school, my friends, and eventually girls.

She bought me my first box of condoms when I started

dating Shelly Lewis.

She read me the Riot Act when I told her I was going to break up with Shelly because there was a hot new girl in school.

And then she drove the getaway car after I'd egged Shelly's house when she cheated on me with that same hot girl's older brother.

That was my mom.

And I loved her dearly, but…

"There is no way I'm listening to you talk about having sex with Dad."

"So, if it wasn't your father, you'd listen?" she asked. "Well, in that case, I saw that fine new waiter at The Porterhouse. Maybe…"

"Annnnd now I'm hanging up."

"I'm kidding!" she called before I had the chance to hit the end button.

Shaking my head, I snubbed my cigarette out in an empty beer bottle and climbed to my feet. "Are you sniffing the cleaning supplies again?"

"Nah, I was trying to make sure you were actually up and getting dressed rather than smoking a cigarette and lounging in the hammock."

I froze and swung my eyes around the balcony, searching for whatever hidden camera she had planted at my house. "Are you watching me?"

"Oh, God, no. I'm not that bored. Besides, I know all about your aversion to clothing. Just because I wiped your butt as a baby doesn't mean I want to see it now."

"Could you possibly make this conversation any more

awkward?" I asked.

"Absolutely. You want me to give it another shot?"

"No." I walked inside, the mid-March heat giving way to my air conditioner.

"Okay, all joking aside. I just wanted to make sure you were up and getting dressed. Porter's expecting you in a half hour."

Smirking, I padded across the wood floor to the hall closet and feigned ignorance. "What? Expecting me where?"

"Tanner Reese, I will hurt you if you pull this crap right now," she snapped in the mom tone that could still cast terror over me despite the fact that I was now thirty-two and not ten.

"Okay, okay. Relax. I'm heading out now." Opting for a waist apron rather than my chef jacket, I tugged it off the hanger and threw it over my shoulder.

"Thank you. And listen, I need you to be on your best behavior. This is really important to Porter. It's important to all of us. Especially Travis."

My smile fell at the mention of his name.

Porter's eleven-year-old son, Travis, was sick. He had been for several years, but it was getting worse. I couldn't count how many times he'd been in and out of the hospital over the past few months. And each and every time, we were all terrified something would go wrong and he wouldn't come home. Porter was desperately trying to secure an appointment with some fancy-schmancy pulmonologist across town—only problem was she didn't treat children.

But there was no way—not when it came to his kids—Porter was taking no for an answer. He'd been calling and begging for weeks, hitting nothing but brick walls, until a few days earlier, he'd made some headway. Somehow, he'd managed to score some face time with the doctor by volunteering The Porterhouse to cater a gig at North Point Pulmonology's Spring Fling.

This would have been amazing except for the tiny little detail that The Porterhouse didn't do catering. Especially not at a children's carnival where they had requested we serve hot dogs and freaking burgers. I mean, for fuck's sake, we'd been voted one of the top restaurants in the country and received four stars from *The New York Times*. I was waiting on our Michelin stars while Porter was out shopping at Costco for the lowest price on economy buns.

But it was for Travis, so I was on board one hundred percent. Though putting my name on a grocery store hot dog was pushing it.

In the most unlikely Reese brother fashion, Porter and I made a compromise—without running the Ninja Warrior course.

Waygu burgers, grilled chicken breasts, and lamb kabobs. I'd agreed to man the grill, and Porter was to handle the prep work. He'd gathered every sous chef we had to prep and package my mom's famous bacon ranch pasta salad and a French potato salad I'd whipped up on the fly.

It was going to cost us a small fortune, but if it helped Travis—okay, fine. And Porter—I'd have signed over the entire contents of my bank account.

But that didn't mean I wasn't going to give my brother immortal hell first.

"I'm dressed, Mama. I'm actually headed out now," I said, wedging the phone between my shoulder and my ear before nabbing my keys from the bowl my interior decorator had insisted I needed next to the door. She wasn't wrong.

"Thank God," she breathed across the line.

Her relief was a tad insulting, albeit deserved.

"I'm not a total jackass, you know?"

"I never said you were. Though your punctuality is definitely in question."

"Yeah. Yeah. Yeah. So you've said a time or four thousand." I jogged down the stairs, walked to the front door, and slipped on a pair of brown dress boots, not bothering to lace them or adjust my jeans. Then I raked my hand through my blond hair, tousling it into disarray. Such was fashion. Women were required to look like they'd walked off the catwalk at three a.m., but a man could pull off sleep-mussed, just-rolled-out-of-bed in the middle of the day.

Or…at least *I* could.

"Listen, I gotta go. Do me a favor and call Jackie and tell her all about your night with Dad and get it out of your system. Otherwise, I'm stepping down as your favorite son and will be looking for a new date to the opening of Ramsay's new restaurant in a few weeks."

"You wouldn't dare!" she hissed. "You know that man is going to be your stepfather one day."

Yeah, my mom was a nut.

"I'll be sure to let Dad know that next time I see him."

She laughed. Chances were my dad already knew about her crush. He knew she was a nut too. It wasn't exactly a trait she could hide for thirty-six years.

"Okay, baby. Get going. Porter is really depending on you. Love you, Tootsy."

Yes. My mom called me Tootsy. It was short for Tootsy Pooter Southern Gentleman. So fucking what? She'd been calling me that since birth. Why? See the aforementioned nut part. And again: I could have given a negative amount of fucks…

Oh, who was I kidding? I hated that nickname. Despite trying since I was old enough to realize I'd like to one day get laid, I'd never been able to make her stop using it. I'd given up after the first tabloid got ahold of it. Much to the *Enquirer*'s chagrin, women thought it was adorable. I'd had to hire an extra bodyguard for events after that story broke.

"Love you too," I replied while arming my security alarm and heading out into the four-car garage.

"Call me and let me know how it goes."

"Will do. Bye, Mama."

"Bye, Toots."

I hung up and then momentarily waffled between the S-Class and Range Rover before opting for speed over power. I folded my six-foot-three frame into the sports car then dialed his number as the garage opened with a quiet purr.

"Where the hell are you?" Porter snapped in greeting. "I asked you to be here *early*."

Yep. He was in full-fledged panic mode. As soon as I got there, I'd take over and send him out to grab a snow cone or cotton candy or whatever the hell they served at a spring fling. But for now…I was going to fuck with him.

"Ah, yeah. Listen about that. Sorry, I can't make it today. Angie needs me."

"What!" he boomed. "Who the hell is Angie?"

I bit the inside of my cheek to stifle a laugh as I backed

out of the garage, navigating the brick horseshoe driveway. "You know...*Angie*."

He didn't know because I'd just made her up.

"No. I don't. You promised me you'd be here."

"Yeah, but her dog died. And she's a total wreck. You know how to cook, right?"

It was safe to say he didn't. Like, at all. If it didn't go in a microwave, Porter couldn't make it. And even if it did go in a microwave, more often than not, he still found a way to ruin it.

"Are you kidding—"

"Hey, I gotta go. Good luck today."

"Tanner!"

He was still yelling when I severed the connection. For good measure, I turned my phone off and flipped it onto the seat beside me.

Was it the nicest thing to do? Probably not. But trust me, Porter wasn't the nicest to me, either. Giving each other shit and arguing were the only things we had in common.

Honestly, this was a good bonding exercise for us.

At least that's what I told myself as I sped down the highway, laughing as I drove.

FIVE

Rita

"WHERE'S GREG?" CHARLOTTE ASKED AS SHE ARRIVED at the folding table I'd decorated with dozens of construction paper flowers and glitter garlands.

It was finally the big day: The North Point Pulmonology Spring Fling. I'd started the tradition a few years back, thinking it would be nice to see our patients and their families out of the office when they weren't sick—and for them to see us when we weren't poking and prodding at them or, in my case, arguing about billing. We donated all proceeds to charity, so honestly, it was a win-win.

But, alas, this would be my final year.

It had been over two weeks since I'd found out about Greg's affair. Two long, agonizing, and confusing weeks. I wasn't eating or sleeping well. And while lying in bed, questioning every decision I'd ever made, was one hell of a diet plan, it sucked in all other areas. The initial shock of his infidelity was starting to fade, but resentment that I'd wasted so much of my life with a man like that was running thicker than ever. The worst of it being that some of my anger had turned inward.

I wasn't to blame for Greg's inability to keep his dick in his pants. Like any sane and rational person, I knew that on a very basic level. But that didn't stop my brain from firing off dozens of "If only I'd…" thoughts over the last few weeks.

To keep those niggling feelings quiet, I'd tried to keep my distance from him. But this was a virtually impossible task. We worked in the same office and he had a key to my house no matter how many times I'd threatened to castrate him if he used it.

He had fresh flowers on my doorstep every morning.

He delivered me lunch from one of my favorite restaurants every day.

And the new hot-pink Jimmy Choos I'd been subtly dropping hints about for months had miraculously appeared on my desk—complete with the matching handbag.

All of this meant my trash can got flowers every morning, one of the nurses got lunch every day, and my shoe and purse collection got a new addition.

What? They were Jimmy Choos! I wasn't a monster.

As shameful as it was, those sweet little gestures were starting to wear on me. They reminded me of the kind and charming guy who'd spent weeks trying to get my number when I was in college. With those memories muddling my resolve, it would have been all too easy to let him back in.

But I couldn't.

Not now.

Not ever.

Before my emotions had a chance to breach my carefully crafted smile, I cleared my throat and told Charlotte, "*Dr. Laughlin* is spending the day in the dunking booth."

She tsked her tongue against her teeth. "I thought we discussed the human dartboard?"

Sighing, I rocked back in my metal folding chair and crossed my legs. "I decided it might be a tad too violent for the kids."

"Yeah, but the dunking booth isn't nearly as satisfying to watch."

"I don't know about that." I leaned in close, partitioning off my mouth, and whispered, "I filled the tank with ice water and paid the pitchers from the local high school baseball team to rotate through the line for a few hours."

"Niiiiice," she praised.

My lips stretched, and I prayed she couldn't see the agony simmering beneath the surface. "If he's going to fire me, I'm going to earn it."

"What are you talking about? He's not going to fire you."

"Oh, please. How long do you think he's going to keep his ex-wife employed after I take him to the cleaners in divorce court?"

"I don't care what happens between you two. He's *not* firing you."

I reached across the table and squeezed her arm. "You're sweet, honey. But it's bound to happen. And I'll be honest, I'm not sure I can spend my days watching him parade around with whatever nurse he's got his eye on next."

She scoffed. "There isn't a woman in that office who

would touch him with a ten-foot pole after the shit he and Tammy pulled on you. Besides, that office is half mine. You aren't going anywhere."

God, that felt good knowing that someone still had my back. Though it didn't change the facts. Moving on couldn't be done while standing still.

I shot her a warm smile. "And I appreciate that, but, Charlotte, it's time for me to move on. A man you love treats you like that, you don't sit around pining after him." I smoothed down my respectable, but still form-fitting dress, which I may or may not have worn just to torture Greg, and finished with, "You put on your tightest little black dress and your best pair of heels and *strut* into the future." My voice caught, but my smile never faltered. "Life sucks sometimes. You and I know that better than anyone else, but we only get one."

Her face suddenly paled and I regretted saying that immediately. I should have known better than to compare our lives. I had not become best friends with a woman like Charlotte Mills without learning to walk the sensitivity tightrope.

But if I apologized, it would only make her feel guiltier and more embarrassed. So, going against my natural inclination to fix and meddle, I held my breath and silently waited for her to lead us out of the awkwardness.

After several seconds, she sucked in a deep breath and replied on an exhale, "Enough heavy for one day."

"Yes. Yes. You're right." I offered her a tight smile. "Go on. Get out of here and have some fun."

She started away when suddenly I remembered why I'd

called her three times yesterday and threatened to burn her house down if she didn't show up today. I'd promised the catering guy a one-on-one with my best friend.

"Oh, wait, Char!"

She turned to face me. "What's up?"

"Do me a favor and take this over to the guy at the grill?" I thrust an empty pickle jar in her direction. "He needs a way to collect the tickets for lunch." I smiled—attempting to keep my enthusiasm locked away.

When her body locked up tight, I knew I'd failed.

"Why are you looking at me like that?"

"Like what?"

She pointed at my mouth. "Like *that*."

"I don't know what you're talking about?" I lied.

She was going to kill me. That much I was sure of, but I'd lost any sense of fear when the blond-haired, blue-eyed, gorgeous specimen of a man Porter Reese had shown up an hour earlier to cater the Fling. He had it in his head that he was going to convince Charlotte to treat his son. This would *never* happen, but after one glance at his muscular shoulders, his scorching grin, and a bare ring finger, I'd hoped that maybe he could convince her of something else—like maybe to get naked with him.

I pressed the jar into her hand. "You should go talk to him."

We both turned to look in his direction, finding a cloud of smoke billowing high in the air. Scrunching my nose, I sent up a prayer for the sake of our patients and staff that The Porterhouse was really as good as the Yelp reviews had insisted.

"What the hell is he doing?" she asked.

I nudged her shoulder. "I don't know. Go ask him."

She swung a murderous gaze my way. "Are you trying to set me up with that guy?"

"Dear God, no." I slapped a hand over my heart. "I'm about to reenter the dating world for the first time in nine years. I can't afford to risk that you'll praying-mantis a hot one like that." This wasn't totally a lie, but trust me when I say Charlotte needed a man far more than I did. And when I caught sight of Greg watching us from the dunking booth, pain and betrayal stabbing me in the chest, I decided that maybe men should be off the table for a while. "Stop being so damn suspicious," I told her. "He looks like he could use some help, and I'm smart enough to know that you're about to find somewhere to hide for the next hour until you can leave. So do us all a favor and do it over there." I gave her a rough shove in his direction. "Go make sure there will be *edible* food to serve people and then you have my full permission to leave in two hours."

"One hour," she countered.

"One and a half."

"One hour, Rita. I need to get up to the hospital."

I rolled my eyes. "One hour and fifteen minutes."

She extended a hand toward me. "One hour and I'll pay to keep the baseball team until five."

Now that was an offer I couldn't refuse. "Deal."

I watched her long, dark hair sway as she walked away. Then I cringed when orange flames shot up from the grill.

Okay, so maybe Yelp had been wrong.

I was Googling the nearest burger joint, just in case,

when I heard her soft voice.

"Hey," she said, drawing my attention up. Tammy fucking Grigs was staring back at me.

With narrow eyes, I gave her a slow once-over. Her long, brown hair was down, flowing over her shoulders in waves. Pearl studs decorated her earlobes, and a classic black maxi dress clung to curves she had clearly been hiding beneath her scrubs.

She didn't look anything like she had the last time I'd seen her.

The gray was gone in her hair, and the crow's feet around her eyes had been covered with makeup.

Her brows were sculpted.

Her nails were manicured.

Her entire look was polished from head to toe.

It was all I could do not to throw up right then and there.

She looked exactly like a woman Greg would date now.

Because she looked a lot like me.

"Can we talk?" she asked.

Nope. Nope. Nope.

"You need to leave," I hissed.

She lifted her hands in surrender. "Please, Rita. I'm not here to cause trouble."

Blood thundered in my ears as I rose to my feet and repeated, "You need to leave!"

But she didn't leave…and her next two words changed my life forever.

Life is weird. People spend so much of it searching for something.

Keys.

Remotes.

Phones.

Love.

Happiness.

Security.

And just when you think you've found it all, the universe laughs, snatching it away and sending you right back to the start.

But everyone knew for there to be a start, there had to be an end.

The end of my marriage had come the day I'd found Greg's texts with Tammy.

The end of our relationship had come when I'd kicked him out of our house.

Then the end of any lingering ties, past or future, had come when I'd sat in Charlotte's office after finding out that my philandering soon-to-be ex-husband hadn't given me a STD…or a child.

But I'd been wrong on all accounts.

The real end of Greg and Rita Laughlin came on a warm Saturday in March at The North Point Pulmonology Spring Fling.

And it came from Tammy fucking Grigs's mouth.

"I'm pregnant."

My stomach dropped and the Earth tilted as her words struck me like a physical blow. My heels sank into the grass as I stumbled backward. At the last second, I found purchase on the corner of the table and miraculously stayed upright.

She rubbed her flat belly and smiled weakly. "Greg told

me you've asked him to work things out. He's such a good guy that he hasn't had the heart to tell you about the baby yet, you know…after what happened." She pointedly flicked her gaze to my stomach.

My empty stomach that had once held my child before we'd miscarried. The pain seared through me, but Tammy continued.

"Anyway…woman to woman, I felt like you deserved to know."

Utterly confused, I blinked at her.

Words were coming out of her mouth, but none of them made sense. I wasn't trying to convince Greg to work things out. He was the one who had spent the last two weeks attempting to schmooze his way back into my good graces. It had been wasted effort from the start, but what could he have possibly thought was going to happen if and when I found out he'd gotten her pregnant? That I was going to sit on the couch, knitting baby blankets for his illegitimate child?

Fuck.

That.

I shouldn't have been surprised by this sudden revelation. Not that Greg had knocked her up and then kept it a secret or that Tammy had shown up to rub it in my face. The two of them clearly deserved each other.

But as much as I wanted to deny it—it still hurt like hell.

She took a step toward me, keeping her voice soft and low. "For what it's worth, I'm truly sorry, Rita. We didn't plan this thing between us. But sometimes, love happens when you least expect it."

I opened my mouth to say something, but I had no idea

what was going to come out. I hoped I was a strong enough woman that it was going to be a colorful variation of "go fuck yourself," but I feared it might also be a precursory croak before I burst into tears.

I'd lost everything because he couldn't keep his dick in his pants. And, now, he was going to walk away with a new woman and a fucking baby? A family. Everything he knew I wanted.

How was that fair?

Suddenly, the man of the hour joined the conversation.

"Rita," he called, jogging over. "Is everything okay?" His shoulders shook with a shiver as water dripped off his soaking-wet clothes.

My baseball team had been doing their job, and it pissed me off that this bitch had robbed me of the ability to bask in my evil handiwork.

"Just *great*," I ground out.

Greg turned his nervous gaze on Tammy. "What are you doing here?"

She smiled up at him. "I just wanted to stop by and—"

"She came to tell me about the baby," I announced, masking my pain with a heavy dose of annoyance.

He winced, his head cranking to the side like I'd slapped him. And God, did I want to slap him.

"Congrats," I chirped, turning to walk away. The anger and emotion swirling inside me caused tears to prick at the backs of my lids. But there was no way I was giving either of them a front-row seat to my impending breakdown.

Roughly, he caught my arm before I could make my escape. "I was going to tell you. I swear. I'm not even sure if it's mine."

"What the hell, Greg?" Tammy yelled.

He ignored her and moved closer, his front becoming flush with my back.

"Let me go," I demanded, fighting against his hold while trying not to make a scene. The last thing any of us needed was to incite more office gossip.

Greg refused to let go, and I winced when his fingertips bit into my arm. But his words were what caused the most amount of pain.

"Rita, please. I love you."

As crazy as it was, a part of me believed him. In his own warped way, he did love me. And with his fingertips searing against my skin, I wanted to take that love, twist it into something dark and dirty, and then torture him with it until he was broken and ruined on his knees.

Just. Like. Me.

And in my next breath, it was as if God were a scorned woman who understood exactly how therapeutic revenge could be.

Because she sent me an angel.

He was tall and lean, but the muscles of his pecs strained against his designer white T-shirt. Don't ask me how I knew that it was designer. It just was. Or maybe it only looked like it was because his hard body could make anything appear expensive. His hair was tousled and sandy blond, but it was trimmed and clean like he'd spent an exorbitant amount of money to make it shaggy. Dark denim hung low on his tapered hips, traveling down long, muscular legs before falling haphazardly into unlaced boots.

I froze, unable to draw breath into my lungs, when his angry, blue eyes met mine then flashed up to Greg.

"Get your hands off her, asshole."

Dear merciful Lord, the man was *gorgeous.*

SIX

Tanner

THE SWEET SMELL OF COTTON CANDY DANCED IN THE AIR as I folded out of my car. Remixed pop songs performed by children echoed through the packed parking lot. For a moment, I almost felt bad for having screwed with Porter when he was staring down a crowd like this. I loved to give my brother shit, but not at the risk of an angry mob of children declaring mutiny.

For fear of being forced to tell my mother about my brother's untimely demise, I tucked my apron into my back pocket and picked up the pace. I beelined for the small group of people who were standing around a table that I swear Roy G Biv had decorated himself.

When I got within earshot, I opened my mouth, a request for directions poised on the tip of my tongue, but they died the moment I saw her.

"Let me go," she bit out, pained emotion carved in her

smooth features.

The tall, balding man moved into her space, his front flush with her back, and whispered something in her ear.

I slowed, studying her reaction while trying to figure out what exactly was going on. It could have easily been a lover's quarrel, but even still, the dick shouldn't have had his hands on her. And when her face screwed tight, her lips pursing like she was fighting back tears, I decided not to wait to find out.

"Get your hands off her, asshole," I called, jogging over.

"Mind your own business," the man growled while *not* letting her go.

I planted my hands on my hips. "Yeah, see. You have your hands on a woman. That's kinda the business of every man here. Especially mine since I heard her tell you to let go." I flicked my gaze to our damsel in distress and found her staring at me with wide eyes and a slack jaw.

Oh, great. This was about to get awkward.

It wasn't unusual for people to recognize me. It was far more prevalent when I was in New York or LA, where everyone was on the lookout for the next famous face to walk past. But since we'd opened The Porterhouse and my house had officially been added to the Places To Visit In Atlanta Guide online, it happened a good bit when I was local too.

Some fans froze and stared from afar.

Some lingered, whispering and giggling until they found the courage to approach.

Some screamed and yelled, snapping a million selfies before I had the chance to smile.

And then there were the ones who had absolutely no concept of personal boundaries and threw themselves into my arms, lap, or car the moment our eyes met.

But never had anyone reacted the way the blonde did as she broke free of the man's hold.

"Oh, honey, you came!" she said, launching herself into my arms.

I narrowed my eyes and peered down at her in confusion. But considering that this woman was fucking beautiful, even if she did look like a senator's trophy wife with her angled bob, pearls, and a knee-length black dress that hugged her in all the right places, I didn't set her away. I was a gentleman like that.

"Well, hello there," I crooned.

She tilted her head back, resting her chin on my pec and somehow shifted closer, the toe of her sexy, red heel brushing my boot to the point that our legs were practically intertwined. "Any chance you'd be willing to play along?" she whispered.

I twisted my lips. "With what?"

Her deep, green eyes turned worrisome as they searched my face. Then almost inaudibly she asked, "Are you married?"

"Not that I know of."

Her nose scrunched adorably. "Fiancée? Girlfriend? Friends with benefits?"

My gaze fell to her plump lips. "You offering or asking?"

"Who the fuck is this guy?" the man rumbled, reminding me that the prick was still standing there and had unfortunately not fallen into a sinkhole.

And then a wide and entirely fake smile tipped her lips as she turned, using my wrist to guide my arm around her shoulders. She wasted no time plastering her front to my side.

"You missed me, didn't you?" she purred. "You couldn't get enough of me last night, so you showed up today for a little more." She pushed up onto her toes, her soft, silky lips brushing my cheek. "Don't worry. I missed you too."

My eyebrows shot up, but swear to God, the way her breasts pressed against me made my cock stir. "Did you now?"

She nodded, and despite having no idea what the fuck was happening, I watched with rapt attention as her pink tongue peeked out to dampen her lips.

Okay, so this was *definitely* different than the usual fan reaction, mainly because she wasn't looking at me like she was a fan at all.

She was nervous, but not because of me.

Up close, the spark glittering in her eyes wasn't recognition—it was…desperation?

Sure, she was hot, and she smelled amazing: like honey and citrus. And the way she fit against my side—and probably under me too—was nothing short of perfection. But I didn't think she knew who I was. And that might have been the biggest turn-on of all.

"Holy shit, are you…" a woman asked, pulling my attention away from my mystery girl.

"Tanner," I finished for her, purposely leaving off my last name.

She slapped a hand over her mouth and muttered, "Oh, wow."

The man with thinning, brown hair, who I belatedly noticed was sopping wet, turned a murderous gaze my way. "Any chance you could take your hands off my wife, *Tanner*?"

Son of a bitch. Why did the hot one have to be his wife? I gave the mousey brunette with too much makeup a perusal. She was more his speed. Plain. Simple. Forgettable.

Nothing like my—er, *his* blonde.

I started to remove my arm from her shoulders. Porter would have hidden creepy dolls in my house again if I'd gotten into a brawl over a married woman whose name I didn't know while he was busy trying to woo a doctor into treating Travis.

Shit. Porter.

"I need to go," I rushed out. "Can you tell me where—"

"Your wife?" My blonde laughed loudly. "That's a joke, right?"

Then my whole body locked up tight, causing me to rock back onto my heels. And not because of her sudden outburst, but rather because she'd caught my hand and guided it to rest on her ass.

Her tight, firm but supple, *incredible* ass.

I bit my lip and fought the urge to flex my fingers, drawing her sweet ass into my palm.

And then I lost that battle in spectacular fashion—groaning and everything—right in front of her fucking husband.

Christ, Porter was going to up his game to include clowns after this shit.

"I should go," I mumbled without moving—and maybe, possibly, definitely giving her ass another squeeze.

Shit. She really had a great ass. I was still holding it and I already missed it.

"Tanner, honey," my blonde said, her voice dripping with sugar—and poison. "This is Greg, my soon-to-be *ex*-husband, and his *mistress,* Tammy, who came all the way down here today to share the joyous news that she is expecting his child." Her hand landed on my stomach, fisting the front of my shirt as she seethed, "Isn't that so exciting?"

This explanation definitely shed light on why my blonde was seconds away from mounting me in the middle of a children's carnival, but it only left me more confused.

"Wait, wait, wait. What?" I asked incredulous. "You cheated on my girl with *her*." Little Miss Forgettable's mouth fell open, so I quickly amended, "No offense, Tammy. I'm sure you're a lovely woman, but man, Greg. What the hell were you thinking?"

His jaw went hard, ticking at the hinges. "This doesn't involve you."

"Actually, I think you've got that backward." Holding his challenging stare, I gathered her tighter into my side. "From what I can tell, this doesn't involve *you* anymore."

My blonde peered up at me, her green eyes sparkling in the sunlight, a bright smile of appreciation softening her entire face—still not a fucking hint of recognition.

Yes. She was using me to make her ex jealous.

But she was using *me*, not celebrity Tanner Reese.

I shot her a wink that drew a blush. Fuck, that was cute.

She was hot, classy, *and* cute. Seriously, this Greg guy was a dumbass. Though I had every intention of capitalizing on his stupidity.

But, first, I had to help Porter.

"Listen, I need to get over there to cook the burgers, but—"

"You're dating the burger guy?" Greg asked like a pretentious prick. "Are you kidding me?"

I barked a laugh. "Wow, you are going to feel like an idiot when you look me up later." I paused, feeling a tad bit pretentious myself, but I didn't give the first fuck.

Gorgeous soon-to-be ex-wife aside, knocking up your mistress was seriously bad form. There was no use hiding my identity. She'd find out eventually. And if it came with the added bonus of making Douchebag Greg feel like the dumbass he was, then I was all for it.

"It's Tanner with two Ns, and Reese—R-E-E-S-E. Maybe you should write that down. You don't seem to be the brightest bulb." I tipped my chin to his new woman. "Again, no offense, Tammy."

"A little taken," she replied snottily.

I shrugged. "Meh. You were sleeping with a married man. You probably deserve it."

My blonde giggled, and when I flashed her a teasing grin, she returned it, adding a warm squeeze of gratitude around my hips. Still, not a hint of recognition on her face as she peered up at me like I was her hero.

Me. Not Tanner Reese.

After my last—and somewhat current—dating fiasco with Shana Beckwit, I'd sworn off women. Okay, fine. That's a lie. My mom and my attorney had made me swear off women for a while. And I'd made it, like, a solid eight weeks too. However, if this woman was newly single and back on the market, I wasn't about to pass up the first shot.

After glancing up to make sure the bastard was still watching, I fit my arms into the soft curves above her hips. "You were right. I did miss you. I mean, after you did that thing with your tongue last night." I closed my eyes and moaned to sell it. "Woman, that was something special."

"You were…pretty incredible too," she forced out, barely able to contain the humor.

"I was, wasn't I? What was your favorite part?"

She bit her bottom lip. "I…enjoyed it all."

I playfully rocked her from side to side. "No, come on. Be more specific or I won't be able to repeat it tonight." I smirked, quietly imagining all the very real and not-at-all made-up things I could do to her that would make her forget all about Douchebag Greg.

"Oh, for fuck's sake," he growled, but I never tore my gaze off her emerald eyes.

Seductively, she slid her hands up my arms, resting them on my pecs, her eyes heating even as her smile stretched. "Oh, honey, you can do whatever you'd like to me tonight. But don't you need to grill those burgers first?"

Shit. Fuck. Damn. I did.

I blew out a ragged breath, willing my libido to slow its roll. For now, anyway.

After retrieving my phone from my pocket, I lifted it in her direction and announced, "So, I got a new phone today."

She tilted her head to the side in question but took the phone. "Okay?"

"Because ya know…we've been going at it like rabbits for what, weeks—"

"Days," she corrected.

I nodded. "Right. *Days.* Obviously, after that much sex, I would have your number. But silly me. I broke my phone and now need you to program your digits in so I can call you when I'm on my way at, say…eight. You know, so I can do all those horrible, filthy things to you tonight. Again, tonight…I mean. Because, you know, I already did them to you last night." I swayed my head from side to side. "And probably the night before too. Maybe even the night before that. Shit, it's been so good all the days are just blending together. "

She grinned up at me, wide, sexy, and fully amused. "You mean they couldn't back your new phone up using the cloud? How badly was it damaged?"

Fuck. Me. I didn't even know her name yet, but this woman was going to end me. I had been rambling like a teenage boy about imaginary sex and she'd decided to give me shit.

She was hot, classy, cute…and a ballbuster.

I hadn't even known I had a type until that moment.

"Well…" I drawled. "Funny enough, an alligator ate it."

Her sculpted eyebrows shot up in surprise. "And that affects the cloud?"

"Well, yeah. Haven't you seen the warnings on the news? Something about their stomach lining and terrorists. One gator could singlehandedly take down our entire cellular infrastructure."

Her shoulders shook, but she managed to keep the laughter silent. "Gators and terrorists. That does sound scary."

Unable to stop myself, I leaned down, brushed my nose with hers, and whispered, "Terrifying."

Her smile faded, and her breath hitched. But much to my elation, she arched her back, pressing her curves deeper into my front.

Oh, fuck yeah.

Greg.

Was.

An.

Idiot.

As if he'd heard me, he let out a frustrated groan. "All

right, enough of this shit. Rita, we need to talk."

Rita.

My blonde's name was Rita.

Rita.

Rita.

Rita.

Oh, yeah. Lou Bega had definitely been onto something in "Mambo No. 5."

"No. We really don't need to talk," she retorted, stepping out of my reach.

I hated the loss immediately, but when she handed me back my phone and prattled off ten numbers I couldn't memorize fast enough, I got over it.

"Greg, you need to get your tail back over to the dunking booth," she said, floating with the grace of a dream in heels to a chair behind Rainbow Bright's table. "There's a line forming."

"I don't give a damn about the dunking booth." He took a long step toward her, one I immediately mirrored on instinct.

But Rita didn't seem to be the least bit threatened. With a bored, poised elegance, she sank down as if she were assuming her throne and not sitting in a cold, chipping metal folding chair. "That's funny because I don't give a damn about you, Tammy, or your precious little love child. Go away. Both of you. Live your life, and leave me out of it. Tammy, he's all yours." Pressing a perfectly manicured hand to her chest, she looked the woman right in the eye as she said, "My condolences."

I smiled, my chest filling with more pride than I'd known I could feel for a person I'd just met.

Getting cheated on was hard. Hell, I still resented Shelly

from when I was in the eleventh grade. But I couldn't imagine finding out your spouse had not only stepped out, but also created a child. And, despite the fact that she was using a fake relationship with me to torture him, she was doing it with such a classy, savage bitchiness that I couldn't help but be impressed.

Okay, and maybe a little scared.

But mainly impressed...and turned on.

Greg hung his head and pinched the bridge of his nose. "Rita, I—"

"Go," she clipped, shutting down all further conversations when a family walked up to the table.

Greg looked devastated as he watched her seamlessly slip into professional mode, smiling, welcoming, and explaining the ticketing system—all the while not paying him the first bit of attention.

Porter was going to kill me, but I waited until Greg had sulked away, Tammy hot on his heels, before leaving her. Rita was talking and laughing with the family, not giving me a chance to cut in to say goodbye.

It didn't matter though.

I had her number.

And we had a date scheduled for later that night.

So, with a smile on my face, I headed toward the plume of smoke that did not bode well for my Wagyu burgers.

I spotted Porter at the grill just in time to see a woman with long, black hair racing away from him.

SEVEN

Rita

"YOU SURE YOU DON'T WANT A DRINK?" I ASKED SIDNEY while twirling the stem of a wine glass between my thumb and forefinger.

"Nah. I'm good. I have to drive home. Though I need *you* to keep drinking so I can properly ply you with alcohol until you spill all the sordid details of your hot new guy."

I rolled my eyes.

Sidney Day had been my second best friend for years. I loved that woman, as did the majority of the male population. She was tall, dark, and bombshell even under her scrubs. But she was also happily married—if such a thing existed anymore—to an equally tall, dark, and gorgeous detective.

She was also Greg's head nurse, his current biggest enemy, and my partner-in-wine when Charlotte wasn't available. Which, it should be noted, was never—at least not voluntarily. However, Sidney was always up for an excuse to drink, eat cheese, and gossip. Which was why she'd shown up at my front door, holding two bottles of wine and the most elaborate charcuterie board I'd ever seen her make, demanding that I fill her in on my relationship with Atlanta's most eligible bachelor—Tanner Reese.

"I already told you there are no sordid details. I didn't even know who he was until after he walked away."

Yeah. I was an idiot.

While I wasn't exactly a fan of The Food Channel, I was—and always would be—a fan of beautiful, muscular men, and I made it my business as a woman to learn the names, faces, and abdominals of those included in that elite subsection of the population.

I'd seen Tanner doing shirtless cooking spots on daytime talk shows, such as whipping up easy-breezy tabbouleh with the likes of Ellen. I'd also seen him, shirtless and ripped, on the cover of magazines at the grocery store.

Yet it had taken three women stopping him to pose for pictures on his way to the grill for his identity to finally click in my head.

I'd never felt like such an ass in my life. He probably thought I was insane. And the saddest thing was he wouldn't have been wrong in that assumption. I was losing my freaking mind. I didn't know what I'd been thinking, grabbing him like I had. Asking him to play along with my stupid game to make Greg jealous. But he'd been so sweet about it that, for a few minutes, I'd forgotten we were playing a game at all.

"Girl, that's another thing," Sidney said. "Do we need to get your eyes checked?" She curled her long legs underneath her on the couch, pointedly issuing me an are-you-freaking-crazy slow blink that made me giggle. "I mean, you *saw* him, right? And he touched your ass. And he held you with his bulging biceps. Oh my God, Rita. Tell me what his abs felt like."

I shifted uncomfortably, crossing and uncrossing my socked feet on the coffee table. "They felt like abs." *Gloriously rippled, contoured muscles made in Heaven*. I kept that to myself and focused on suppressing a memory-induced moan.

After Porter had taken off after Charlotte—who had not surprisingly refused to treat his son—I'd been forced to help Tanner with lunch.

Luckily, it had helped sell our relationship to Greg, who had been staring daggers at Tanner from the dunking booth.

Even luckier, Tanner had been so busy cleaning up the mess his brother had made at the grill that he hadn't talked much.

Then I got even luckier when, an hour later, I was able to duck out of the Fling without anyone noticing.

And then, luckiest of all, I found out that *The Golden Girls* was available on Hulu, so I spent the afternoon in bed, preparing for my future as the single and jaded Dorothy Zbornak.

"I don't understand," Sidney said. "I heard that he was super into you and he went off on Greg for cheating and everything."

"Who told you that?"

She shrugged. "Beth."

"And how did Beth hear… Wait, she still talks to Tammy?"

Her chocolate-brown eyes crinkled with apology. "Several

of the nurses do. And word travels fast when it comes to you dating a fine-ass man with his own TV show. I'm not going to lie, I love Kent, but I'd give up sex for a year if he'd learn how to cook."

"I'm not sure that should be your selling point when you try to convince him to attend culinary school." I tipped my glass up for a long sip while mentally crossing Beth off my Christmas card list. Though I did enjoy the fact that it had looked like Tanner was super into me.

She eyed me suspiciously "So there's *really* nothing going on with you and Tanner Reese?"

I set my glass on the end table and swiped a piece of Asiago off the wooden board. Nothing soothed an aching soul like cheese. Except maybe chocolate. And wine. And sushi. Okay, fine, and carbs in general.

"Sorry to disappoint, but my interactions with the mystical shirtless beast were limited to me throwing myself at him, sexually assaulting him, and him taking enough pity on me to help me torture Greg. However, the good news is, unlike Greg, who I'll have to see again to sign our divorce papers, and Tammy, who I will no doubt run into one day while she's carting around Greg's spawn, I'll never have to face Tanner again. Though, on the off chance I do, I did check his Instagram when I got home and he hadn't posted a pic of himself at the police station, filing a restraining order against me, so I think I might be in the clear."

"Damn," she whispered, absently lifting a grape to her mouth before thinking better of it and exchanging it for a cracker with Brie. "I was hoping you were keeping a hot, blond secret from me."

"I should probably get a divorce before I start keeping a hot, blond secret."

"Fuck that. Greg didn't offer you that courtesy. You sure as hell don't owe it to him in return."

The knife in my stomach twisted. "No. He didn't, did he?"

She flashed me a tight smile, and then we both fell silent. She went for another cracker, while I stared into space, my mind drifting back to the Fling, only instead of thinking about Greg and stupid pregnant Tammy, it was Tanner who came to mind.

His smile—warm and playful.

His eyes—warm and mischievous.

His arms—warm and comfortable.

Shaking off the memory, I moved for a subject change. "So, what's new with you?"

She finally gave the poor discarded grape a try, frowning before following it up with a pinch of mini chocolate chips. "Meh. Not much. Kent got a new surround sound system yesterday. It's become his sole mission in life to see if he can turn it up loud enough to rupture his eardrums. I left him a copy of the alphabet in sign language before I left in case he was finally successful while I was gone."

I let out a loud laugh. "Wow, how thoughtful of you."

"I know. I know. Wife of the year."

We both laughed until my phone on the table beside me lit up, catching my attention. I'd turned the ringer off after Greg had texted me for the twentieth time, stating that we needed to talk. The man was making me crazy. I'd blocked his number, so now, his messages were coming from random email addresses and what I assumed were a zillion dollars in prepaid phones.

Unknown: Hey sexy, what's your address? I'm walking out the door in five.

Picking it up, I rolled my eyes and muttered, "Fucking Greg." Though I couldn't figure out why he'd asked for my address. With my luck, he'd confused my number with the mistress he was cheating on his pregnant mistress with.

Sidney leaned toward me to see the screen. "What the hell is wrong with that man? Doesn't he need to be out helping Tammy shop for clothes with elastic waistbands, hemorrhoid cream, and nursing pads for her leaking nipples?"

I smiled huge at the thought.

And *that* was why I loved Sidney Day. Charlotte might not have been the kind of woman to help me build a dummy and burn it in effigy.

But Sidney absolutely was.

Me: Try searching for I Will Neuter You in your GPS then take your first left at the cliff and drive off of it. M'kay. Thanks.

Sidney fell over to the side laughing, and I was quick to join her. I shouldn't have responded. I'd been strong and steadfast about ignoring him the last few weeks, but two glasses of wine were currently roaring through my veins, not only making me a little brave, but a lot bitchy too. Less than a minute later, my phone lit with another message.

Unknown: No such luck. The only thing that showed up for I Will Neuter You was a restaurant in Wisconsin, which I have to admit I find rather disturbing.

"Oh, hell no!" Sidney dove to grab my phone, but I snatched it out of her reach. "Give me that. This fool does not get to make jokes now."

"Sid, stop." I giggled. "Yes. We hate him, and we will take that out on the voodoo doll you constructed including actual hair you cut from the back of his head when he wasn't looking, but he's technically still your boss. I know you're planning that cruise to the Bahamas this summer. Kent will frame me for murder if I get you fired."

She righted herself on the couch and glared at me. "Damn it, I need to find another job."

"We both do. But until then, I'm in charge of sending Greg scathing text messages."

She groaned. "Fiiiine."

Me: You know what I find disturbing? You texting me all freaking day. We are over. You made your bed. Don't think you can come crawling back to me because you've got fleas.

Unknown: All day? This is the first time I've… Oh, wait. You don't think it could have been that terrorist alligator, do you? Dammit, I told you they were dangerous.

It was the most ludicrous, nonsense text he had ever written.

And then it wasn't.

"Oh my God," I breathed, a tsunami of realization slamming into me, pinning me in place, and stealing my breath. Chills exploded across my skin.

Greg hadn't written that text at all, but suddenly, I knew

exactly who had. If I tried hard enough, I could still feel his strong arms wrapped around me and that million-dollar grin aimed down at me like a spotlight.

My stomach dipped as I imagined his long fingers gliding over the screen of his phone as he'd typed that message out to me.

To *me.*

Tanner Reese was texting *me.*

For ninety-nine percent of the population, this would have been the greatest day of their lives.

For me, it felt like someone had set the room on fire, my whole body heating with embarrassment.

"What?" Sidney asked, once again sidling up close to read the screen as message after message started rolling in.

Tanner: I should probably come over and do a full sweep to make sure those texts didn't cause a security breach in the cloud.

Tanner: I'm not sure if I told you this, but the only weapon we as a country have against the terrorist alligators is a naked woman.

Tanner: Really, it's our patriotic duty as Americans to see this thing through.

Tanner: Obviously, I think it would be best if we grabbed some dinner first. A person can't go to naked war against terrorist alligators on an empty stomach.

Tanner: But first, I'm gonna need that address.

"What the hell is that dumbass talking about?" she asked. "Is he having some kind of stroke?"

He wanted my address. Holy shit. Tanner freaking Reese wanted my address.

Sure, I'd given him my number, but I'd thought it was all part of the show. I'd never considered while I was downing a pint of ice cream and watching Blanche insult Rose that he'd actually use it.

In case I hadn't mentioned it before…he was *Tanner freaking Reese*!

Women around the world would compete Spartan-style to land themselves on his radar. And he wanted *my* address because he wanted to take *me* to dinner before *we* got naked and did our patriotic duty of fighting terrorist alligators *together*. Yes, I knew how stupid that last part sounded, but the first part included the words naked and together. That was more than enough to send my nerves into a frenzy.

Tanner: By the way, this is Tanner. Not your bag of burning manure ex Gary.

Sidney gasped, sucking all the oxygen out of the room. But it didn't matter. I wasn't breathing anyway.

Tanner: Or was it George?
Tanner: Grant?
Tanner: Whatever. It doesn't matter. Soooo… Address?

I was still staring at the phone, my jaw hanging open and my heart in my throat, when Sidney shouted like he could hear her via text.

"Three Fifty-One Stony Bridge Drive!"

"Hey!" I objected, saying it like he really had heard her and, instead of giving my address to the most gorgeous man I had ever laid eyes on, she'd given it to a serial killer who wanted to wear my skin for a suit.

"Hey, what?" Grabbing my shoulders, she gave me a firm shake. "What the hell are you waiting for? Give the man your address."

I glanced at the phone then back to her, repeating the process as my mind struggled to catch up. But nothing was making sense.

He was *Tanner Reese*—mouth-watering, larger-than-life television personality who was so mouth watering and larger than life that people referred to him with *both* names.

And I was Rita. Just boring Rita. Yes, I was attractive—fabulous, really. But no one called me Rita Laughlin. And short of the one time I was interviewed by the local news, I'd never been on TV.

Two-named Tanner Reese had no reason to want anything to do with one-named Rita.

"Why does he want my address?" I breathed.

"Uhhh… Best I can tell"—she reached over my shoulder and used a finger to scroll up a few messages—"to take you to dinner, get you naked, and then wrestle alligators. Which I'm hoping is y'all's secret code word for hot, sweaty sex." She gave me a teasing side-eye. "You little liar, pretending you don't have any sordid details about Tanner. Psh."

I ignored her and kept staring at the phone, waiting for the *Haha, just kidding! This is actually Greg* to pop up.

In that moment, I didn't know what I was feeling.

Excitement?

Disbelief?

Flattery?

An unsettling amount of lingering embarrassment?

Some wicked combination of all of the above?

But no matter what, I couldn't convince my fingers to type a response. What the hell would I even say? In the two whole weeks since I'd shut the door on my marriage with Greg, I'd never mentally prepared for the possibility that a man would ask me out again so soon.

And it was safe to say I'd never, never-never-never, thought that man would be Tanner Reese.

If I responded now, my knee-jerk reaction would be practical, something like, *Oh, honey, you are too sweet. But I'm not ready for anything like that. Best of luck to you in the future.*

It would have been the safest option for my already bruised ego and heart. I hadn't been able to go toe-to-toe with a mere mortal like Greg. What the hell did I think was going to happen with a demigod like Tanner Reese?

But the more I thought about it, my lips pulling up into a smile from just thinking about him, the more I wanted to take that risk.

Screw Greg. I'd spent years trying to be the woman he wanted me to be. And look where it had gotten me. Maybe I wanted to be chewed up, devoured, and spit out by a man like Tanner. As I remembered when he'd held me against his hard chest and brushed his nose against mine, chills radiated over me from head to toe. It kind of made me want to scream out Three Fifty-One Stony Bridge Drive too.

Before I had the chance to decide, I got another text.

Tanner: P.S. I know you're reading this. You might be the last person in the world who has read receipt turned on. So, on the off chance that you are doing something filthy that requires the use of two hands, I'm going to call instead. Feel free to put me on speaker and carry on.

My whole body jerked when the phone started ringing. "Oh shit! Oh shit Oh shit. *Oh shit*!"

"Yesssss!" Sidney hissed, her hands in fists and pumping in the most ridiculous victory dance. It made me super happy for her sake that she was already married to a hot man.

"What do I do?" I cried.

Casually sliding her finger across the screen, she accepted the call and smiled. "You say hello."

"What the hell!" I whisper-yelled, shooting her a glare that I hope scalded her flawless skin.

"You can thank me later with all the sordid details." Using my hand, she guided the phone up to my ear. "But first, give the man your address."

With no other choice, I closed my eyes, steeled myself for what was possibly the best or worst decision of my life—excluding marrying Greg, of course—and nervously croaked, "Hello."

EIGHT

Tanner

"OH, THANK GOD. I WAS STARTING TO THINK THE alligator already got to you," I joked, tossing my phone onto the passenger seat when my car switched our conversation to hands-free. "Listen, I'm pulling out now. What's your address?"

"I…uh… Yeah. Look, Tanner, I'm not sure I should—" I heard some rustling on the other end then a muffled, "Ow, shit. Stop pinching me! Ow. Ow. Ow. Stop!"

My head snapped back and my eyes narrowed as if they could see what I was hearing. "Is…everything okay?"

"Oh… Yeah. Sorry, my friend is here. But she was just leaving. Hang on."

I got more muted and urgent chatter, including what sounded like a woman yelling something about a stony bridge. There was a slam and then complete silence.

I glanced at my dash to see if the call had been dropped.

"Rita? You still there?"

"I'm here!" she chirped. "Okay, sorry about that. She has some issues. If you know what I mean."

I did *not* know what she meant, but we'd have plenty of time for her to explain over dinner. "Listen, can I get that address?"

"My address?" she parroted as though it were the first time I'd asked and not—literally—the fourth in so many minutes. "Tanner, I don't think that's a good idea."

"Then you would be wrong because it's an excellent idea." I sighed, stopping at the large gate at the entrance of my property, and leaned back in my seat.

It had been a while since I'd had to convince a woman to go out with me. Hard-to-get was a game I had no time or desire to play. This was probably why I ended up with overly eager nutcases. Maybe it was time for a change. For as many times as I'd thought about Rita over the course of the day, I'd be willing to make an exception for her.

I'd done some digging after Rita had tucked tail and snuck away while I was still on the second lunch wave. I could barely contain my laughter when I'd caught sight of her trotting away in those sexy red heels. With pink cheeks and shifty eyes, one would have thought she was headed to rob a bank, not making a break from a children's carnival.

According to the countless women who had stopped by for pictures, autographs, or a flirty chat, her name was Rita Laughlin, soon-to-be ex-wife of Greg Laughlin, balding, boring, and completely average MD. She had been born in Midtown, gone to college at Emory, and married the douchebag seven years earlier. She currently lived in a large and well-decorated house in Buckhead that the majority of my new friends hoped she got when she "took him to the cleaners."

To hear them tell it, she was kind, generous, and honest to a fault. *Definitely not bad qualities.*

She loved sushi, wine, cheese, and yoga. I hated sushi, but three out of four weren't bad. What? Yoga was great for my core.

And some woman named Beth had told me a riveting story about Rita's drunken dance moves at last year's Christmas party. From the way she'd told the story, I was positive it was supposed to be insulting. But what my good pal Beth didn't know was that not only had I seen her conspiring with Tramp Tammy before heading my way, the idea of Rita dancing—drunk or not—was far from a turn-off. *Huge fucking stamp of approval.*

Smiling at the thought, I turned left. I lived at least twenty minutes from Buckhead. This gave me a full twenty minutes to work my magic.

"Yes, your address, babe. We made a date for eight, remember? I'm nothing if not punctual."

"It's currently eight fifteen."

My gaze jumped to the clock. Damn, how had it gotten so late? I really shouldn't have taken that call from my attorney while I was getting dressed. Nothing good ever came from an after hours, eight-hundred-dollar phone call. And since this particular call had been about Shana's latest bullshit, it was even worse than I'd expected. For half a second, I'd considered calling Rita and canceling, but she was a far better distraction than drowning myself in a bottle of Belvedere while Porter cracked jokes about my God-awful taste in women.

Scrambling for an excuse that didn't make me look like a total jackass, I said, "You didn't specify Daylight Savings Time or not." Yep. That was the best I could come up with. Maybe this was why I didn't like women who played the hard-to-get game. I sucked at it.

"Does a person *need* to specify that?"

"Apparently."

"Riiiight," she drawled. "Anyway, maybe I should take a rain check on tonight. My life is kind of a mess right now."

"Come on, Rita. You can't get a rain check. It's not even raining."

She laughed softly. "You know what I mean. You're sweet, honey. And I do appreciate you letting me accost you today. I also would like to formally apologize for that. That wasn't right."

"It wasn't wrong, either. You won't find me complaining when I pick you up in a little while—this being after you give me your address."

She sighed. "Tanner, don't be silly. You're sweet, really. But I'm letting you off the hook."

"Who says I want to be let off the hook? You agreed to a date tonight. So I'm taking you up on that legally binding verbal agreement."

"Legally binding verbal agreement?" she asked, incredulous.

Shaking my head at myself, I turned onto the highway. Eighteen more minutes. I had better get to work. "Okay, fine. Let's say this isn't a date but rather just me taking you out to dinner to say thank you for the very pleasurable accosting you gave me today. No hooks. No semantics. Just dinner. Though, just so you know, I won't take being further accosted off the table. But totally your call."

She laughed again, and my chest swelled as I flexed my hands around the steering wheel.

Oh, yeah. I was making headway.

"I don't know. Today was such a train wreck."

"Excluding the part where you met me."

"After the ass I made of myself, it was probably *including* meeting you. You were so nice to come cook for us today, and that was how I treated you. On behalf of the whole office, I really want to say thanks again to you and Porter for not only donating the food, but also your time. I heard rave reviews."

Shit, she was changing the subject. Next up would be saying goodnight. Then hanging up without giving me that address. *Time to turn it up a notch.*

"I wouldn't go so far as to say the *whole* office. I doubt your ex is thanking me for anything right about now. I dropped three hundred bucks on tickets for the dunking booth while my guys were cleaning up. You know, I was never much of a baseball player, but I kept him in the water a fair amount."

She sucked in a sharp breath. "Shut. Up. You did not."

I smiled smugly even though she couldn't see it. "I sure as hell did. It was a charity thing, right?"

"Oh my God, Tanner." Her melodic laugh drifted across the phone, causing my mouth to stretch even wider. "You bought twelve hundred balls and threw them at my ex-husband?"

"Well, it wasn't nearly as heroic as that. There was a cage protecting his face. But if it helps at all, I got five in a row and pretended I was waterboarding him for you."

"Wow. Who knew unsanctioned torture methods could be so romantic?"

God, I loved that she got my sense of humor.

"I try. I try," I replied.

"I would have given anything to see his face. You know he seriously believes we're dating, right?"

"Well, that's fantastic because we *are* dating. Or at least I'm trying to take you on a date. And as soon as you give me your address, I'll show you the pictures I took too."

She gasped. "You took pictures?"

"Yep." I popped the P. "Pictures or it didn't happen, right?"

I heard some rustling on the other end of the line like maybe she was crawling under blankets, and while bed was my second favorite place in the world—second only to being inside a woman while inside said bed—I didn't see her issuing an invitation for me to join her. "Did you just get in bed?"

"If, by bed, you mean carrying a glass of wine out back to swing in the hammock, maybe."

I bit my bottom lip, my head falling back against the headrest. For most men, this would have been an innocuous statement. But for a hammock connoisseur like myself, this was the normal guy equivalent of her saying that she liked to give blowjobs during halftime.

"You have a hammock out back?"

There was a delay in her response, which was followed by a subtle kiss of her lips on what I assumed was a wine glass. "Don't knock it until you try it. It's one of the most underrated luxuries in outdoor furniture."

"Oh, I'm not knocking anything. Rope or quilted?"

"Mayan, actually."

"Oh, sweet heavenly baby Jesus, she's beautiful and knows her hammocks. I've never been so turned on in my life."

She giggled, pausing for another sip. "You know, if you leaked this hammock fetish to the press, you could probably increase demand by five million percent and singlehandedly lower the country's unemployment rate."

Okay, so at some point during the day, she'd figured out who I was.

But! Even with this knowledge, she was trying to *avoid* a date with me and was not elbow-deep in planning our televised wedding. This was a definite plus in my book.

"Yeah, but then, when I talked to beautiful women like yourself, I'd have no idea if the hammock was your idea or a ploy to impress me."

"Jeez, that's sad, Tanner," she said, her sweet Southern accent like a wave rolling over my name.

I'd meant it as a joke, but it was the absolute truth when it came to dating. Once early on in my career, I'd done a rapid-fire interview about my personal life. One of the questions had been: What would your ideal woman order on the first date? Truth be told, the only thing I hoped my ideal woman would order was something *she* wanted. I didn't factor into that. But I'd been on my last question in my last interview of the last day of a month-long press tour. My face had hurt from fake smiling, I'd been in desperate need of a shower, a smoke, and sleep, and my mind had been mush, so I'd prattled off the first thing that had come to mind: shrimp and grits.

That one little answer somehow made it onto my Wiki page, and after that, every woman I'd taken out ordered shrimp and grits. One of them even had a shellfish allergy and nearly ended up in the hospital. And this insanity was not limited to women outside of the spotlight.

I'd once gone on a date with America's princess of pop, Levee Williams. We'd hit it off at a charity event. For one of the most famous women in the world, she was a surprisingly nice girl, gorgeous, and funny as all get out. But the first time I took her out? One guess what she ordered.

I was at the end of my rope with dating and lost my freaking mind before storming out like an asshole. That night, as I was reporting shrimp and fucking grits as an error to Wiki, I noticed that her page listed it as her favorite food. I'd never had the balls to contact her again, and I once hid behind a palm tree on Rodeo Drive when I heard the clamoring of paparazzi calling her name. But that's neither here nor there.

In short, while finding a woman was all too easy, dating was hard.

But that wasn't about to stop me from trying with Rita.

"Yeah," I replied. "You know what else is sad? Having to beg a woman for her address so you can pick her up and take her to Lenox Circle Station."

"Shut the front door," she breathed.

Warmth filled my chest as I smiled. "I will not. Then we wouldn't be able to get to Lenox."

The Porterhouse was one of the most sought-after restaurants in Atlanta. We were always packed, and The Tannerhouse hadn't even opened yet and it was booked a year out. But Lenox Circle Station was where Atlanta royalty dined. And I happened to have a huge in—like, say, my best friend being the chef and him owing me so many favors because his wife loved me that I was practically drowning in them. It wasn't usually my scene, what with my neck being allergic to ties and all. But it's not like I could have taken a woman like Rita, who wore a little black dress and pearls to a kids' carnival, anywhere else for our first date. I'd considered cooking her a private dinner at The Tannerhouse but decided against it on the off chance that she asked me to make shrimp and grits and I was forced to throw myself into the oven.

"Holy shit. You got us reservations at Lenox? I heard they turned Beyoncé away last month."

I barked a laugh. "Did I mention I got the chef's table in the kitchen for us?"

"Oh. My. God. Shut the front door!" she exclaimed in a high-pitch squeal. "Is this your idea of foreplay? Because I am so okay with it."

"Imagine how I felt with all the hammock talk."

She didn't just laugh—she *laughed.* Rich and melodic, filled with honest-to-God amusement that couldn't be faked. And in a world where everything was faked for my benefit, it was the most intoxicating sound I'd ever heard.

I passed the first exit for Buckhead and instead headed toward The Commons, which were anything but common. They were lush houses on Lake Oconee. If she had a hammock out back, I was banking on the fact that there was something in her backyard that she wanted to overlook. At least that's why I lounged on my balcony.

"Say yes," I urged.

"I don't know, Tanner."

"Rita. Stop thinking and say yes. It's dinner. Just dinner."

She let out a resigned sigh that shot intoxicating victory through my veins. "What time do we have to be there?" she asked. “Because it’s going to take me a solid six hours to get ready for Lenox.”

I flicked my gaze to the clock; it was now eight thirty. “Eight. But as long as we’re there by nine, it should be fine.”

“No!” she cried. “I’m in yoga pants and a tank top. I’ll never be ready in time.”

“I guess I could try to reschedule,” I quasi-lied. Kevin wasn’t going to turn me away—ever—so there would be no *trying* about it. But I *really* didn’t want to reschedule.

“I’m warning you. It’s not going to be pretty, Tanner. But no way I’m passing up an opportunity to sit at the chef’s table at Lenox.”

“Or a date with me, right?” I teased.

“Yeah. Sure. That too.”

My face split into an epic grin.

She let out a huff. “Okay, I live in The Commons at Buckhead.” *Bingo.* “Three Fifty-One Stony Bridge Drive. How long do you think it will take you to get here from your house?”

I chewed on the inside of my cheek as I turned into her neighborhood. “My house? Like maybe…twenty minutes.”

“Okay. It’s going to be touch and go, but I’ll do my best. See you soon.”

She had no idea just how soon that really was.

I could have driven around, giving her time to get dressed. But then I would have missed seeing her life-altering ass in yoga pants. I didn’t know Rita well, but I had enough experience with women to know she would probably kill me for showing up early.

Meh. Worth it.

Two minutes later, I was laughing to myself as I walked

up to the navy-blue door of her brick two-story home. It was nice, in the newer part of The Commons right on the lake. Clearly, Greg did well for himself.

I did better.

After straightening my skinny baby-blue tie and buttoning my gray Dior Homme jacket, I cracked my neck, shoved one hand into my pocket, and knocked.

She opened the door in the next beat.

I blinked.

Once.

Twice.

Thrice.

If I'd wanted a show, that was exactly what I was getting.

My mouth fell open as I gave her a very slow head-to-toe—then back again. "What the hell kind of witch-craftery is this?"

Note to self: Not the best way to greet a woman I'd like to potentially see naked one day.

Her green eyes glittered like emeralds as she smoothed her hands over the shallow curves at her hips. "What? What's wrong with it?"

Nothing. There was absolutely nothing wrong with it.

She looked spectacular. And *that* was what was wrong with it. It was like she'd walked out of hair and makeup on the set of a classic Hollywood film. Every one of her short hairs were in place, curling at her chin as if they too were drawn to her plump, crescent lips. Her eye makeup was subtle, but her pink cheeks and long lashes carried all the drama. She was just as classic and gorgeous as she had been at the Fling. Maybe more so in that ruby-red strapless dress. It was simple in the way that allowed her body to be the star. It hugged her large breasts before flaring out at the bottom, the pleated hem flirting with her shins.

My mouth dried as my gaze made it down to black, mile-high, strappy heels, which still left her several inches shorter than I was.

I was usually an ass man. Though I could understand the appeal of a nice set of legs.

But, on this woman, while all of that was spot-on, it was the idea of tracing my tongue over her exposed collarbone and up her delicate neck that forced me to distract myself by mentally converting grams to ounces.

Just kidding. I hadn't measured anything since culinary school. But you get the point.

"Holy fuck, you look incredible," I told her.

A bright white smile split her lips. "I could say the same about you. But I won't because I think you already know."

I scowled teasingly. "You said you were wearing yoga pants and a tank top."

She shrugged, tipping her head to the side. "And you said you were twenty minutes away."

"Did you willingly start our soul-searing, blazing-romance-of-the-ages with a lie?"

She lifted a single manicured nail in the air. "Whoa, easy there, Nicholas Sparks. First of all, we are just going to dinner at Lenox. I'm going to need you to tuck that soul searing in your back pocket for a while. This is not a date, remember? Secondly." She turned her finger toward her face. "This is today's makeup and hair and I literally just stepped into the dress and shoes one minute ago. So no lying involved." She cocked her head to the side. "At least not on my side."

I stepped toward her, not even waiting for her to invite me in.

Her body got tight and she inhaled sharply when my hands landed on her hips. For the briefest second, I couldn't decide if this reaction was in surprise or discomfort. We'd had more physical contact earlier in the day, but the last thing I wanted was to misread the situation.

"Rita," I whispered.

Her head tipped back, the color of her cheeks now matching her dress. "Yeah."

It was a thoughtless response *and* an answer to my unspoken question. In the next blink, she swayed into me, her hands resting on my pecs.

Oh. Hell. Yes.

I dipped low, and sweeping my lips across her cheek, softly stated, "I wasn't lying. I was just hoping to catch you in yoga pants. It sounded sexy, but I have to say… This dress and those heels… Mmm. They are definitely better."

Her fingers spasmed, digging into my chest, and the breath she'd drawn in exited her lungs on a sweet sigh. "Okay, but I need ten minutes to touch up my makeup."

I leaned away so I could see her face again, my eyes going straight to her mouth as I rasped, "Okay then. Point me to the hammock."

NINE

Rita

I COULD DO THIS.

I could so do this.

At least that's what I was chanting to myself less than an hour later, while sitting at the chef's table at the Lenox Circle Station with *Tanner Reese*, trying not to freak out.

This was after *Tanner Reese* had spent fifteen minutes chilling in *my* hammock before kissing *me* on the cheek and telling *me* I looked gorgeous, then guiding me to his Mercedes with his large hand gently resting on the small of *my* back, opening the door for *me*, rounding the hood while digging the keys from his pocket thus giving me a David Beckham worthy side profile of his ass in that suit, and then folding in to drive *me* to said chef's table at the Lenox Circle Station.

It took every ounce of willpower I possessed not to text that enormously long run-on sentence to every person in my phone, including Greg and Tammy.

Instead, I took a sip of wine.

Adrenaline and excitement had long since burned off the bottle I'd consumed with Sidney, causing a breach in my alcohol-induced armor and allowing my nerves free reign on my date.

Holy shit. I was on a date. I'd made him promise that it wasn't a date, but we both knew it was.

With *Tanner Reese*.

I took another long sip of wine and glanced around. Our table for two that evening was tucked away in the corner of the kitchen. The space was small, only a short counter, a four-burner gas stovetop, and an oven were across from us so we could watch the chef cook, something that I assumed was more for my benefit than Tanner's. He was probably more accustomed to being the one doing the cooking rather than watching.

There was a flurry of activity happening around the corner in the long galley kitchen we'd walked through when we'd arrived. It was very much what I'd assumed the back of a restaurant would be like, the sounds of metal clanging, people calling out orders, the occasional shout. But in our little nook in the back, we were secluded from the action. Tanner had asked me if the table was okay, stating that he'd specially requested for the chef's table to be moved so we could have some privacy without all the heat and noise. And knowing that Tanner wanted said privacy with me, I thought it was better than okay.

Our waiter and wine steward had stopped by several times in the few minutes since we'd arrived, but I'd yet to meet the chef.

"You like wine," Tanner said with a devilish smirk from across the small table.

I set the stem of my glass on the crisp, white tablecloth. "I haven't met a wine I didn't like."

He chuckled, quieting when Kevin Story—another man who was double-name worthy—came strolling over in a pair of chef whites, wiping his hand on a towel at his hip before extending it for a shake.

"Mr. Ab-tastic, so glad you could finally join us."

Tanner rose from his seat and clasped his hand. "Mr. One Beer Too Many, I'd apologize for being late, but I was busy denying your wife's request for naked selfies again." His playful, blue eyes flicked to mine. "I'm kidding. I'd never send naked selfies. Partially because I'm a man of morals, and partially because I don't want to be the one who clues Jade in on the fact that real men have two balls unlike her husband here."

Quietly laughing, I stood up as Tanner waved a finger between us.

"Rita, this is Kevin Story, my mortal enemy or best friend depending on the day you ask me. Kevin, this gorgeous woman is Rita Laughlin. Please keep the drool in your mouth. Even if you weren't married to a woman you don't deserve, Rita would be completely out of your league."

Kevin chuckled and extended his hand. "Nice to meet you, Rita Laughlin."

I flinched at the use of Greg's last name, but no way I was wading into the mess that was my life in front of Tanner's friend to explain that, as soon as I could get a judge to recognize my divorce, I was changing my name back to Hartley.

"Nice to meet you too," I replied. "I've heard such amazing

things about your restaurant."

"They're all lies," Tanner hissed. "This place should be condemned."

Kevin boomed a loud laugh that echoed off the stainless-steel equipment. "How does a woman like you put up with this asshole?"

"I… Uh, well, this is our first date. So I'm not sure yet."

"Oh, so it's a date now?" Tanner smarted.

I rolled my eyes. "We both know it's a date."

Mischief lit his face. "Yeah, I know. I just really enjoyed hearing you say it."

Kevin's handsome, but aging, face crinkled at all the corners. "Your *first* date?" He swung a disbelieving gaze to Tanner. "And you brought her here? So I could witness this?"

"Kev, don't," he groaned.

"Don't what?" I asked, flicking my gaze back and forth between the two men.

Suddenly, Kevin lifted his hand up to his ear, pressing two fingers against the shell as if he were wearing an earpiece. "Oh, wait. I think someone in the kitchen is trying to reach me. What's that you say? We have an unexpected menu change tonight?"

Tanner's head fell back between his shoulders as he stared up at the ceiling. "Dammit, Kev, stop. I actually like this one."

Warmth settled in my stomach. He actually liked this one. *This one* being me.

Kevin's only acknowledgement was to use his other hand to pat Tanner on his toned stomach as he kept talking to no one. "Yes, okay, I can hear you. Go ahead. So, in addition to the chef's menu tonight, we are adding shrimp and grits as an entrée. Did I hear that correctly?"

"You are such a prick," Tanner muttered.

"Okay, I got it." Kevin dropped his hand, disconnecting the imaginary call he'd been on, and asked, "So, Rita, any interest in shrimp and black truffle grits tonight? Mine are world famous."

Tanner's head snapped up, those Caribbean-blue eyes landing on me with a tangible weight that sent a chill down my spine. For the first time since I'd met him, the happy-go lucky guy with an arsenal of wit and humor was gone. Honestly, he looked nervous.

And it made me nervous.

His brows drew together as he held my stare. The palpable tension in the air was lost on his friend, smiling at me like a used car salesman.

Four eyes, all of them blue, two of them heart-stopping, bored into me as I tried to figure out the answer to a question that I somehow knew was far bigger than what I would be eating for dinner.

Greg loved shrimp and grits, so I'd cooked them a lot. And through the years, I'd gotten quite good at it. I imagined Kevin Story's would be better, but regardless of why this question was so important, there was only one answer.

"Thank you, but I don't like grits. I know. I know. How does a woman born and raised in the great state of Georgia not like grits? And I honestly don't know. My mother spent a lot of years attempting to sway me, but it never took. Now, if you manage to master the art of shrimp and black truffle Cream of Wheat, I'd be interested in getting the recipe."

Kevin's smile grew exponentially, but Tanner just stood

there staring at me, his chest rising and falling with heavy breaths.

Shit.

Clearly, I'd made the wrong choice. "Look, I—"

"Marry her," Kevin said without tearing his eyes off me.

My head snapped back. "I'm sorry. What?"

Tanner nodded, his eyes glued to me. "I'll send you an invitation." He became unstuck and moved toward me, ushering me back into my chair before taking his across from me. There was still no smile on his face or the lively flicker in his eyes I'd become accustomed to, but his shoulders sagged with visible relief.

Relief I did not share. "Marry who? Because you know I'm kinda sorta already—"

"Relax," he whispered, reaching across the table to cover my hand with his own.

It was a simple gesture, and like most things with Tanner, it was warm and entirely nice. And for reasons I'd never be able to explain outside of magic or hypnotism, it soothed the nerves ricocheting inside me almost immediately.

"Tell me, Rita," Kevin said. "Has Tanner cooked anything for you yet?"

I licked my lips and tore my attention off my date. "No. We actually just met today."

"Excellent." He winked. "I might have a shot at impressing you now."

He looked at Tanner, who was still staring at me, but his lips were quirked arrogantly, a flirty dimple making an earth-quaking appearance.

With his hands linked behind his back, Kevin bent in

something of a half bow. "If you'll excuse me, I'm going to wash up. I'll be back to get started in a moment."

Confused, amused, and thankful for the space, I straightened in my chair when he disappeared around the corner.

"Wow," I breathed, looking back at Tanner. "You were not wrong. I can't decide if you two were mortal enemies or best friends today."

He turned sideways in his chair, crossing his legs knee to ankle before lifting his wine to his lips. But he did all of this without releasing my hand. "I'll tell you another time when I'm not fighting the urge to kiss you."

My breath hitched, and heat bloomed in my face—among other places.

Tanner Reese wanted to kiss me.

And God, did I want to let him.

When his sexy smolder became too much, I cut my gaze to the table, unable to hide my smile as I polished off my wine. Tanner was quick to refill it, and by the time I met his gaze again, his one-sided smirk had reappeared.

Moments later, Kevin reemerged, but unlike the first time, it was all business. And as the sounds of pans sizzling and the scent of garlic and rosemary filled the air, Tanner got down to business as well.

"So, tell me about yourself, Rita." He leaned back in his chair, his hand sadly sliding off mine.

I shouldn't have wanted it back as badly as I did.

I was a married woman for Pete's sake.

Yeah, married to a man who cheated on me and got his mistress pregnant, I reminded myself. Greg and I were done. I was allowed to enjoy myself with the company of another man if I wanted to. And I currently wanted to do a whole hell of a lot of enjoying with Tanner Reese.

My stomach fluttered, and I took another sip of wine. "What do you want to know?"

"I don't know. That seemed like the required first date question."

I leaned forward on my elbows and whispered, "Which was why I gave you the required first date answer. You'll have to be more creative than that if you want to get the goods on me, Reese."

His eyes sparked, burning like an inferno. Deep and filled with promise, he whispered, "Oh, I can be very creative, Rita."

The molten heat rolling off his words hung in the air, causing a chill to pebble my skin. One he did not miss. A gentle arrogance lit his handsome face, that dimple dancing as he held my gaze until I feared I was melting right in front of his eyes.

While it was true that I didn't have a ton of experience with men—Greg had been my first and only in pretty much every category—I was no delicate wallflower.

He might be two-named Tanner Reese.

But one-named Rita could be creative too.

Leaning back in my chair, I folded my hands on the table and taunted, "Prove it."

"You prove it," he retorted.

"I didn't say I was creative." *At least not out loud.* "I don't have anything to prove." My tongue snaked out to dampen my lips and I took a great pleasure as he watched the movement with hunger etched on his face.

We stared at each other.

Me trying to be sexy and mysterious.

Him actually being sexy and mysterious.

And we stared some more.

The tension between us building.

Nerves rolling in my stomach.

My palms starting to sweat.

But neither one of us actually did anything "creative."

We just *stared*.

And that was when I realized how freaking awkward silently staring at someone could be.

Finally, Tanner broke the silence. "I can't keep this up much longer. My eyes are starting to burn. Any chance we can…maybe…agree that being creative is hard, and let's just be cliché until we get to know each other a little better?"

A bubble of laughter sprang from my throat. "Yes. I can totally do that."

Like a sleepy little boy, he used his balled-up fist to rub his eyes. It totally wasn't fair that he looked hot even doing that.

"So, Rita, tell me what you do in your free time besides mopping the floor with school children across the country in staring contests?"

I giggled. "Oh, you know, the usual. Rock, Paper, Scissors. Thumb wrestling. Slapsies."

He stopped rubbing long enough to peek up at me. "Slapsies?"

"Come on. You know, Slapsies."

He shook his head. "Nope. Can't say I do."

"Seriously?"

"Seriously," he confirmed.

I huffed and put my hands out, palms up. "Give me your hands."

Eyeing me skeptically, he scooted his chair around the table until our knees were only a few inches apart and put his hands out, mirroring mine.

"No. Like this." I turned his hands over and then slid mine underneath. "Okay, now, you have to try to jerk your hands away before I can slap one of them."

"Ohhh yeah. I know this game. Porter and I used to—"

Smack!

"Ow!" he shouted, yanking his right hand away, but it was too late. I'd gotten him good.

"Annnnnd that's how you play Slapsies."

He narrowed his eyes, shaking out his hand before placing it back on top for round two. "That was messed up. I wasn't even ready yet."

Smack!

"Shit!" he yelled, shooting to his feet, his left hand being my latest victim. "What the hell, woman? You didn't say go."

I beamed up at him, fighting back laughter. "No one ever says go in Slapsies. It would defeat the purpose if you knew it was coming." I pushed my hands toward him. "Round three?"

"I think I'm going to pass, Cheaty McCheaterson."

"Fantastic," I deadpanned, pouting my lips before smiling up at him. "The great Tanner Reese is a sore loser."

I expected him to smile back, and for the most part, he did. His mouth was curled up, but something strange passed over his face. A wince, maybe? I couldn't tell. Whatever it was, he hid it well.

I didn't have a chance to harp on it because Kevin cleared

his throat, stealing our attention. He was leaning over a pan, using a spoon to drizzle butter over what I hoped and prayed were seared scallops for us because they smelled divine. In a bored tone, he said, "I'm so glad I volunteered to do this tonight so I could watch you two ignore twenty years of culinary excellence in order to play a game of Slapsies."

My whole body locked up tight, ice hitting my veins. *Shit.* Maybe that was what Tanner's wince had been all about. I must have looked like a fool and probably embarrassed him. Tanner was a professional chef after all. And freaking Kevin Story was standing not ten feet away, preparing our dinner.

And I, one-named Rita, was playing Slapsies.

Oh. My. God. I was usually so good at reading the room. Maybe I was drunker than I'd thought.

"I'm so sorry," I breathed, my cheeks flashing red. And that had nothing to do with the sudden rise in temperature since Kevin had turned the burners on.

"Don't apologize to him," Tanner scolded, settling back in his chair, But he didn't move it away. He did, however, reach out, take my hand, intertwine our fingers, and rest our joined hands on his thigh. "I'm the one you physically maimed, and not in the way a man hopes a beautiful woman will physically maim him on a date." He smiled, flirty, charming, one hundred percent Tanner Reese. And he gave my hand a squeeze like he could read my embarrassment.

Which, let's be honest, my face was on fire, so it probably wasn't hard.

But Tanner was holding my hand. With his magic, calming, reassuring hand.

And he was smiling at me like he thought I was cute.

Most importantly, he was holding my hand and smiling at me like he was truly and genuinely happy just to be sitting with me.

And this scared the absolute shit out of me because I knew I was truly and genuinely happy just to be sitting with *him*.

I made a weak attempt to pull my hand away, but Tanner was having none of it.

And as contradictory as it made me, I liked that he was having none of it.

Turning in his seat, he used his other hand to slide his plate and his fork to the spot adjacent to me, a waitress quickly rushing over to help him in this task.

Okay. So I guessed we were sitting next to each other now.

It might have made me a seventh grader, but he was holding my hand in the best hand-hold of my life *and* we were sitting next to each other like he couldn't get close enough. My stomach did an Olympic gymnast pass of somersaults.

Even as all of this once again terrified me.

He leaned toward me, his warm breath fluttering across my skin as he whispered, "And besides, I don't care what this guy tries to tell you. Twenty years of culinary excellence my ass. Hand on the Bible, this asshole includes three years in high school when he was a fry cook on his resume."

"Oh, fuck off!" Kevin interjected. "At least I had a job and wasn't sitting at home, holding hands with my mommy. How does that work when you're with a woman, Tanner? Does the umbilical cord reattach itself every morning?"

I let out a soft laugh—not so much at what Kevin had said, but rather that Tanner had put his chin to his chest and was shaking his head.

"Jesus Christ, Kev."

"What?" He feigned innocence. "I figured you'd have already introduced her to Mama Reese. I didn't know you were allowed to date without her approval."

"So, I'm guessing you're close with your mom?" I asked, thinking it was really freaking sweet if he was.

"Close?" Kevin answered. "The man is worth millions and he'd probably still live in the basement if his dad would let him. Those two are inseparable."

Tanner shrugged. "My mom's amazing. I'm not going to lie. We're tight. Kev's just jealous."

Yeah. I was right. Totally freaking sweet. Greg and his mother spoke twice a year. Once on her birthday. Once on his. He didn't even call the woman on Mother's Day. She wasn't incredible though. She was actually a super pretentious snob who'd raised a pretentious asshole. But everyone deserved a call on Mother's Day, so that responsibility had fallen to me. I distractedly wondered if it was going to fall on Tammy now. And then I giggled at the idea of Daphne Laughlin meeting Tammy Grigs for the first time. God, they were going to hate each other.

"His mom *is* amazing," Kevin parroted. "It's a shame she got stuck with a son like this one. But everyone knows Porter is her favorite anyway."

Tanner lowered his voice as he whispered, "Would you be willing to give me an alibi for tonight on the off chance that Kevin washes up on the shores of the lake?"

Smiling wider than I knew possible, I whispered back, "Sure, honey. As long as it's not *my* lake. A dead man in the water would really decrease my property value. *And* my hammock view. Though those scallops smell amazing, so if we could forgo murder until after I've eaten, I'd be much obliged."

His face transformed into what could only be described as awe. It might have been the only thing in the world that was even more tremendous, outstanding, and astonishing than the natural beauty of Tanner Reese's smile, and it stirred something inside me.

It was small. But I felt the stir all the same.

He glanced down at the table, then back up at me, repeating this three times before he stopped and stared.

There was nothing awkward about the staring this time.

And when his thumb started rubbing circles over the back of my hand, his warmth engulfing me, traveling through me, and then burrowing in deep, I finally felt myself relax.

And not because of the wine.

I could do this.

I could so do this.

TEN

Tanner

DINNER WAS INCREDIBLE. AND NOT BECAUSE—DESPITE HIS unfortunate personality—Kevin Story was an amazing chef.

No, dinner was incredible because Rita was incredible.

We'd eaten, polished off the wine, and held hands more than I had since middle school.

It was nice being with her.

Okay, that's not completely true. It was *fun* being with her.

Rita was a smartass who did not pull punches even when the jokes were at my expense. She and Kevin had ganged up on me more than once while he was preparing our dinner. I should have hated it. But I fucking loved every second of seeing her interacting so naturally with my friend. It wasn't forced or overwrought. Honestly, Rita didn't seem like she was trying at all.

So either she was the world's best con-woman and I was

going to wake up to find she was second in line behind Shana to sell a story about me to a tabloid or Rita was a genuine person on a date with a man who liked her a hell of a lot.

After Kevin said his goodbyes, whispering another, "Marry her," into my ear before leaving us to dessert, I found out that Rita and I had a lot more in common than a quick wit.

We'd been born in the same hospital, albeit two years apart. (I was older. She'd pointed that out at least twelve times. In a cute way though.)

We were both a Leo, but she'd quickly informed me that she didn't buy into the horoscope bullshit because her arch nemesis from ninth grade was a Leo too.

Her favorite color was red. And after seeing her in that dress and staring at her lips all night, it was quickly becoming mine too.

Our high school football teams had played each other every year. Sure, she'd been a cheerleader and I had more than likely only attended the games to make out with a girl under the bleachers, but we'd both been there.

And surprisingly enough, we even knew a few of the same people. Chris Tobin—a random guy I'd graduated with who I hadn't spoken to in years—was her older brother's best friend. Okay, so that one was a stretch.

But! That same big brother, Jon, owned the company that had completely renovated my house when I'd bought it.

I mean, what were the chances?

Atlanta had to be the smallest big city in the entire world.

And there was a very solid chance that I'd just found the most incredible woman in the whole city.

It was past midnight when I rested my hand on the curve of her lower back and guided her out of the restaurant. We'd both stopped after glass two of wine, but while my metabolism had burned it off quickly, I could tell that Rita was still feeling the effects. This meant she forgot to play hard to get and instead tucked her arms against her chest and pressed into my front when the cool wind whipped around us as we waited for the valet.

Fuck, she felt good. All soft against my hard and the perfect height in those heels so my chin could rest on the top of her head. I drew her in close, pretending it was only to help block the wind. But the truth was I could have stood outside that restaurant for the rest of the night.

We rode back to her place in comfortable quiet. She occasionally smiled over at me or commented on the song on the radio, and I kept my hand on her dress-covered thigh, replying to those glances with a gentle squeeze, wishing I didn't have to let her go.

Dinner wasn't enough.

Though I had a feeling it wouldn't have been enough if I'd booked us a fourteen-day cruise to Alaska—or somewhere equally cold so she'd never want to leave the room. But even in that little mental shoulda-woulda-coulda, we didn't spend those fourteen days naked and in bed. I didn't even know what Rita looked like naked and in bed.

But I knew how much I loved talking to her.

Laughing with her.

Verbally sparring with her.

I liked the way her body sagged when I took her hand.

I liked the way her nose crinkled when I teased her.

I liked the way she didn't laugh at everything I said, so when she did, it was a gift.

I liked the way she looked at me—like I was incredible too.

And I liked the way she *didn't* look at me—like *I* was the gift.

Yeah. It'd only been one date.

But I was fucked—and not in the literal sense.

I stood in front of a camera every week, taking my shirt off and smiling with all the confidence in the world. But with this woman, I couldn't even gather the courage to ask her back to my place for a drink.

Because fuck me. Fuck me. *Fuck me.*

I *liked* her. A lot.

And that was exactly why bile started crawling up the back of my throat when I pulled into her driveway and found a silver Jaguar parked next to her BMW SUV. One that had most definitely not been there when I'd picked her up.

"Oh, shit," she breathed as I put the car into park.

A light at the front of her house came on, and I prayed they were motion-sensored. But no such luck. The front door swung open and the silhouette of a man holding a highball glass appeared within. He casually propped his shoulder against the jamb and crossed his legs at the ankle.

Greg.

Fucking fucking *fucking* Greg.

"Oh, shit," Rita repeated, this time with a whole lot of pissed off replacing the bitchiness.

It was only that pissed off in her voice that kept me in the car. Greg was not my competition. He was a nuisance. Not to mention an idiot. Something I'd known when she'd told me that he'd cheated on her back at the Fling. Something I knew even more after having spent the last four hours with her.

He was also not something I wanted to deal with when he was standing inside her house after midnight with a drink in his hand. I did not have the PR capital to spend on getting arrested tonight. Per my attorney, I was supposed to be lying low. I didn't think waking up to my mug shot on TMZ was what he had in mind.

"Does he still live here?" I asked.

She swung her head my way so fast that I feared she'd given herself whiplash. "Hell no. I kicked his ass out weeks ago."

"But he's still got a key, and after finding out about us today, he decided to show up tonight and be a dick," I deduced.

"*God*, I hate him," she groaned. "I had a really good night. He does not get to show up here and ruin it." She jerked the door handle, but I caught her arm before she had the chance to swing it open.

"So don't let him ruin it," I implored.

"What the hell am I supposed to do? Go inside and yell, 'Honey, I'm home'? Maybe scooch over in the bed so Tammy can sleep in the middle of us?"

If I wasn't so pissed that she had a jackass like Greg in her life, I would have laughed. But I didn't think laughing at her was going to get me a yes to my next question.

Grabbing my balls—not literally because that would have been weird—I rushed out, "Come back to my place. We can have another drink." I waggled my eyebrows. "Maybe swing in the hammock."

Her face got soft, all the pissed off fading away. "Oh, honey. That's really sweet of you. But I couldn't."

Shit. Rejection stung. But I'd convinced her to go out on a date with me. I could work some magic on this too. "And why not? You said it yourself: We had fun tonight. And if you go in there now, he's going to erase all of that with more of his bullshit. It was bad enough he got to be a part of the way we met. Don't let him be a part of the way tonight ends too."

She looked away. "I don't know, Tanner."

I lifted my hands, palms up. "Well, I do. I'm not asking you to sleep with me. I swear to you that is not part of this. I mean, you are a beautiful woman and I would definitely like to have sex with you eventually." I winked. "But the whole drive here, I was trying to figure out how to keep you for a little longer." I motioned toward the door. "Maybe the douchebag is a sign."

Her lips curled. "A sign, huh?"

While I was already grabbing my balls—again, not literally—I snaked a hand out, catching her at the back of the neck, and pulled her toward me. Her breath caught, but she came willingly.

I rested my forehead against hers and begged, "Come on. Say yes."

She chewed on her bottom lip, swiveling her head to glance at the door without breaking our connection. "I would like to see your hammock. You know, just so I can see how it compares to mine."

Victory sang in my veins. "It's a *really* good hammock."

Her eyes fluttered closed, and then she brushed her nose with mine, bringing her lips painfully close.

I could have done it. I could have kissed her until the

windows steamed.

But I didn't want a fucking kiss in her driveway.

I wanted to take her back to my house. Get her someplace where she was only mine, without that moron looking on.

I wanted her laughing in my hammock with my arms around her. I wanted her curled in close like she'd been while waiting for the valet.

Mainly, I just wanted more time with her.

Gliding my hand up to cup her jaw, I pleaded, "Say yes."

We both jumped when Greg suddenly appeared beside the car and knocked on my window. "Get the hell out of the car, Rita."

Clenching my teeth, I turned a thunderous glare his way.

I would not go to jail.

I would not go to jail.

I would not go to jail.

Ah…fuck it.

I reached for the door handle, but it was Rita who caught my arm this time.

"You know what. You're right. Let's go back to your place. This asshole does not get to ruin this for me. I let him have seven years. He does not get one more minute."

I don't know why, because I knew she was in the process of getting a divorce, but it felt like a punch to the stomach knowing she'd given this guy seven damn years. I'd had one date with her and was fighting like hell to get one more *hour*. If I'd had seven years, you can bet your ass she would not be sitting in another man's car in my driveway.

She'd be in my arms. In my fucking hammock. Laughing and smiling up at me while I frantically thought of ways to keep that smile aimed at me for another fucking seven years.

Fuck this guy.

"You sure?" I asked her as a courtesy, but I was already putting the car in gear.

Confidence brewed like a summer storm in her green eyes as she replied, "I'm positive. Let's go."

That was all it took.

Throwing one arm around the back of her seat, I reversed out of her driveway.

"What the hell are you doing?" Greg yelled, jogging beside us. "Rita, get the fuck out of the car."

She laughed, wild and carefree, giving him a finger wave.

I only gave him one finger.

Then, much to my excitement, her hand came down and landed on my thigh.

It was probably a show for her ex.

I should have cared that it was a show for her ex.

I didn't, but only because she'd left it there—her thumb tracing sweet circles until I couldn't take it anymore and intertwined our fingers—long after we'd left Greg in the proverbial dust.

"Holy shit," Rita breathed as we drove down my oak-lined driveway. The motion lights came on as soon as we hit the brick horseshoe. "Holy. Shit," she repeated more slowly when my white, old-South plantation home appeared in front of us.

I loved that house. And not just because it was mine, bought outright with cash when I was only thirty. It had the most kick-ass top and bottom wraparound porches, giving me a full three-sixty view of the property. And that's not even to mention the six bedrooms and five bathrooms I wasn't currently using but had high hopes that I would in the not-so-distant future. It had taken quite a bit of renovating to get the kitchen the way I'd wanted it. But those upgrades allowed me to film in my home rather than traveling back and forth to The Food Channel studios in New York, so it had been worth every penny.

"Wait until you see the backyard." I clicked the garage door open and guided us inside, cutting the engine before it had fully closed.

"It gets better?" she asked in a tone filled with wonder.

I went to smile, but it occurred to me that it had become a permanent fixture on my face since I'd first picked her up. Reluctantly releasing her hand, I tipped my chin to the garage door leading to the house. "C'mon."

I hurried around the hood, but she was already out of the car, her high heels clicking on the concrete as she made her way to me. The second she got close enough, she hooked her arm through mine and leaned in close, causing my perma-grin to stretch.

After using my key to open the door, I hit the alarm and then guided her through the mud room to the wide-open living room. My downstairs was impressive. It was what my interior designer called "the showroom." Three bedrooms, a dining room, and a sitting room all decorated in classic minimalism with dainty furniture that had absolutely not a touch of my personality anywhere. I didn't care. Short of filming in the kitchen hidden on the other side of the stairs, I didn't use that space anyway.

With her head craned back, admiring the massive crystal chandelier that I'd thought was overkill from day one, she said, "Wow, Tanner. This is gorgeous."

It was. But it wasn't me.

"Let's go upstairs." I started us toward the split staircase.

She pulled us up short. "Uh…how about we stay down here for a while."

Shaking my head, I chuckled. "Relax. I live upstairs. There's a den with a TV. According to my interior designer, a television ruins the aesthetic of a room, so I wasn't allowed to mount one down here. There's also another kitchen that actually has food and wine and not just lighting and cameras." I swung my arm out toward the closed double doors on our left. "Though, if you'd prefer to awkwardly stare at each other again, that useless sitting room is perfect for it."

"You have *two* kitchens?"

She followed when I once again started us toward the stairs.

"I'm a chef. What did you expect?"

"Right. Of course," she murmured.

However, when we got to the second floor landing and hung a right, I knew it wasn't what she expected at all.

"*This* is your second kitchen?"

Yeah. It could be said that my kitchen upstairs wasn't exactly what a person would consider luxurious. But it was all me.

Reluctantly releasing her, I walked around the two-seater bar and retrieved a bottle of Chardonnay from the fridge. "Were you expecting more?" I asked with a smirk, knowing good and damn well she had been.

She lifted her fingers about an inch apart. "Maybe a little. I think we had that same range at my house before we upgraded. And while I am no slouch in the kitchen, I am far from a chef."

I got busy with the cork-and-pour routine while she settled on the stool closest to the end. "My mom does too. I've promised her a Viking for Christmas this year. I've been holding out because it's going to piss my dad off. He'll have to cut out a cabinet to make it fit. But she's been begging for it." I slid a glass of wine her way before pouring my own.

"Can I just say that I think it's adorable that you're close with your mom?"

I propped myself on a forearm at the corner of the bar so I was facing her. Close enough for the citrus scent of her hair to put a spell on me, far enough away that I could resist the overwhelming urge to kiss her… Maybe. Possibly. Shit, I was going to fail.

It was strange having her there. And not just in my house. Dozens of cameramen, assistant cameramen, boom operators, and sound guys were in and out of my front door on a daily basis. But rarely did anyone go upstairs. I could count on two fingers the amount of women I'd brought home with me—only one if I didn't include Andrea. I didn't date much when I was in Atlanta. I could barely get a woman to look at me without stars in her eyes in that city.

But life in the spotlight was crazy like that. It made me a different person, and not because I was some diva with a mile-long rider. Honestly, in the years since *Simmer* had taken off, I hadn't felt like I'd changed at all. But the world looked at me differently. And because of that, I was expected to act differently. I wasn't allowed to have a bad day, or flip someone off when they cut me off in traffic, or even just eat grapes as I walked around the grocery store. (Relax, I always paid for them.) When I left my house, anything and everything I did became a representation of who I was as a brand—not a man.

Judgy Judys were everywhere, waiting for me to step out of line. Sometimes those Judgy Judys were masquerading around as my friends. Or worse, my real friends became the Judgy Judys, selling me under the bus for five minutes of fame.

Having any kind of private life was next to impossible. So when I "dated," it went a lot like this: She ordered shrimp and grits, we'd go back to her place or whatever hotel I was staying at in New York or LA, and they'd leave the next morning with stars still in their eyes but without the promise of a second date. I was a nice guy. These women knew the score. Or at least they accepted the score because without it nothing came after shrimp and grits. This system had worked well for several years.

Cue Shana Beckwit, the only woman I'd attempted the illusive "more" with.

Also cue the restraining order, a new set of tires, a photo of me lounging in bed covered by a thin blanket that did nothing to hide the outline of my cock two minutes post-orgasm floating around the internet, and a PR firm working overtime to keep the rest of her bullshit out of the headlines.

So yeah, maybe bringing a woman back to my place and trusting her with the most vulnerable part of my brand—i.e. me—wasn't the smartest idea in my current situation. But there was exactly a zero percent chance that I was going to pass up an opportunity with Rita.

And I had to admit, seeing her casually sitting on my stool made me happier than I'd thought possible a few months ago.

I touched the rim of my wine glass to hers. "Adorable wasn't what I was going for tonight."

She leaned forward on her elbows. "Then what were you going for?"

Honest. Free. *Real.*

Dramatically, I sucked in a deep breath. "Clearly, a savage warrior in my patriotic duty against terrorist alligators."

"I think you may have missed the mark," she whispered back. Then she pursed her lips, the slightest hint of humor peeking out at the corners.

Like a moth to a flame, I swayed toward her.

I was going to do it. I was going to kiss her. I was going to kiss that fucking smile right off her sexy face, swallow it, turn it into a moan, and then swallow that too.

Instead, I nearly stumbled off-balance when she suddenly stood and rounded into the kitchen. I couldn't decide if it was a pointed move on her part or shit for timing on mine. She didn't give me long to think.

"So, explain this kitchen to me," she asked, trailing her finger down the brown-and-taupe-veined granite beside the single-basin sink. "There are dishes in the sink and fingerprints on the fridge, so obviously, you use it. But that stove is electric. I figured you'd want something fancier. Was it like this when you bought the place?"

I could have said yes, let the question die in the water

without exposing anything real about myself no matter how innocent it might be. But I really liked the idea of being myself with this woman.

"It makes me feel like I'm at home," I confessed. "Growing up, I had top-of-the-line nothing. I learned to cook on electric and it's kind of nostalgic for me now. I'm also a single guy, so let's be honest. By the time I leave the restaurant or finish filming, I'm too tired to cook for myself. But if the urge strikes me, I have an enormous chef's wet dream downstairs." I shrugged. "So, when I asked to have this kitchen added upstairs, I just wanted it to be comfortable." I waved a hand around the small space. "And this is what I picked."

I had no idea what happened after that. It was the strangest thing. One second, we were causally sipping wine and chatting, and the next, the air in that room became too heavy to breathe.

Puzzled, I narrowed my eyes on her. "Rita?"

She didn't reply—at least not with words. Her smile faded, and her shoulders rounded. Her green eyes grew distant before lighting with something I couldn't quite figure out.

Sadness. Regret… Hell, what was that?

Instinctively, I reached for her hand, but she pulled it away.

Then, in a broken whisper, she gave it to me. "You could have had anything in the world and you picked something that made you feel like home?"

And then I'd wished she'd stop giving it to me.

"I think I picked Greg because I wanted something that

didn't feel like home." She slapped a hand over her mouth as though she were trying to force the words back in.

I didn't understand her confession, but the mortification carved into her face was plain as day.

Darting past me, she mumbled something about a bathroom.

"Rita, wait."

But it was too late. She was power-walking through my den, straight to the hall.

I jogged after her, rounding the corner in time to see her yank the linen closet open. She quickly shut it before throwing the door to the guest bedroom open.

She kept her gaze aimed at the floor and snapped, "Jesus. Where is your bathroom in this mansion?"

"Next door on the left," I answered.

She hurried inside, shutting the door with an urgency just shy of a slam, leaving me in the hall. Alone and with my stomach in knots, I prayed that this wasn't the dramatic ending to the best first date I had ever been on in my entire life.

ELEVEN

Rita

With shaking arms, I leaned on the sink. "What the fuck was that?" I asked myself in the mirror.

Not surprisingly, my refection didn't answer.

I'd been wrong. I couldn't do this. Not while keeping the hurricane brewing inside me at bay.

I shouldn't have gone home with him. I should have thanked him for a lovely dinner. I should have apologized *again* for putting my hands on him at the Fling, and I should have gotten out of his car, gotten in my car, driven to a hotel so Greg couldn't find me, and spent the night—and quite possibly the rest of my life—hiding under the blankets.

There was a knock at the door. "Rita?"

I sucked in a shaky breath, turning on the water before calling back, "I'll be out in a minute."

"Please," he said. It was followed by a thump on the door that I thought was his head. "I'm sorry. Whatever I said, I...

Shit. I don't know. You have something against an electric stove?"

My stomach wrenched. He was trying to crack a joke. He'd been nothing short of incredible all night, and I'd acted like a nutcase dumping my shit on him. Yet there he was, standing outside of *his* bathroom door, issuing blind apologies for something he couldn't possibly understand.

Why did he have to be such a good guy?

I turned the water off and faced the door as though I could see him standing on the other side. "There's nothing to apologize for, silly. I just needed a minute."

There were several beats of silence before he said, "You want to talk about it?"

I smiled sadly. Yeah. He was a *really* freaking good guy. "Not particularly. I just… Give me a minute, okay? I'm dying to see that hammock."

"Okay," he replied, but the shadow of his feet never disappeared from the bottom of the door.

"Tanner, please," I begged. "One minute. That's all I need."

"Okay," he repeated, his feet finally disappearing.

Putting my ear to the door, I listened to his dress shoes against the hardwood fading into the distance.

Once I was sure he was gone, I sank to my butt, pulled my legs to my chest, and tackled the insurmountable task of getting my shit together. "What the hell are you doing?" I whispered to myself. "You're on a date with a freaking amazing man and you bring up Greg? Seriously? Fucking Greg? You think he brought you up while he was in bed with Tammy? Goddamn it, Rita. Get it together."

Tears filled my eyes. Fantastic. My makeup was going to

streak down my face like a horror show if I didn't pack this crap away.

It shouldn't have happened—me breaking down.

Especially over Greg. He didn't deserve those tears.

But if I really thought about it, those tears weren't for him.

They were for me.

There was just something so beautiful in the honesty of Tanner's kitchen. Seriously, I'd seen low-budget, one-bedroom apartments with bigger and nicer kitchens. But he'd wanted something that made him feel like he was at home.

I'd never felt like that. There was nothing worth remembering about the way I'd grown up. And now, thanks to Greg, there was nothing worth remembering about the life I'd made for myself after that, either.

I was starting over at thirty and I didn't even know who I was anymore. Or maybe I'd never known because I'd stupidly allowed Greg to dictate so much of my identity. That hurt. Really badly because I'd always prided myself in being a strong and independent woman. But I had literally married a man because he was nothing like my father. And he could provide me with a life that would ensure I didn't end up like my mother.

"I loved Greg though," I argued with myself, not wanting to believe the emotional epiphany my subconscious had felt the need to share with me while I had been standing in the middle of Tanner Reese's kitchen.

Seriously, could my life get any more embarrassing?

Yes. The answer was yes.

"Do you *still* love him?" came from the other side of the door.

I screwed my eyes shut, hoping if I concentrated hard enough that I could disappear. "Oh, God," I croaked.

His voice came from somewhere low, like maybe he was sitting down too. "There's no wrong answer, Rita. I just want to know what I'm up against here."

Jesus. This man.

Did I love Greg Laughlin?

Did I *love* Greg Laughlin?

Did *I* love Greg Laughlin?

"Love is weird," I told the empty room.

"That's not a no," he replied, so soft that it was barely audible through the door.

And it wasn't. It absolutely wasn't a no.

It also wasn't the whole truth.

I needed to shut my mouth, stand up, open that door, call a cab, and never look back. I had no business being on a date with Tanner Reese or anyone else when I couldn't answer a simple question like *do you love another man?*

But as kind as he'd been to me, I owed him an explanation, even if I was such a coward that I said it from the other side of the bathroom door. "I didn't have the best life growing up, Tanner. My mother had a pretty serious pill problem she refused to acknowledge. My brother and I spent most of our childhood in the back seat playing stupid games to keep ourselves entertained while she did God only knows what to score her next fix."

"Shiiiit," he rumbled.

"Sorry. I probably should have warned you tonight that I'm something of a Slapsies master. I had *a lot* of practice over the years."

"Open the door, Rita."

I was nowhere near ready to face him yet. "My dad was always around but never really *around,* if you know what I mean. He never had much, but Jon and I loved going to his house because he had a backyard we could run around in."

The doorknob clicked like he was testing it again. "Rita, please."

I shook my head and kept going before I lost my courage. "Dad married some woman and moved to Alabama when I was ten, leaving me and my brother behind with my mom, and never looked back." I dried my eyes on the backs of my knuckles and laughed sadly. "And yes, I have been out of the dating game for a while, but I do realize this is not a first date conversation. At least not if you want a second date. But I needed you to have a little back history on me in order to truly understand my answer about Greg."

His voice was sharper, more desperate, when he repeated, "Open the door, Rita."

Ignoring him, I said, "Sometimes love isn't a factor in whether you should or shouldn't be with a person. And I can tell you with an absolute certainty that I *should have never* been and *will never again* be with Greg Laughlin. I made a stupid decision fueled by a shitty past when I married him. Hindsight being twenty-twenty and all. But when you told me about your kitchen, how you picked it out because it reminded you of home, a light bulb came on in my head. I think I made the decision to marry Greg because he *didn't* remind me of home. And for seven years, I let him shape me into a woman I don't recognize anymore, and I'm not altogether certain if I even like the person he made me. But I let him do this all because his version of me was so much better than who I thought I could be. Rita Laughlin with all her pearls and heels is nothing like the girl in dirty clothes in the back of that car, playing games with her brother."

"Wow," he replied, and it sounded a lot like sarcasm, making me feel even more stupid than I already did for confessing that to him.

I started to push to my feet, ready to bolt—to where, I didn't know—but he suddenly stopped me.

His voice was thick as he stated, "I don't know who I am anymore, either."

I froze, turning my head to the door. "You?"

"Yeah. *Me.* I wish I could be the kid in my mom's kitchen all over again. Don't get me wrong. I love my job. It's all I've ever wanted to do. But then I started hosting *Simmer* and shit got weird. I was no longer *me*. I was chef Tanner Reese, this freaking joke who took his shirt off on TV every week. The money is fantastic, but God, it's such a head fuck. My parents weren't like yours. They've been married for over thirty years and I think the only thing they love more than each other is me and my brother. And when you grow up like that, experiencing that kind of love up close, you assume that's what you'll have one day. It's funny because I spent my twenties hoping I *wouldn't* find that woman. I was out having fun, discovering who I was." He chuckled, deep and sad. "I thought it was like a switch. When I was done living the fast life, I'd just flip the switch, find my wife, start a family, and settle down." He whistled low. "Boy, was I wrong there. I know you're just getting back into the dating scene, and I don't say this to discourage you, but it's a fucking blood bath out here. And for me, having a public persona, it's a nightmare. My last girlfriend makes Greg look like husband of the year. She lied to me at every turn, sold intimate pictures of me to the highest bidder, and is currently in the works with a major publishing house to write a tell-all about our relationship. And according to a few leaked chapters, it's a pure work of fiction, including some pretty detailed—and completely made-up—mentions of me, hookers, and cocaine that could potentially cost me my job at The Food Channel if my lawyers can't stop her from publishing it first."

My heart stopped. "Holy shit, Tanner. That's terrible."

"Yeah. But you want to know what's worse? There's a part of me that wishes she would publish it so I could go back to working at the restaurants and be regular old Tanner again."

Suddenly, my stomach wrenched, and not only did I feel like a fool for hiding out in his bathroom, I felt like a complete and total asshole for how I'd been treating him. "Oh my God. I did that to you too," I rushed out, chills exploding across my skin.

He laughed. "You writing a tell-all about our first date on toilet paper in there?"

"No, but I used you at the Fling to make Greg jealous. If it's any consolation, I didn't recognize you until after you had walked away. I just thought you were a really sexy guy who would make his blood boil."

He chuckled, and I heard his head thud on the wall beside me. "Don't worry about that. Grabbing your ass was not torture. Besides, I could see it in your eyes that you didn't know who I was. I think that's why I was so hell-bent on taking you out tonight. Stupid as it might sound, I was thrilled that you were using my looks to make him jealous rather than some societal fascination that deems me important because I'm on TV."

My lips lifted at the corners in something vaguely resembling a smile. "TV or not, you're a very good-looking man, Tanner Reese."

"Douchebag Greg's version of you or not, you're an amazing woman, Rita Hartley."

I sucked in a sharp breath at his use of my maiden name. It was something so small, but hearing it come from his lips (even from the other side of a bathroom door) made tears prick the backs of my eyes. "How do you—"

"I asked around about you after you took off today. You've got a lot of people who care about you in that office. They filled my ears with nothing but how great you are. Though stay away from Beth. She's a raging hemorrhoid."

The tears spilled out as a laugh sprang from my throat. "Yeah, she is."

Neither of us said anything for several beats. What else was there left to say? Oh, right.

"I'm not ready to date yet," I confessed.

"Don't say that," he grumbled. "Come on, Rita. There's something here. I know you feel it."

I did. Absolutely. But it changed nothing. "Maybe one day, we could… Shit, I don't know. I've got a lot of stuff to work through."

"So let me help."

I scoffed. "You're sweet, honey, but—"

"No buts. Look, I've got issues too. *So* many issues. I've actually been legally advised not to get into a relationship right now. But I really think we could be onto something here.

Maybe it's nothing and it will all fizzle over the next few weeks. But dammit, I want to try. Tonight was the most fun I think I've ever had with a woman."

"Me too," I replied before amending. "Like, with a man though."

"You talking about me or Kevin?"

I sniffled and managed to croak out a sarcastic, "Obviously Kevin."

"Smartass," he muttered. "What if we just…take it slow. No strings. No pressure. Just two people having fun and see where it goes."

"I can tell you where it's going to go: up in flames."

"Maybe. But maybe not. And I don't know about you, but I haven't had a lot of 'maybe not' people in my life. So all I'm asking is that you say okay and spend some time with me. Who knows? Maybe I'll run you off the good old-fashioned way by leaving my toenail clippings on the coffee table or forgetting to flush the toilet."

"Okay, ew."

He chuckled. "Don't worry. I have a housekeeper."

"Housekeeper or not, toenail clippings are my hard limit, Tanner."

"Then I vow, right here and now, to never clip my toenails again."

I scoffed. "I'm not sure that's helping your case."

He laughed again and it felt like I'd been wrapped in a blanket. "Say yes," he urged. "Nothing serious. We don't even have to call it dating. We're just two unspeakably sexy people who enjoy sarcasm, staring contests, and Slapsies and also happen to like holding hands and hanging out."

I smiled, allowing my chin to drop to my chest. All of that did sound pretty great. Maybe I was fighting this thing with him because dating was a scary word for me in my current predicament. But "hanging out" sounded manageable. And hanging out with Tanner? Well, that sounded amazing.

I didn't tell him any of that and instead retorted, "The alliteration in that sentence made my head hurt."

"For the record, only one of us likes grammar jokes. And spoiler alert: It's not me."

I barked a laugh. Yeah. Spending time with Tanner would *not* be torture.

"Say yes," he pressed.

Fuck it. What could it hurt? I'd smiled more that day than I had in months. And that's including before I'd found out about Greg's affair.

I'd had fun with Tanner. I had a lot of shit headed my way over the next few weeks and probably months until my divorce was finalized. It'd be nice to have a little fun mixed in.

"Okay, but we keep it casual."

He quickly replied, "I can do casual."

"Then…okay. I'm in."

His voice smiled as he repeated, "Okay?"

"Yeah, Tanner. *Okay*."

He blew out a loud exhale. "Good. Listen, now that that's settled, you gonna come out of there so I can hug you and then show you my hammock, or should I just put my hand up to the door so we can do the prison glass palm-to-palm thing?"

And that was the exact moment when I realized that Tanner Reese was more than a good guy.

He was one of the best.

Laughing, I stood, dusting imaginary dirt off my dress. I glanced at myself in the mirror. My eyes were red rimmed, and my mascara was streaking my cheeks.

I definitely looked like I'd been crying.

But for reasons that were almost as magical and hypnotizing as Tanner's hand-holding abilities, the hollow ache in my chest had disappeared, so I didn't *feel* like I'd been crying anymore.

Before opening the door, I used my fingertips to clean up under my eyes. It didn't do much to fix my face, but I couldn't bring myself to care what I looked like anymore.

I was just me. Take it or leave it.

And Tanner had made it clear that he wanted to take it.

I found him in the hallway, still wearing his suit, sans the coat and tie. His back was pressed against the wall beside the door, and his long legs were stretched out in front of him.

"I knew the hammock would get you," he teased with a megawatt smile as he climbed back to his feet.

The moment he was fully vertical, I moved into him, wrapping my arms around his waist and pressing my face into his chest.

One of his hands went to the back of my head, his other arm hooking around my waist. But it was his lips at the top of my head that sent the warmth radiating through my entire body.

It wasn't exactly a kiss.

It wasn't exactly not a kiss, either.

But whatever it was… It was incredible.

"I'm glad you told me all that," he murmured into the top

of my hair. "I'm always here to listen if you want to talk, Rita. Even if you need to do it in my bathroom."

I smiled into his chest. God, how was he not running for the hills after that? And how was I not engulfed in a fiery inferno of embarrassment, but rather comfortably engulfed in the warmth of his arms?

"I'll keep that in mind," I replied.

We stood there, in the middle of his hall, holding each other in a simple embrace that was more intimate than I would have thought a hug could be a mere twenty-four hours earlier.

But twenty-four hours earlier, I hadn't known the wonder that was one-named Tanner.

He kept his lips in my hair in the kiss/nonkiss as he said, "Can I ask you something?"

I snuggled in closer. "Yeah."

"This goes against casual."

"Already? God, you are terrible at this."

He chuckled. "Spend the night."

My body got tight, but he kept going.

"I'm not trying to get you into bed. I just don't want to take you back there tonight. Your ex is a douchebag, and while he might be harmless, I don't like the idea that he was waiting for you to get home. I've had enough crazy exes to know that is seriously uncool."

"I know," I whispered. "I need to change the locks."

"You *really* need to change the locks, babe. But there's nothing you can do about that tonight. So stay. I'll give you a T-shirt to sleep in and everything. It's a really good one too. I hear someone famous once wore it."

I tipped my head back and rested my chin on his chest.

"Any chance I can just get one of your T-shirts instead?"

His eyes flared before they hooded. "Fucking hell, that man is an idiot."

And then I lost sight of him altogether.

Because his mouth came down on mine.

His lips swept mine before pressing in deep. It wasn't a wild and frenzied kiss filled with scorching passion. His head didn't slant. His mouth didn't open.

It was soft, simple, yet overflowing with complexities.

Slow and gentle.

Painfully brilliant.

And, as I was learning, it was pure Tanner.

When he pulled away, he dropped his forehead to mine, his lips curling up into a lazy smile. "Is that a yes?"

"Something like that."

"That's a yes," he murmured, coming in for another all-too-chaste kiss.

Did I want Tanner to sweep me off my feet, his mouth sealing over mine, his hands roaming my body as he pinned me to the wall right there in the hallway? Probably more than I should have.

But there was something inherently nice about having him hold me. No pressure. No overthinking. No considering if I should or shouldn't. There was no right or wrong.

There was just us.

I don't know how long we stood there, his blue eyes boring into mine, my greens straining not to blink.

He finally relented and looked away. "I'm never going to win one of those, am I?"

I shrugged. "Probably not."

My stomach swooshed as he found my mouth again. This time, I only got a lip touch—albeit a pretty spectacular one.

And then he backed away, caught my hand, tucked it into the crook of his bent arm, and led me outside.

His hammock was better than mine—but only because he was in it with me.

TWELVE

Tanner

I was on my back, one leg outstretched on the hammock, one foot on the ground, gently pushing against the wooden slats to keep us swaying, and the most content smile I'd ever felt stretching my lips.

She'd fallen asleep over an hour earlier with her head on my shoulder, her front snug against my side like we were two puzzle pieces, and her legs wound around mine in the most uncomfortable way possible.

But I didn't dare move.

If I did, she would have stirred, purring like a kitten before tipping her head up to sweetly kiss the underside of my jaw.

I'd purposely done it a few times, my chest tightening with each touch of her lips.

And then it had become too much.

Predominantly, because it wasn't enough. Nowhere close

to enough.

I wanted to wake her up and force her to keep talking. I wanted to kiss her again, this time sweeping my tongue with hers. I wanted her on top of me, flush head to toe. I wanted to trace my fingers over every inch of her body as she writhed beneath me.

I wanted as much of her as I could possibly get.

But not at the risk of losing her.

She wasn't ready for what I wanted from her. But I'd wait.

For Rita… I. Would. *Wait.*

Because over the last few hours, as I'd held that unbelievable woman at my side, talking and laughing, getting to know each other until she finally fell asleep, she'd done it with her head on my shoulder, her front snug against my side like we were two puzzle pieces, and her legs wound around mine in the most uncomfortable way possible…

And with her hand over my heart.

Not my abs.

I'd always heard that it was the little things that mean the most in a relationship.

And, in that moment, I understood that more than ever.

Her hair was a mess.

Her makeup was smudged.

She was wearing my T-shirt, baggy and loose. She hadn't tried to tie it up into something sexy.

She hadn't asked for a tour of the house.

She hadn't asked to see my bedroom.

She was so damn content to be swinging on a hammock with me on my porch that she'd fallen asleep mid-conversation.

And she'd done it with her hand over my heart.

Not my abs.

Yeah. Life was all about the little things.

And, in just one night, it made me realize that Rita was one of life's *big* things.

THIRTEEN

Tanner

ON MY TWENTY-FIRST BIRTHDAY, I'D GONE SKYDIVING. I'D never forget the terror or exhilaration of standing in the doorway, looking down at the ant farm that was Atlanta from that height.

And, in the eleven years since I'd taken that faithful leap, I'd never experienced anything quite like it.

That is until I folded out of my car in front of North Point Pulmonology on Monday morning after Rita had not responded to a single one of my texts after I'd dropped her off at her house on Sunday morning.

She'd woken up bright and obscenely early, asking that I take her home. Her rush to leave was definitely not what I was used to. Women usually made every excuse in the book to hang out with me for the day.

Not Rita.

She was dressed, her heels tapping down my stairs while

I was still trying to use every excuse in the book to keep her there for the day. She'd bought exactly none of them.

Hell, the woman wouldn't even let me cook her breakfast. That was an offer that had *never* been refused.

I'd loved that she'd refused.

I'd loathed taking her home.

Greg had thankfully been gone when we'd pulled up at her place, but I'd still hated the idea of leaving her there. More accurately, I'd hated the idea of leaving her period. But she hadn't invited me in. Though she had brushed her smiling mouth against mine and promised me she'd call me later.

A promise she had *not* kept.

We'd agreed on casual. Call me naïve, but I assumed that meant responding to texts that thanks to her read receipts, I knew she was reading. I wasn't as much upset or put off as I was worried that she was rethinking our little arrangement. Giving her some space to get her head straight was probably the smartest move I could make.

But patience had never been my strong suit.

So there I was, pulling a crazy-ass Shana Beckwit and showing up at her job unannounced at eleven thirty in the morning under the guise of *I just so happen to be in the neighborhood, so how about lunch?*

Lunch was casual, right?

My nerves were thrumming like an electrical current as I walked to the front entrance. Sucking in one last breath that did nothing to calm me, I pushed my sunglasses up to the top of my head, slapped on an award-winning smile, and walked inside.

It was a nice office, excluding the picture of Douchebag

Greg hanging on the wall, of course. Strategically, I avoided eye contact with the handful of people in the waiting room as I approached the check-in window.

Just as I got close, a nurse wearing pink-and-purple scrubs swung a door open and called, "Mr. Thom—" She froze the minute our eyes met. "Holy shhhh…oot." She clutched a medical file to her chest and did the fish-out-of-water mouth thing a few times before finally stammering, "You're… You're Tanner Reese."

Fuck.

I offered her a tight smile and a chin jerk, praying she was the gape-from-afar type of fan, before carrying on to the receptionist, who was luckily not peering at me like a snack. "I'm here to see—"

"Rita," the nurse finished, and this time, when my gaze landed on hers, her mouth was no longer hanging open, but rather curled into a sly smile. "You're here to see *Rita*." The stars had faded from her eyes as she extended a hand my way. "I'm Sidney, Rita's number-two bestie."

Sighing with relief that she *probably* wasn't about to throw herself into my arms, I took her hand and teased, "Number two, huh?"

She gave me a firm shake before releasing it. "She's got a history with Charlotte, and I've got a guy I like to spend time with, so it works for both of us. I was at her house before your date on Saturday night."

"Ah, the crazy friend with issues. So nice to meet you."

She waved me off. "Don't listen to Rita. I'm only crazy when *she's* being crazy. Like when she was trying to talk herself out of going to dinner with a certain man you may know.

You're welcome, by the way."

A wry smile tipped my lips. So I had an in with bestie number two. *Score one for Team Reese.*

"Any chance you'd be willing to work that crazy again and convince her to have lunch with me?"

She blinked. "Convince her? Did she say no?"

I lifted one shoulder in a half shrug. "I haven't asked her yet. Maybe you could let her know I'm here so *I* can convince her?"

"Oh, I can do you one better. It's all about the element of surprise with Rita." She paused, pressing her lips together before adding, "Or cheese. She responds well to that too."

Jesus, this woman really was crazy, but I kind of loved that Rita had friends like her. It made more sense with how well she'd gotten along with Kevin.

I glanced down to see a shiny band on her ring finger. *Damn.* She would have been perfect for Porter.

Making a show of patting my pockets down, I smarted, "I think we're going to have to go with surprise today. I left the Gruyere at home."

"You'd do better with Asiago," she returned.

And Rita liked Asiago. Excellent insider information that sealed the fate of where I was taking her if and when she agreed to have lunch with me.

Pushing the door wide, Sidney slanted her head in invitation. "Come on, Tanner Reese. I'll take you to her office."

Despite the usually off-putting use of my full name, I got to stepping.

It wasn't a long walk, but during those nerve-racking seconds, I practiced what I was going to lead with.

Things I came up with that wouldn't make me look like a stalker: nothing.

Seriously. I was terrible at this crap. This was why God had graced me with the abs-and-smile package. He had known I couldn't handle the responsibility of chasing a good woman.

I felt Sidney's gaze land on me.

"Are you…okay?"

"Yeah. Of course. Why?"

She barked a laugh. "I'm not going to lie. Seeing a man like you freaking out over my girl is doing some really good things to my romantic side."

I leveled her with a weak scowl, but it only made her laughter intensify.

We stopped at the end of a hall, and the sound of Rita's voice floating out from the other side of the door caused my mouth to split into a goofy grin.

"Oh, wow," Sidney breathed. "That smile is even better than the freak-out."

Nervously brushing my hair off my forehead, I replied, "You tell her about either and I'm canceling your reservation for the opening of The Tannerhouse next week."

"My reservation?" She gasped. "Shut up!"

"My way of saying thanks for getting crazy on her Saturday night. Fair warning: Bring your man with you or I'm going to try to set you up with my miserable brother, wedding ring or not."

"As very exciting as your 'miserable brother' sounds, I'll bring my guy."

I dipped my chin, sucked in a deep breath, and lifted my hand to knock, but Sidney beat me to it.

"You have to know the code or she won't answer."

"The code?"

Her pretty face scrunched. "After Dickhead Greg saw you two together the other night, he's been pacing this hallway any free minute he finds. Don't worry. I've done what I can to keep him preoccupied. I just dumped a stack of charts on his desk for review." She glanced around the hall and then finished in a conspiratorial whisper with, "Some of them aren't even his patients."

Yeah. It was safe to say that I really fucking liked that Rita had friends like Sidney.

"I call him Douchebag Greg," I told her, flashing her an appreciative grin.

"I'd call him a lot worse if he didn't sign my paychecks."

Shit. I hadn't thought about it, but he probably signed Rita's paychecks too. That was no doubt going to turn into a shit show soon enough. However, I wasn't in the position to convince her to find a new job. At least not yet. We'd get there though. Provided she went to lunch with me. Those same nerves ignited inside me again.

"So, what's the code?" I asked, attempting to use my non-existent x-ray vision on the door.

She pointed at her mouth. "My voice. My husband, Kent, is a detective. He loves me so much that he'd probably cover for me if I, say, accidentally tripped and somehow dropped a box of rat poison in Greg's coffee, this being done after he asked me to get a message to Rita for him. Fun fact: Greg knows this. Rita too. So voila, the code was born. Watch this." She knocked. "Rita, open up. It's me."

My back shot straight when the door swung open and my

blonde appeared. She had a phone pressed to her ear, the curly cord stretched out across the office behind her. Today, she was wearing a simple black pencil skirt with a blue silk blouse tucked into the top. More pearls around her neck. Another pair of black heels. But her lips? They were pink this time.

I had no idea what she was going to say about me randomly showing up at her office. And as her green gaze slid to mine, I was standing on the ledge of that plane all over again, knowing it was either the best or worst decision I'd ever made.

My heart was in my throat, and blood thundered in my ears, but all I could get out was a whispered, "Hey."

I waited, holding my breath as her eyes flashed wide. And then she put me out of my misery with a mesmerizing smile.

"Hey," she mouthed, waving with one hand for us to come in while still holding the phone to her ear. "Okay, Mr. Simmons. Let me look back at our records and I'll get back to you ASAP. Right. Uh huh. Okay. I'll give you a call back this afternoon. Okay. Sounds good. Talk to you then. Buhbye." She backed up to the desk, sinking onto the edge while blindly attempting to hang up the phone.

Through it all, her eyes—and her smile—remained glued to me.

She was happy to see me.

Genuinely.

Relief surged through me like a tidal wave.

"Look who I found roaming the halls," Sidney said when Rita finally managed to land the receiver in its base.

Rita glanced at her for only the briefest of seconds before asking me, "What are you doing here?"

"Not stalking you. That's for sure." Yes. That was what

came out of my mouth.

She laughed musically.

Yes. That's what came out of *her* mouth.

While God had not given me the wherewithal to chase a good woman, he had sent me a good woman who thought this inability was funny. I could work with that.

Sidney nudged me with her elbow, and I nudged her back before adding, "And to see if you wanted to maybe go to lunch."

"Yeah. Sure," Rita chirped. "I'm starving."

My smile got bigger.

So did hers.

Which, in turn, meant mine got bigger than big.

"Awww." Sidney rested a hand over her heart. "Look at you two, grinning like a bunch of weirdos. I'm going to leave you two to this awkward moment of bliss." Flinging a hand out, she slapped my shoulder with the medical file she'd been holding. "My last name's Day. D-A-Y. Day. Like…of the week. What time is my reservation at The Tannerhouse?"

Rita's eyebrows shot up. "Your reservation?"

I kept my gaze locked on Rita as I replied to her friend, "You tell me."

"Seven? Table for four? My sister may never speak to me again if I get a table and don't take her. So, obviously, I need to ignore her and invite Kent's brother and his wife."

"Done," I confirmed.

She turned on a toe, calling over her shoulder, "Enjoy your lunch." And then she closed the door.

Rita stood off the corner of the desk as soon as we were alone. "Sorry about her. I told you she has issues."

Ambling forward, I closed the distance between us. "Yeah, but you also said you'd call me. And that didn't happen, so..."

Her face filled with apology as she looped her arms around my hips like it was the most natural gesture in the world. And for the way it warmed my chest, I hoped maybe it was.

"I know and I'm so sorry," she said. "Yesterday was a tad crazy. I didn't want to unload on you after I'd already unloaded on you the night before. But I swear I was going to call after I got off work today." She smiled, sweet and stunning. "But you stopping by is better."

That felt good, especially after I'd nearly talked myself out of going to her at least a dozen times. But something she'd said did *not* sit well with me. "Define crazy?" I mirrored her position, our arms crossing as I linked my hands at the small of her back.

She gave me a squeeze. "How about we talk about where we're going to lunch instead?"

"Rita," I pressed.

"Tanner," she mimicked in the most ridiculous deep rumble that sounded nothing like my voice. But it was cute...and a little annoying.

"Talk to me," I urged.

"Please refer back to the 'I didn't want to unload on you' comment."

I bent at the knee to bring us eye level. "That's what I'm here for. I unload on you. You unload on me. If I need to sit out in the hall so you can do it from the other side of the door, I can make that happen."

She gave my chest a patronizing pat. "Trust me, honey. You don't want any part of the last twenty-four hours of my life."

"Try me."

"Or you could take me to lunch and forget I said anything."

"*Or* you could talk to me."

Her gaze cut off to the side. "Tanner, It's just… I don't know. Maybe we should save the drama dump for a day in the distant, *distant* future."

"First, I like that you're thinking about our distant, distant future."

She rolled her eyes.

"Secondly, I made it pretty clear the other night that I want to explore this thing with you. And despite your inability to reply to my texts—which, from here on out, I'm going to assume was driven by a medical condition and not your desire to talk to me—I seem to remember you saying you want to explore this thing with me too." I gave her a gentle shake, and begrudgingly, she gave me back her eyes. "We're in this together, remember? You slept in my hammock, Rita. Snored in my face and everything. If that doesn't say together, I don't know what does."

Slapping my chest, she laughed, "Shut up. I did not."

"No. You didn't. But as a testament to how much I like you, it would have been okay if you had."

"Well, I can't say the same. You better pray you don't snore in *my hammock*."

"Hey!" I feigned offense, but I couldn't hide my laugh, so I doubted that it packed any heat. "I drama dumped on you. It's only fair…"

"Okay, okay, fine." She blew out a resigned sigh and then dropped her head to my chest so I couldn't see her face. "Your brother is a jerk."

My chin jerked to the side. "Porter? What did he do?"

"He took Charlotte on a date."

"Damn. He's terrible at that crap. Where did he take her?"

"I don't know and it doesn't matter because it's not happening again. But she was pissed at me for kinda-sorta hooking them up, so after I got home yesterday, I listened to her yell at me for a while, and then, while I was trying to find some carbs in my fridge to commiserate with, I realized he stole my fish."

"Porter stole your fish?"

"No," she impatiently told our shoes. "*Greg* stole my fish. And I know what you are thinking. It was just a stupid fish. But it was *my* fish, Tanner."

Greg.

Fucking Greg.

Where was a bubbling volcano in need of a human sacrifice when I needed one?

"Fuck him. I'll buy you a new fish. A whole aquarium full of 'em."

"Please don't," she whined, rolling her forehead back and forth on my chest. "I could barely remember to feed the one I had. It's just the principle of it."

"Did you confront him about it?"

"Yeah. I called him and of course he denied taking it. But I still lost my shit and we argued for over an hour. It was stupid and I played right into his hand by reaching out to him even if it was only to yell at him. But damn, who steals a freaking fish?"

"A dick," I replied curtly. "And he's the worst kind of dick, babe, because he's the kind that has just realized he's losing the best thing he'll ever have. Trust me, it's going to get way worse before it gets better. Change your locks. Avoid him as much as possible. Though, working in the same office with him, this might be difficult."

Her hair fell into her face as she tipped her head to the side to peer up at me like a shy child. "My brother is changing the locks today and I'm looking for a new job. I've got a few leads."

"Good. Let me know if there's anything I can do to help with that. In the meantime, how much longer until you can finalize the divorce?"

Groaning, she lifted her head off my chest. "There's a mandatory thirty-day wait in Georgia, but fortunately and unfortunately, my brother went through something eerily similar with his ex, so we were able to get Greg served pretty quickly. Less than two weeks left now, but that's assuming he doesn't try to drag it out." She screwed her eyes shut. "God, do you have any idea how embarrassing it is to tell you all of this?"

Brushing the hair off her face, I allowed my fingertips to trail down the soft slope of her jaw. With gentle pressure, I tipped her chin up. "Why is talking to me about your life embarrassing?"

Her eyes opened and immediately focused over my shoulder. "I… I don't know. Have you seen you, Tanner? Airing my dirty laundry in front of a guy like you is a little, well… intimidating."

I tried not to let the "guy like you" comment sting by

assuming she was referring to my good genes.

"So this is about looks? Have you seen *you*, Rita? Trust me when I say I am *not* stalking you for your dazzling personality. Honestly, you scare me sometimes. But you have a nice ass, so here I am." I winked to be sure she knew I was kidding.

She glared at me, unimpressed. "I'm serious."

"Fine. Then seriously, Greg is a dick, but whatever bullshit he does or doesn't pull doesn't reflect on you. You have nothing to be embarrassed about." I paused. "Well, except for the fact that you mounted me when we first met. I can't wait to tell our kids about that one day."

"Talking about children is not casual!" She shoved at my chest. "I should have hit you harder when we were playing Slapsies."

Refusing to let her go, I stole a peck at her lips. "See. Scary."

"You're ridiculous."

"Maybe. But you can talk to me. I told you that the other night and I meant it. You can even look at me when you do it too." I swirled a finger around in front of my face. "I promise you won't see anything but understanding up here."

Her face got soft. "You're a sweet guy, Tanner."

"I know."

"And so humble," she deadpanned.

I tsked my teeth and shifted her deeper into my front. "Aw, shucks. Now, you're just flirting."

Her eyes were twinkling with humor, but her face remained stoic. "Are you going to take me to lunch or what?"

"I don't know. Are you going to unload on me instead of ignoring my texts from now on? You're giving me a complex with all the chasing I've had to do in the last few days."

Her sexy mouth fell open in mock horror. "You? A complex?"

I nodded, bending to nip at her bottom lip. "I know. I know. It's hard to see past all of my raw sexual magnetism. But believe it or not, I have feelings too."

"Oh, yeah," she purred. "And what are those feelings right now?"

Unable to hide my smile, I dropped my mouth to hers and whispered, "Asiago mac and cheese."

Her lips parted, a gasp fluttering out. "Dear God. Who's flirting now?"

"Me. Absolutely. Unquestionably. Me. Christ, it's been three days and you're just now catching on to this?"

When she burst into laughter, face-planting into my chest, her arms folding around my hips as she hugged me, I realized how wrong I'd been.

The terror and exhilaration of jumping out of a plane at fourteen thousand feet had nothing on the pure adrenaline-fueled high of finally finding a woman like Rita Hartley.

FOURTEEN

Rita

I WAS SITTING ON A RICKETY WOODEN BENCH BESIDE A FOOD truck in downtown Atlanta when Tanner Reese changed my life. My arteries and waistline probably did not view this change as being for the better. Though my taste buds and stomach adamantly disagreed.

Eight words: Asiago mac and cheese topped with crispy prosciutto.

An actual, honest-to-God tear leaked from my eye after the first bite.

My life was never going to be the same after that twelve-dollar paper bowl of heaven. Tanner had gotten Greek mac and cheese, so his was topped with gyro meat, feta, and Kalamata olives. Mine was better and we'd both known it as soon as they had been placed at the pick-up window.

Since he'd paid, I'd been kind enough to feed Tanner a bite of mine between my cheese-induced moans. However, I hadn't offered him the same generosity when I'd caught him trying to sneak a second bite and had therefore been forced to stab him with my plastic spork.

What? It's not like I broke the skin or anything.

Food-induced violence aside, lunch with Tanner went a lot like dinner had gone with Tanner: Fun. Easy. Comfortable.

We laughed a lot.

He held my hand every chance he got.

He stared me in the eye, listening intently to everything I had to say even as a herd of women congregated near our little bench, waiting for their moment to catch his attention. If he noticed them, he never let on. And when he took my empty bowl to the trash before I had the chance to embarrass myself by licking the bottom, he offered his clamoring audience a panty-drenching smile and stated, "I'm trying to spend some time with my girl today. I'll pop back by for pictures later this week. Yeah?"

Their disappointment was palpable, and I had no idea if he was actually planning to keep his word about popping by later in the week (and if he was, if he'd be willing to pick me up a to-go bowl of carby deliciousness). But the fact that Tanner didn't want to take his attention off me long enough to sign a few autographs or pose for a picture? Well, that was taking the sweet that I'd already known existed inside that man to a whole new level. And, for a woman whose last relationship had ended with her husband in the bed of another woman, there were no words for what that did to the bruises inside me.

Tanner didn't just act like I was special to him with words. He actually followed it up with actions.

After lunch, Tanner drove me back to the office with his

hand anchored to my thigh. The amount of dread swirling in my stomach when he'd put his Mercedes into park was almost comical. I'd taken a two-hour lunch break, but I still wasn't ready to go back to the real world yet.

He must have felt the same, because the second I reached for the handle, he rushed out, "You want to hang out tonight?"

My stomach dipped and heat filled my cheeks as I slowly turned back to face him, a resounding *yes* poised on the tip of my tongue.

But the word never made it past my lips when I got a good look at him.

He was just as gorgeous as he had been on those magazines in the grocery store, maybe more so up close. But it was the pinch of his eyebrows and the pained crinkle on his forehead as though he were staring down the barrel of a gun that struck me the hardest.

Tanner Reese. Freaking Fracking *Tanner Reese*, who I now knew was also just one-named Tanner but no less hot, no less successful, and no less talented—though he was surprisingly more vulnerable than his flashy counterpart—was staring back at me, timid as a teenage boy who'd asked his crush to the prom.

Jesus, my life was surreal.

"Tanner, honey," I said, reaching for his arm.

He caught my hand, lifting it to his mouth to kiss my palm before saying, "Come on, Rita. Don't make me work for this one."

So I didn't. "My place. Say, seven?"

An epic smile split his handsome face. "Your place?"

I shrugged. "I have the better hammock."

"Oh, please."

"Take it or leave it, Reese."

He gave my hand a tug, dragging me in for a lip touch. "Oh, I'm taking it, Hartley. But let's make it eight. I have a meeting with Porter at The Tannerhouse tonight. But even if you forget how your phone works again. I'll still be there. Possibly in your bushes, peering in your window, but there nonetheless."

A laugh bubbled from my throat. And it felt so amazing after the last few weeks of emotional upheaval.

After another of his signature lip sweeps, I climbed out, shut the door, and headed inside, my steps light, my stomach fluttering, and the craziest high pulsing through my veins.

Not surprisingly, Greg was waiting for me when I reached my office.

Also not surprisingly, I slammed the door in his face, locked it, and spent the day tying up loose ends, all the while fighting the losing battle of keeping my mind from drifting back to a pair of ocean-blue eyes.

The TV droned in the background as I sat on my couch, scrolling through a local staffing website. There were several doctors looking for a new office manager. But I wasn't sure I wanted to do that anymore. Short of my years waitressing in college, my experience was limited. But this was my chance for a fresh start. Even if I had no idea what that entailed.

Giving up, I closed my laptop, set it on the end table, and checked my phone.

There were at least a dozen new messages from Greg.

Since he'd found out about Tanner, his messages had been coming more frequently, and the tone of them swung like a church bell between anger and desperation.

Some of them stated that Tammy's baby wasn't his—as if that would matter.

Some of them were profuse apologies, begging me to give him a second chance.

Some of them were insults about Tanner.

And some of them were long streams of consciousness with the general idea being that I was a gold digger who had never loved him because I was quitting on our marriage at the first sign of trouble.

Call me crazy, but having six months of unprotected sex with another woman who eventually fell pregnant was a little more than the first sign of trouble, but whatever.

The hardest part was that he still believed he could fix us. And that did not bode well for me. As long as he saw even the tiniest flicker of hope for our marriage, he'd never sign those divorce papers.

Therefore, I was stuck in some weird purgatory for stupid women who had given up everything for a no-good man. But as my doorbell rang, I got up to answer it with a smile on my face because, in my purgatory, I had the witty Tanner Reese to keep me company.

I pulled open my front door, my smile fading as I drank him in.

Tanner was definitely hot. No mistaking that. But he was also pretty. Like movie-star pretty. He had a strong jaw and an angular nose that made him purely masculine, but his light eyes and his long lashes softened his face. And that smile?

Forget about it. It was charming and flirty, yet somehow innocent and gentle all wrapped up in a gleaming white package.

I knew he was thirty-two, but he looked like the type of guy that should have been out chasing the latest up-and-coming twenty-something actresses in Hollywood.

Instead, he was on *my* front steps, grinning from ear to ear, ready for a boring night of sitting on my couch. Or at least that's what I'd thought we were doing when I'd gotten dressed. He, however, was in a pair of dark slacks, tapered at the ankle, and a white V-neck T-shirt covered by a snug gray button-down cardigan. (Yes, a freaking cardigan like the world's sexiest Mr. Rogers impersonator.) His sleeves were pushed up, revealing muscular forearms, and his pecs cut at hard angles through the thin fabric of his sweater.

He was downright edible *but* entirely overdressed for a night of *hanging out.*

Raking his gaze over me, he fired off, "What the hell kind of witch-craftery is this?"

I curled my lip and leaned against the jamb without inviting him in. "Why do you always ask me that?"

"Uh…because Saturday night, I raced over here in hopes of finding you in yoga pants and a tank top and you were wearing a little red cocktail dress. And tonight, I rushed over here thinking about that little red cocktail dress and hoping it had a strapless sister only to find you in yoga pants and a tank top."

I giggled as he took my hand and spun me in a circle.

"Not that I am complaining because I was right about your ass in yoga pants, but this is hardly going to cut it for The Port."

My body turned to stone. "The Port?"

His hands found my hips. "Oh, that's right, baby. You didn't think Lenox was the only ace up my sleeve now, did you?"

"Ace? No. But The Port is more like a two of clubs in my deck."

"What?" he exclaimed. "Wait, you do realize I don't mean, like, a real port. The Port is a private bar downtown."

I stepped away, allowing him space to enter. He turned around, clicking the locks on a gunmetal-gray Range Rover before following me in.

Leaning around him, I twisted the deadbolt. "The Port is not a bar, Tanner. It's a nightclub for rich people, and I'd rather be shot out of a cannon into a pool of hungry sharks than brave that place. Besides, I thought we were just hanging out tonight."

"Yeah. At The Port."

"Uh, no. That is an excursion that should be limited to New Year's Eve when I momentarily forget that I'm not twenty-two, so I put on a tiny dress, drink too much overpriced wine, and then dance the night away."

He stuffed a hand into his pocket and grinned. "Oh, so you do see why I want to take you there."

I rolled my eyes, sauntering into my living room, very aware that he was probably staring at my butt. "It's a school night, honey. I have to work tomorrow. I can't afford to spend the next two days hungover, sore from head to toe, and paying the price because I am actually a boring thirty-year-old with a bedtime of eleven."

He followed behind me. "Okay. Fine. Where do you

normally hang out? Let's go there."

Swooping my arm out to the side, I did my best Vanna White wave across the length of my couch and then dramatically sat down. "Club Rita."

"Club Rita?" he repeated, incredulous.

"Yep." I patted the leather cushion beside me. "It's Atlanta's most exclusive nightclub. But don't worry. I know the owner, so I was able to pull a few strings and get you an invite tonight."

One side of his mouth crept up. "Is there a bar at Club Rita?"

I pointed toward the kitchen around the corner. "Sure is. I picked up some beer and wine on my way home from work today. I wasn't sure what you'd want, so I grabbed a couple things."

Something strange sifted through his features when he asked, "You stopped on your way home from work to pick up beer?"

"Yeah," I drawled suspiciously. "But if you want something else, we can run out and grab it."

His Adam's apple bobbed as he swallowed. "So this is what you meant by hanging out. Sweats. Beer." He hooked a thumb over his shoulder. "Maybe a little TV."

"Yeah," I breathed when an odd sense of unease settled over me.

He drew in a deep breath, his shoulders pulling up toward his ears, and planted his hands on his hips.

And then he held it.

Just. Held it.

His chest puffed, full of air. He aimed his gaze down my hallway at nothing in particular.

My nerves rumbled as I tried to get a read on his face, but all I could see was his profile.

My pulse quickened, a heat rising in my cheeks as I slowly stood up. "I mean, if you'd rather go out, I guess I can get dress—"

I didn't finish before his head snapped my way, his blue eyes blazing like a wildfire, melting the rest of my sentence.

"You're wearing yoga pants," he whispered on a rushed exhale.

I looked down at myself. They were actually a pair of black-and-pink leggings cropped above the ankle and riding so low on my hips that they would have been a nightmare to do yoga in. But they were soft and tight. They made my ass look fabulous and were the closest thing that existed to sexy lounge wear. I'd paired them with an equally soft pink tank I probably could have worn to the gym if I'd been desperate, but a sports bra would have ruined my subtle cleavage.

When I'd been standing in my closet, trying to figure out what to wear on a "hang-out date," it had been the most obvious choice. Classy. Comfortable. Flirty.

Now…I just felt odd.

"Tanner, I—"

I got absolutely nothing else out because, in the next second, he was across the room, both of his hands cupping my face as he pulled me up to his heavy and demanding mouth.

I moaned when his lips parted, his tongue twisting and tangling with mine. It was a desperate duel, raw and needy. It was so unlike the sweet Tanner usually gave me, but the pure brilliance of it threatened to take out my knees.

Using his hips for balance, I shifted closer until our bodies were flush, my breasts molding to his front. The brush of his hard chest against my nipples as I pushed up onto my toes sent sparks to my clit. My entire nervous system ignited with frenzied need. The feeling was so overwhelming that I momentarily lost purchase of his mouth on a panted, "Oh, God."

"Fuck, woman," he mumbled, raking my bottom lip with his teeth. "You are so goddamn hot."

And then I was off the floor, dangling with his arm hooked around my back as he carried me the last few steps to the couch. Gently, he laid me down first, pausing long enough to strip his cardigan and shirt over his head in one swift movement.

"You know how many women have put on fucking yoga pants when they knew I was coming over?" he rasped.

My breath caught as I got my first real look at the sculpted beauty that was Tanner Reese's body, but it was his ravenous gaze locked on mine that made heat pool between my thighs.

I traced my fingertip over the ripples of his abs as he stared down at me for several agonizing seconds. I was fully clothed as he raked his molten gaze down my body, but my nipples tingled as I squirmed as though the flick of his eyes were a tangible tease.

"Tanner. Please," I breathed, tugging at his arm, unable to take his scrutinizing gaze and the lack of his touch for a second longer.

His lips twitched devilishly before he answered my plea. His body came down, covering mine, forcing me deeper into the couch, and all at once my mind checked out, desire overtaking me.

He gently rocked on top of me, providing enough friction

to ignite the fuse inside me.

"Tann—"

He kissed me again, rough and punishing, breaking it only long enough to answer his own question. "None, Rita. Abso-fucking-lutely none. But you. You wore these fucking pants without any hesitation."

I clawed at his back, trying to get closer. "I just thought—"

He silenced me with another kiss, volcanic waves of pleasure crashing over me with every roll of his hips.

Pushing up onto a hand beside my head, he slid his other under me, going straight to my ass. God, he was such an ass man. I would have laughed, but I was too preoccupied fighting down the climax building inside me as he ground against my core.

"What about how many of those women have assumed I was going to sit on their couch and watch TV, drinking beer that she'd picked up on the way home from work instead of taking her to some very public and stupidly expensive bar?"

I gasped as his long, thick erection, devastatingly still covered by his slacks, stroked against my clit.

I couldn't take it anymore. My head was spinning, and the pressure of my release was climbing closer and closer to the edge until it was the only thing I could focus on.

I didn't care that I was still dressed; he hadn't even bothered to take my shirt off. Or the fact that Tanner and I had never discussed sex. Hell, up until ten minutes ago, he'd never properly kissed me. But, right then, with his hips rolling between my legs, I wanted him so fucking badly that I didn't care if the only foreplay I got was him snatching my pants down before he drove into me, stealing the orgasm from my body on the first thrust.

Okay, maybe I did care.

Because that was exactly what I wanted.

To feel him inside me, stretching and claiming.

His teeth at my shoulders, rough and demanding.

His hands at my breasts, kneading and plucking.

The blunt head of his cock, jerking as I milked him through my release.

My head was a mess these days. But Tanner had made one thing clear.

It was my body he was desperate for.

It was me he'd been chasing for the last few days.

It was me he couldn't get enough of.

Fuck that Rita Laughlin person. Tanner Reese wanted *me*.

And I wanted him to take it.

"Oh, God, honey. Please." I went for the button on his pants, but he grabbed my wrist, pinning it above my head.

He continued his torturous rhythm with his hips, rolling and circling, as he dropped his forehead to mine. His lips peeled back off his teeth as he spoke into my open mouth. "Fuck. You're going to come, aren't you?"

I was. I absolutely was.

Embarrassed, but not nearly enough to stop myself, I closed my eyes and turned my head away.

His hot breath flittered over my skin, igniting the sparks inside me into a raging inferno.

"Oh, fuck. You are," he groaned. "Fuck, Rita. Give that to me." He pressed in deep—or what would have been deep if he had actually been inside me—and demanded, "Give it to me. Let me watch how fucking beautiful you are when you come."

He punctuated it with a nip at the hinge of my jaw.

The sharp twinge of pain severed me in two, my climax tearing through me with the deafening roar of a freight train, wrecking me in its wake.

I was spiraling out of control. Higher and higher, my whole body wound so tight, I prayed for the crash. And like a boulder dropped over the edge of a cliff, I crumbled. The fall back to Earth was no less catastrophic—or extraordinary.

And he kept moving. Kept rolling. Kept stroking. Kept fucking me through our clothes.

I writhed beneath him, my body quaking and my breathing shuttering. Through it all, Tanner bit and sucked his way up and down my neck, his talented tongue swirling and soothing the marks he was surely leaving behind.

When I was thoroughly wrung out, I relaxed into the couch, languid and sated. My arms fell away from his back, sagging at my sides, and finally, his relentless rhythm gradually slowed to a stop.

As the sexual fog dissipated, the gears in my mind started turning again.

Specifically, the part of my brain that controlled post-dry-hump mortification.

I flicked my lids open, hoping I was waking from some kind of orgasmic dream.

But nope. The first thing I saw was his bicep, flexed beside my head.

"Oh. My. *God*," I whispered.

"Holy fuck, Rita," he rasped like he too was spent.

Okay. Okay. Maybe I wasn't alone. "Did you…"

He chuckled, nuzzling my cheek with the tip of his nose.

"No. That was all you, babe."

"Oh, God," I croaked. The heat that only seconds ago had been coursing through my veins was now creeping into my face.

"Tomorrow..." he started, pausing to shift to the side. He wedged his back against the couch, rolling me to tuck into his front.

Burying my face in his chest, I finished the thought for him. "Tomorrow, we are going to have couple's electrical shock therapy in hopes of erasing that from both of our memories forever."

He rested his hand in the curve of my hip and gave me a gentle squeeze. "I see the blood hasn't returned to your head yet. I'll give you a minute to recover. Because there is no fucking way I'm ever letting anyone take that away from me. Tomorrow, I'm forking over my life savings to buy a mountain and then I'm paying someone to carve every single detail of the last ten minutes into the side of it so that the sexiness of watching and feeling you come against my cock can be passed down through the ages for all of eternity."

My stomach dipped, and my pulse slowed. At least he thought it was hot and not as totally sad and desperate as it'd felt to me.

"Okay, that's a bit much, honey," I told his chest. "I'm glad you liked it and all, but why don't you just commit it to memory or something?"

His shoulders shook with amusement. "Rita, look at me."

I shook my head. "I'm good. Thanks."

"Baby," he crooned. "Seriously, give me those eyes." He walked his finger up my side before sneaking under my arm for a tickle.

"Tanner, stop!" I half yelled, half laughed. But he ultimately got what he wanted because my head snapped up.

A satisfied smirk decorated his face. "You gotta stop being embarrassed all the time. I didn't just like that, Rita. I fucking loved it." He slid his hand between us, the backs of his knuckles brushing against my nipples.

A gasp escaped my mouth before I could stop it, and it made his smirk turn downright smug.

"I haven't even seen these yet and I already have claw marks on my back. Who else can say that?"

I rolled my eyes. "Men who wrestle bears."

He threw his head back and a rich laugh bellowed out. "Jesus, you have a snarky reply for everything, don't you?"

I placed a kiss in the hollow dip at the base of his neck.

And then I froze with my lips still touching his warm skin when he asked, "It's been a while, huh?"

I sucked in a sharp breath. It hadn't exactly been a while since I'd had sex. Maybe six or so weeks. Good sex? Psh. I couldn't even remember. But it had definitely been a while since I'd come with a man. Greg wasn't known for his sexual prowess—or his selflessness between the sheets. I'd learned to drop my fingers between my legs when we were together if I wanted an orgasm. Something he had not minded; therefore, he had never tried to change. And, given the state of our marriage over the last few months, a couple of late-night quickies had not resulted in an orgasm, much less a mind-blowing one like Tanner had given me without so much as taking his pants off.

"Uh…I guess you could say that," I replied.

He gave me back his eyes, all the humor gone from his face. "I'm guessing since you only found out about the affair a few weeks back that shit hadn't been good with you two for a while?"

I sighed. "Are we really going to waste oxygen on Greg right now?"

He kissed me, letting it linger as he inhaled reverently. "I have no interest in talking about that prick. But I do want to talk about you, and unfortunately, I can't do one without the other, at least not on this topic."

I twisted my lips, dread souring my stomach. Sadly, that was true. Especially considering…

"He's the only man I've been with."

Tanner turned to granite. "I'm sorry. What?"

Softly laughing, I shimmied down to hide my face.

"Nope. Nope. Nope," he said, shimmying down too. "No more hiding. After what just happened, we need to have a little chat about sex sooner rather than later. I'm willing to take it slow, and I'm more than willing to dry-fuck you into oblivion, but if you'd whispered, 'Please, Tanner,' one more time, things would have ended a little different—like, say, with my cock buried inside you."

My breath hitched, those sparks he'd momentarily extinguished at my clit sizzling back to life. I squirmed, pressing my thighs together to ease the ache.

A small smile popped his dimple, letting me know he'd noticed, but he continued talking. "The only thing that stopped me was, well, it was a fucking spectacular show, and also, I don't have a condom on me. So we did what we did, and now, we are going to have a conversation so that, if the mood strikes again in the future, we both know where we're at. And for that conversation, I'm gonna need you to look me in the eye, babe."

I pursed my lips. "Well, aren't you Mr. Responsible."

He pecked my lips. "No one else? Really?"

"We met when I was twenty-one. Married at twenty-three. Separated at thirty. Few weeks later, enter Tanner Reese. So yeah. I haven't had a lot of time for other men."

"And what about before you were twenty-one? No high school or college boyfriend put the moves on you in the back seat of his Ford Taurus?"

I arched an eyebrow. "Did you drive a Ford Taurus?"

He smirked. "Maybe."

Shaking my head, I explained, "When I was in high school, Jon and I took turns on the weekends staying at home to make sure our mom kept breathing while she was passed out on the couch. The back seat of any guy's Ford Taurus was pretty low on my list of priorities. By the time college rolled around, I was up to my eyeballs in student loans, so I had to work my ass off in order to pay for room and board. I didn't even allow myself to think about men because I couldn't afford the distraction. If I didn't graduate, I had no way to pay back the loans. So I kept my head down until my senior year and then met Greg at a bar the first and only time I'd allowed myself to go out." I shrugged. "So here we are."

"So here we are," he repeated. He rested his hand on the side of my face. "Now, walk me through the part of how you became so sexually deprived that I was able to make you come without ever dipping a finger in your panties."

My eyebrows shot up. "Um. No."

"Um. Yes," he mocked.

"That's none of your business, Tanner. And tomorrow, after electrical shock therapy, you won't remember it anyway. So it's a moot topic." I started to roll away, but he caught my hip.

"I'm not asking for specifics about you and Greg having sex. God knows I don't have enough mind bleach for that. But maybe a little insider info on how long shit has been running downhill for you two. I'm just trying to see where I'm at in all of this."

That shouldn't have sucked as much as it did. It shouldn't have even been a conversation we needed to have. Most people would consider it taboo to talk about the ex with the new guy. But, unfortunately, until I got the divorce finalized, Greg was still a part of my life regardless of how much I wished he weren't. This meant he was part of Tanner's life too.

I groaned and stared into his deep, blue stare. "I'm sorry."

"For what?"

"For the fact that we even have to have this conversation. This is why I've been trying to keep a little bit of distance between us. It's not fair."

He narrowed his eyes. "I don't give the first fuck if it's fair. Stop with the distance. I know the score. And I'm still here because I want to be here. *With you.* Regardless of what baggage does or doesn't come with you. I'm only asking questions because I'm trying to gauge how slow I need to take this thing. If you were blindsided by this shit with him and Tammy, the answer is really fucking slow. I don't want to be your rebound guy. But if you two had been falling apart for a while, therefore you've had some time to distance yourself from the relationship, then the answer would be that I only needed to take it a little slow. But if you two were over and done with long before you found out about the other woman and she was just the precipice to get the ball rolling on your divorce, then I need to get the hell up and go grab the condoms from the glove compartment of my Rover."

My chest got tight when he stopped talking. How was he so sweet? I mean, seriously, that could get obnoxious one day.

"Are you ever a dick?" I asked.

His eyebrows furrowed. "I…um, I'm pretty sure it happens on occasion. Why?"

"Because it's going to be really annoying if you're this great all the time. I'm warning you. I've been known to get a tad bitchy sometimes, and it's going to be no fun at all to take it out on you if you always say the right thing."

A Tanner Reese masterpiece split his mouth. "I will definitely keep that in mind and do everything I can to step up my dick game." He paused, twisting his lips. "Wow, that did not come out right at all."

A laugh didn't just flow from my lips. Rather, it traveled through my entire body, soothing the bruises inside me before springing from my throat.

This. Man.

I slid my arms around his neck and dragged him to me for a deep kiss packed with as much gratitude as it was passion.

He hummed against my lips, the corners tipping up into a smile even as I felt his cock thicken between us again.

What I wouldn't have given to be free to fall in love with this man. He was pretty perfect for me.

But right then, I was *not* perfect for him.

Maybe one day though.

And maybe, if I was really lucky, I wouldn't ruin us both trying to get there.

Breaking the kiss, I finally gave him what he wanted to know. "I was blindsided, Tanner. I didn't think he would ever cheat on me. But we were also falling apart for a while before that. I'm harvesting more resentment toward him than I am any brokenhearted emotions. I'm pissed at him, but worse, I'm pissed at myself for allowing him to pull the wool over my eyes for so long. So, as much as I would *love* to tell you to go grab the condoms out of your car, maybe we should just take it a little slow for a while." I sucked in a deep breath. "Though I did kind of leave you hanging on the dry-humping thing, so if you'd like to give it another go so you don't end up with blue balls, I would be willing to lay here and fake moan for you."

Chuckling, he moved in for another kiss. "As very appealing as that offer sounds, what do you say you point me to the beer and we'll watch some TV instead? Are you all caught up on *Game of Thrones*?"

His warmth engulfed me, and I snuggled into his chest, relishing in how easy Tanner made everything. Even the hard stuff.

"Not if there's more than one episode," I replied.

"Are you fucking kidding me!" he boomed, suddenly sitting up. "You haven't watched *Game of Thrones*?"

I turned and put my feet on the floor. "It's not my thing."

His face was hard and red when he stood and stabbed a finger in my direction. "That's bullshit. *Game of Thrones* is everyone's thing. You need to shut it with that blasphemy and turn on your goddamn TV. Right fucking now, woman."

I cocked my head to the side. "Is this you being a dick?"

He blew out a hard breath and planted his hands on his hips. "I figured I'd give it a shot. Is it working for you?"

It wasn't. But *he* was. Every single thing about him was working for me.

And for that reason alone, I smiled like a freaking maniac when he picked up the remote and turned on *Game of Thrones*.

FIFTEEN

Tanner

"THAT'S A LOAD OF SHIT!" I YELLED INTO MY PHONE while pacing my downstairs kitchen.

Andrea was glaring at me from across the room, and at least a dozen cameramen were milling around, attempting to look disinterested.

My attorney, Doug Cross, sighed across the line. "I agree. But unless the judge grants the injunction, Shana can do whatever the hell she wants."

"Stall her," I demanded.

"Or we could buy the publishing rights. By the time you finish trying to stop this, you'll have spent damn close to the three million she's asking for."

"Yes, I'll have paid that money to *you*. I'm not giving that bitch another dime. She's gotten enough already." I raked a hand through my hair.

Andrea clapped loudly, drawing my attention up. "Joan

already left. Don't touch your hair or we'll have to reshoot everything."

Joan was *Simmer*'s one-woman hair-and-makeup department. Considering I was the only person in front of the camera this week, her job wasn't all that demanding. But in my current state of exhausted-and-pissed-off-at-the-world, I was infuriated that she'd left before we'd finished filming.

"And whose fault is that?" I shot back at Andrea.

"Excuse me," Doug said, reminding me that I still had the phone to my ear.

"Not you," I groaned, heading for the back door.

"Five minutes," Andrea called after me in the especially bitchy tone she reserved just for me.

I slammed the door in a petulant response.

After snagging a pack of cigarettes off the small table, I plucked one out with my lips and ignited the tip.

I inhaled deeply, basking in the burn in my lungs as I stretched them to capacity.

It had been a long-ass week.

The Tannerhouse was only days away from opening and Porter had been running me ragged with last-minute shit. It wasn't his fault. He had a lot of stuff going on with his kids and was doing the best he could. But my eighteen-hour days on the set of *Simmer* weren't leaving me much time to pick up his slack. We were both struggling, and on top of that with Shana's shit hitting my fan once again, I was at the end of my rope.

"What can we do?" I asked Doug on a smoky exhale.

"At this point, we start thinking about a defamation case for if and when the book releases. Judge Bernard might not be willing to stop the publication. But I don't foresee any problems proving slander and hopefully winning all royalties."

I closed my eyes and pinched the bridge of my nose. "Fuck the royalties. I'm more concerned with what the hell is going to happen to my career after half of America including the president of The Food Channel reads that I was snorting lines off of a hooker's tits."

"I know. And trust me—we are still working on the injunction, but the judge did not seem favorable today. I think now would be a good time for you to reach out to the network and let them know what's going on. Who knows? They might surprise you."

"Or they might fire me," I muttered before taking another drag. "Christ, this is such a fucking nightmare."

"Just hang tight, okay? We're going to get through this. Nobody's losing their job."

"Right."

"Now, go. Get back to work or you won't be able to afford the obscene bill my secretary will be sending you tomorrow."

"Fan-fucking-tastic." I hit end without so much as a goodbye, and when I turned back to the door, Andrea was standing on the other side, her arms crossed over her chest as she glared at me through the glass.

"What?" I said loudly.

"Can we get back to filming now?" she yelled back without bothering to open the door.

Impatiently, I lifted my half-smoked cigarette in her direction. "Can I get a minute first?"

She flicked me off, rolling her eyes before stomping away.

I took another toxic inhale. It was the first cigarette I'd

had in a while, but it was doing nothing for my shitty mood.

Nothing in the world pissed me off more than Shana Beckwit. I couldn't even think about her without my blood pressure soaring.

On the flip side, there was one woman who seemed to have the most amazing knack for erasing it all.

After opening my texts, I clicked on her name. My face broke into a smile at the sight of her last message.

Rita: Okay. Fine. I'll bring an overnight bag. But I'm not wearing the yoga pants again.

I hadn't responded because, while I had a nostalgic soft spot for those pants, I was also pretty damn curious to see what she'd bring to my house to sleep in.

Over the last week, going slow with Rita had been the most incredible—and agonizing—thing I'd ever done. Our schedules hadn't allowed us nearly as much time as I would have liked, but we'd gone out to dinner twice, and she'd come over once to watch *Game of Thrones*. Which, not to brag or anything, but also to brag a little bit, I'd been right about. She loved it. I was counting down the episodes to The Red Wedding. And not because I was some kind of masochist eager to relive that insanity. But I was sick of listening to her prattle on about a certain someone's abs. And yes, I did see the irony in that.

It was Monday night, and due to the long hours we'd been pulling to finish up the season, Andrea had given everyone the following day off. It had taken a fair amount of convincing since Rita had to work the next morning, but I'd somehow managed to convince her to spend the night with me. The fickle March weather had cooled significantly over the last few days, so sleeping in the hammock again was out. And with the day I'd had, the idea of having her in my bed, even without sex, was the only thing keeping my head from exploding.

After taking one last drag, I snuffed my cigarette out and then typed a message.

Me: What time are you coming over?

She replied almost immediately.

Rita: What time do you want me there?
Me: Now? My day's been shit.
Rita: Aw, honey. I'm sorry. Are you done filming?

I groaned to myself. Fuck no, I wasn't done filming. It was four in the afternoon, and we probably had at least two hours left—maybe more since I'd messed up my hair like a dumbass.

Me: Not yet.

Rita: Okay. How about this? Let's skip Antojitos tonight. I'll come over and we can watch my future husband's abs crusade across Westeros.

Me: No, babe. You've been talking about tacos all week. Antojitos is the best. I'll be fine.

Me: Also, you call that man your future husband one more time and I'm going to tell you how every single episode ends.

I wasn't annoyed. Not in the least. I was actually smiling because I could imagine her sitting at her desk at work, giggling. Christ, I was such a sap. But that woman—that beautiful, smartass, witty woman—was so deep under my skin and I fucking loved every second of it.

Rita: Don't be silly. (On both accounts.) You had a crappy day. I don't need that funk tainting my delicious tacos experience. We'll hang out at your place tonight. You still think you'll be done by seven?

I breathed a huge sigh of relief. I'd have loved to take her to Antojitos, but a night at home with her was exactly what my tired body needed.

Me: Come at six thirty. I can't wait until seven.
Rita: Then I'll be there at six thirty.

Rejuvenated by more than just the cigarette, I tucked my phone into my back pocket and went inside, all of the anger and frustration washing away by the time I hit the massive kitchen.

And then, with one glance at Andrea, who was standing at the mouth of the hall, it all came roaring back—tenfold.

Because she was standing next to Douchebag Greg.

What the fuck was what I thought.

"Are you fucking kidding me?" was what I said.

Thanks to the internet, my address was unfortunately public knowledge, but after buying the place, I'd had a security gate added at the entrance of the property. But on a day while we were filming, dozens of people coming and going, I figured it wasn't impossible to follow someone in.

Andrea backed away from Greg and threw out a palm to stop me. "Chill out. I already called security."

It was safe to assume I did *not* chill out. "Are you seriously fucking standing inside my house right now?"

"We need to talk." He tugged at the collar of the plain-ass white button-down tucked into his plain-ass white khakis. In what world had this man been able to score a woman like Rita?

"And what the hell makes you think that I want to listen?" I closed the distance between us, snapping and pointing for Andrea to move.

Surprisingly, she followed my order.

He shifted his gaze around the room before bringing it back to mine. "Because, if you don't, Rita's going to lose everything."

I stopped only a foot in front of him, a wicked smile pulling at my lips. This asshole had not just threatened her. He hadn't. No fucking way. "I am positive you didn't say that."

"I said it and I meant it." His nostrils flared as he held my stare, but his hands revealed the barest hint of a shake. "I hired a PI. I have pictures of you two together. Pictures of you kissing her, your hands all over her ass." He paused, sucked in jagged breath, and then spat, "She's my *wife*!"

"Your wife? You're delusional, man. To hear her tell it, she hasn't been your wife in a long time. Even before you bare-backed Tammy's pussy and knocked her up."

He gritted his teeth. "According to Georgia law, she is still very much my wife. And you are fucking her for nothing more than sport."

I blinked. As much as I would have adored to be fucking Rita, it sure as hell wouldn't have been for sport. It would have been to see how many times I could make her come over the next hundred years. Meh. I guessed that could have been a sport.

"You have no idea what you're talking about."

He planted his hands on his hips. "I already spoke with my attorney. If I take those pictures to a judge, she'll never see a single penny of alimony from me. Her infidelities will also be considered in dividing our marital property. I swear on my life, Tanner, if you two keep this shit up, I will leave her with nothing but the waitress's uniform she was wearing when she walked into our relationship."

My vision flashed red, and blood thundered in my ears. This. Fucking. Prick.

"Let me see if I've got this right," I said, bumping my chest with his.

He wisely backed away.

"You spent the last six months *lying* to her, *cheating* on her, *breaking* her, and now, you're pissed and making threats, because *she's* trying to move on? For fuck's sake, you got a woman pregnant. What the hell do you think a judge is going to say about that?"

He lifted his pretentious, weak chin. "She's not trying to move on. She's trying to hurt me. You two have the perfect little arrangement, don't you? You get your rocks off inside of my wife, and she's parading you around through my own fucking office to get back at me."

I barked a laugh. "That's not what's happening here, Greg.

But I applaud your abilities to somehow make everything about you. Truly, that's a talent."

"That's exactly what's happening here. You don't know Rita like I do."

I stabbed a finger into his chest. "You need to fuck off with that shit. I may not have had seven years with her, but you don't know Rita like *I* do. If you did, you never would have given her a reason to move on. Your loss. You fucked up." I smirked, leaning in to whisper, "I really appreciate it though."

His face got tight. "Leave her alone. This is your only warning. Walk away, or I swear to you this will get ugly for her."

"Ugly? For her?" I laughed. "How did a dumbass like you graduate from medical school?" I took a step away and threw my arms out to my sides. "Take a look around you. You might have deep pockets, but I assure you mine are deeper. And for a woman like Rita, you have no idea how much I'm willing to invest. Go ahead. Try it. I fucking dare you to file your fancy little pictures at the courthouse. Do me a favor and send me a copy while you're at it." Smugly, my lips curled at the corners. "I love the way her cheeks pink when my hand is on her ass."

His eyes flashed wide, but I didn't let it slow me. This moron picked the wrong day to fuck with me.

"You show up here tonight thinking you're going to throw down the gauntlet? But you failed to consider that I'm going to be the man to pick it back up."

His jaw went hard, and his shoulders rolled back like he might *possibly* have a backbone. I didn't wait to find out.

"From here on out, my attorneys will be handling *your*

divorce from *my woman*. And just so you know, my legal team will gut whatever ambulance chaser you have on retainer. By the time I'm done with you, you're going to be lucky if you get to leave that marriage with your own dick. Now, get the fuck out of my house so I can finish filming my goddamn show. I have a date tonight." I could barely hear through the blood thundering in my ears, but instead of breaking my knuckles open on his face the way I so desperately wanted to, I winked, turned on a toe, and walked away.

I heard Andrea swoop in behind me, a few of the production crew jogging over to take her back. But Greg wasn't going to do a damn thing other than tuck his tail and slither away like some sort of weird stray dog-snake shifter.

I, on the other hand, went back outside, had one more cigarette, and called Doug back to inform him that we needed to add a divorce to his ever-growing list of legal duties.

With a flirty grin aimed at the camera, I tossed my side towel over my shoulder and flexed my abs. "Until next week. Keep on simmering." I winked for good measure.

"And that's a wrap!" Andrea yelled.

My smile fell immediately. "Thank you God!"

"Good job, guys. Pack it up. I don't know about you, but I'm ready to get the hell out of here."

A glance at the clock told me it was six forty. Rita should have been there already. Unlike me, she was never late. I dug my phone out of my back pocket, finding a notification on my home screen.

Rita: I'm here, but there's a ton of cars, so I think you're still filming. I'll be in my car, Googling pictures of Robb Stark when you're done.

I laughed, shaking my head.

Me: You didn't have to wait in your car, crazy. Get in here. I'm done.

The read receipt popped up only seconds before the text bubble.

Rita: I didn't want to interrupt. On my way in now. See you in a second.

My first stop was pulling on a new T-shirt. Topless cooking was only fun on TV. After that, I retrieved the two resting filets I'd prepared during the last episode and hurried to the stove to put the finishing touches on the Asiago cream sauce. I usually let the team take home whatever odd and ends we'd prepared during filming, but tonight, I had other plans for it.

Rita and I had been dating for over ten days and I'd yet to cook for her. Despite that we'd spent a fair amount of time together, we'd mostly gone out to dinner, so I hadn't had the opportunity. Plus, she'd never asked me, so I hadn't gone out of my way to make it happen, either.

But I'd had a bad day and the first thing she'd done was cancel dinner at a restaurant she was looking forward to and offer to come over, sit on my couch, and just hang out. That meant a lot to me, so I was going to cook her a dinner that would blow Antojitos out of the water. It might not have been tacos, but I was going to make damn sure she'd love it all the same.

I was plating the asparagus and mashed parsnips, the room still a flurry of activity as the crew packed up to leave, when I heard Andrea say, "So you are the infamous Rita."

My head snapped up, my smile already wide.

"Um, I guess?" she replied, her gaze finding mine over Andrea's shoulder.

"You were quite the hot topic of conversation on the set to—"

Oh, hell no. Greg's showing up was a conversation I was going to have with Rita when we were alone. The last thing either of us needed was Andrea swooping in and laying it on her with all the finesse of a sledgehammer.

"Medusa!" I interrupted. "Put the snakes away."

Andrea turned to glare at me, but I only had eyes for my blonde.

I gave her a chin jerk. "C'mere."

She flashed Andrea a tight smile, and then her heels were clipping against the hardwood as she navigated the cords and cameras surrounding my kitchen. She was holding a white casserole dish with both hands, a large pink bag dangling from her arm.

"What's that?" I asked.

She set the dish down on the large island and started around to my side. "Dinner."

I froze with the spoon of asparagus halfway to the plate. "What?"

"Dinner," she repeated, glancing at the two plates I was

working on. "What's that?"

My lips quirked. "Dinner." And then something struck deep at the center of me. "You cooked for me?"

She pressed up onto her toes to steal a quick kiss. "You said you had a bad day. I didn't have much time after work, but I decided to save us the trouble of ordering a pizza."

My chest got tight—like, so damn tight I thought there was a solid chance I was going to have a heart attack. "You… cooked for me?" I repeated, incredulous because it was such a foreign concept. If I wasn't at a restaurant, no one besides my mom ever cooked for me. Honest to God, Shana had never even made me a PB&J. I was a chef. It was assumed that I would always be the one in the kitchen.

But Rita had cooked for me. Just like she'd worn yoga pants last week. And asked if we could hang out instead of gallivanting around town. And she had a hammock. And a great ass. And she laughed at my jokes. And she sat in her car instead of barging in when we were filming. Sure, she always beat me at staring contests, but I could get better. And she was beautiful beyond all reason. And a great kisser. And she made the world's best sounds when she was coming. And I was going to throw down the gauntlet with her ex. And and and…

Her small hand landed on my back. "Tanner?"

I gave her a single finger, asking for a second as I doubled over in full-fledge hyperventilation mode. Okay, it was mostly a joke, but it very easily could have been real for the way my chest felt.

"Honey, are you okay?" She doubled over beside me.

"Yes. But I'm having a bit of a moment." I turned my head to see her and dramatically panted, "What's in the dish, Rita?"

Her emerald greens shifted from side to side. "Uh…tuna noodle casserole?"

And she'd made me tuna noodle casserole.

Jesus Christ, this woman had made a professional, world renown chef tuna noodle fucking casserole.

Something deep inside me knotted again.

Oh, yeah. Life was all about the little things.

I blindly reached out for her arm, accidentally on purpose grabbing her boob before finding her forearm. "With or without peas?"

She giggled, replying, "With. Who the hell makes tuna noodle casserole without them?"

Who the hell made tuna noodle casserole at all anymore? Whatever. It didn't matter. She'd made it *for me*.

I didn't stand up as much as I turned, put a shoulder in her stomach, and lifted her off her feet.

"Tanner!" she squealed as I headed for the stairs. "I'm in a dress."

I smoothed a hand down her ass to make sure she was covered—and also to cop a feel.

"Turn off the stove and lock up when you leave," I called to Andrea and the rest of the stragglers as I took the steps up to my real home as quickly as one could with a laughing woman thrown over their shoulder.

I went straight to my bedroom, threw her on the bed, and then followed her down. I caught my weight on my palms at either side of her head, planking above her before gently settling my weight on top of her. Her simple black sheath dress was too tight around her thighs for me to fit between them, so I rolled to my back, taking her with me.

"What are you doing, crazy?" she asked.

"I'm kissing you, for probably the next twenty minutes, so I'm going to need you to clear your schedule with Robb."

Her laugh morphed into a moan as I took her mouth.

And then I kissed her.

Not "casually" or "slow" or anything else our relationship was supposed to be.

No. I kissed Rita Hartley like a woman I not only *could* fall in love with, but one I absolutely would fall in love with.

We just needed to take some time, grow this thing between us into the highest peak it had always been meant to be.

I'd give her time to heal and get back on her feet.

And she'd give me tuna noodle casserole because I'd had a bad day and she'd had an hour after work.

Together, we'd rule the world. Or, at the very least, sit on the couch, holding hands and laughing as it burned down around us.

I was fine with either option because they both included her.

For twenty minutes, I kissed Rita, frantic and needy. Our hands roamed and our bodies rolled, but we never took it any further.

When our mouths finally broke apart, we were both out of breath, but a pair of matching smiles split our faces.

Rita rolled to her back, an arm crooked over her face. "So I take it you're a tuna noodle casserole guy?"

I flipped to my stomach, propped myself on my elbows, and forced her arm away so I could see her. "I've never actually had it."

"Then what was the caveman act about?"

"You cooking for me. No one does that when you're a chef."

Her nose crinkled. "No one?"

"My housekeeper once boiled me a dozen eggs because they were expiring and she didn't want them to go to waste."

"Jeez, that's depressing."

"It was." I hooked an arm over her stomach and dragged her over until she was halfway under me. "But, now, I have you, so it's not anymore." I wasn't talking about the tuna noodle casserole, and judging by the way her face softened, we both knew it. And damn if that didn't stir that something deep inside me all over again. "We need to talk about something shitty. Do you want to do that now or after we eat?"

Her frown caused a crinkle between her brows. "Shittier than why you taste like cigarettes?"

I rolled my eyes. "Great, are you one of those people who's going to lecture me about quitting?"

She offered me a patronizing glare. "My best friend is a pulmonologist. What do you think?"

"Fiiiine," I drawled. "You'll be happy to know that I've been trying to quit for several months and only smoke a couple cigarettes a week now. Sometimes in the mornings. Sometimes when something stresses me out. There? Are you happy now?"

Her shoes hit the floor one at a time, and then her legs tangled with mine. "I'll be happy when that cigarette count becomes zero. But I'm not going to nag you about it. You're a grown man and can give yourself lung cancer if you want."

"And that's you not nagging me?"

With a devilish glint, she whispered, "Oh, honey, you

have no idea how good I am at *not nagging*. But if this shitty stuff we need to talk about isn't your cancer sticks, what is it?"

I sucked in a deep breath and shifted the rest of the way on top of her to cage her in. "Greg stopped by today."

Just as I'd expected, her face got hard and then a waterfall of rage rained down over her. "Here? Like your house?"

Yep. She was going to lose her mind.

"Yeah. Apparently, he had a PI following us. Snapped some pictures. He told me if we didn't break it off he was going to use them to prove adultery so you walked away from the divorce with nothing."

By the time I'd finished talking, her eyes were huge and the storm brewing inside was so powerful that I could almost feel the winds.

"He did not say that," she hissed, squirming beneath me. "He did not *fucking* say that!"

"It's okay. Just relax, I took care of it. Hear me out—"

I would never understand how she did it, but one second later, she'd Harry Houdini'd me and was out from under me and pacing the room. "He cheated on me for six damn months, got her pregnant and everything, and now, *he's* going to claim I'm the adulterer? He can keep it all. I don't want a damn thing from him."

"If he can prove it, the judge could deny you alimony."

"Fuck his money! I never wanted alimony in the first place. I want my car. That's it. He can have everything else. The day those papers are signed, we're done. Forever. I don't want a damn check in the mail once a month reminding me of the biggest mistake of my entire life."

"Rita, babe, come here. I wasn't done talking." I sat up and reached for her, but she dodged my hand as she continued to pace.

"Is your next sentence that he's buried in your backyard and we need to go on the lam together?"

I laughed. She was so fucking cute—and scary. Very, *very* scary.

Standing off the bed, I pulled her into a hug. "I'm going to take care of it, okay? I need you to call your attorney first thing in the morning and have them send over everything they've done so far to my legal team. They're taking over and I want them to be able to hit the ground running."

Her body was still tight, but she rested her chin on my chest as she peered up at me. "What the hell are you talking about? I can't afford your legal *team*. I could barely afford the retainer on my lone attorney whose office is above a cupcake shop."

"A cupcake shop? Seriously?"

She shrugged. "A little chocolate frosting afterward really took the sting out of our appointments."

"Okay," I drawled, giving her a tight squeeze. "It's official. Call Frank Fondant and tell him he's fired. No fucking way you're going against Greg with an attorney who goes home every night smelling like vanilla extract."

"Stop. He's really nice, and so far, he's—"

"Fired, Rita. Effective immediately. And don't give me shit about paying the team. You know good and damn well I'm not going to let you pay."

She pushed out of my arms. "Then I'm keeping my attorney."

"No, you're not."

She crossed her arms over her chest and glowered. "Yes. I really am. This is *my* divorce, Tanner. I appreciate what you're trying to do. I genuinely do. But I can handle Greg. What I can't handle is using you like every other woman you've been with."

My head jerked to the side. "You aren't using me. I'm *telling you* it's happening."

"And I'm *telling you* it's not happening. You just freaked out because I boiled some noodles and dumped a can of tuna in a bowl for you."

I gripped the back of my neck to keep from reaching for her again. "You forgot the peas."

"Right. See. Frozen peas are not the gift you think they are. Neither are yoga pants or simply sitting on the couch with you."

"They are to me."

Suddenly, her whole body softened like I'd transformed into a puppy right before her eyes. "And I love that they are to you because it makes doing something nice for you that much easier. But I also hate that they mean so much because I hate that no one cooks for you, or is comfortable enough with you to wear lounge attire, or content enough to just spend time with you without an ulterior motive. I don't want to be one of those women." She walked over and rested her palms on my pecs. "I will allow you to use your connections to get us into every restaurant in the city, but I draw the line at you spending thousands of dollars on my divorce. That's just crazy town, Tanner."

I stared down at her, noticing for the first time that her lipstick was smudged around her mouth and her hair was disheveled from where my hands had threaded through it while we'd made out like teenagers. It was then that I realized she was more beautiful than any other woman I had ever met, and not because of the way she looked—which at the moment was rather ridiculous.

It was just… That was the exact second I realized I'd found *her*.

I cradled her face in my hands and used my thumbs to clean up the pink smears around her mouth before dipping down to kiss her. "Do you remember when I told you how I'd always assumed that, when I was done living the fast life, I could just flip a switch and find the person I was meant to be with?" I kissed her again. "You flipped that switch. And not because of peas, yoga pants, or hanging out. You flipped it in ten short days because you're *you* and there is roughly a one hundred percent chance that I'm going to fall in love with *you*, Rita Hartley."

Her eyes sparkled with unshed emotion, so I kissed her again.

"But, in order to do that, I need to get your ex out of your life. If he tries to drag this shit out, that is time I do not have you to myself. And that is time I am not willing to sacrifice. So believe me when I tell you that unleashing my legal team on your divorce is purely selfish on my part. Because I want you, Rita. All of you."

She opened her mouth to speak, but I kissed it closed.

"Don't make a joke right now. None of this is funny." I tipped my head, squinting one eye. "Well, except for the part where I'm falling in love with a married woman I haven't even had sex with yet. But I'm sure Porter will spend the rest of his natural life making fun of me for that. Honestly, as long as you're there laughing too, I'm okay with it."

This time, she kissed me. "Oh, Tanner." She guided my hands down to her mouth, where she kissed one palm and then the other. "You really suck at casual, honey."

I grinned. "Only with you."

"Okay. I'm going to admit that you are kind of freaking me out right now, but I'm choosing to chalk it up to you being weird."

"Fair enough. Now, say yes to my legal team."

She cut her gaze away. "Fine. Call your fancy attorneys and tell them they've got the job. But only because I don't want to waste time arguing with you. Whatever you were cooking downstairs smelled really good and I'm starving."

My smile was unrivaled as I went in for another kiss. All I got was her palm in my face.

"Tanner. Food. I need to stress-eat about everything you just said."

Yeah. I'd found her.

Rita and I spent the night on my couch watching *Game of Thrones*, my legs propped on the ottoman, hers propped on top of mine. She moaned as she ate filet with Asiago cream sauce, and I grinned like a Cheshire cat as I ate tuna noodle casserole, peas and all.

SIXTEEN

Rita

"PLEASE," I CRIED, FISTING THE TOP OF HIS HEAD.

I was on his bed, one week later, my hips swiveling as his tongue swirled my nipple, but not one damn thing was playing between my legs.

Catching his hand, I guided it down to my panties.

He groaned and it vibrated deliciously against my nipple. But that was all I got. That was all I *ever* got with Tanner. And on this particular Saturday morning, I was at my wit's end.

Over the last week, we'd been doing our best to find time together. Per my—Tanner's—attorneys, we'd been staying low profile so as not to give Greg any more fuel while they worked their magic.

This meant no more hanging out at my place, impromptu lunches, or dinners out—not even Antojitos. It also meant I hadn't gotten to attend the opening of The Tannerhouse.

It sucked, but Tanner had hired a security guard for the

gate at his place, so when he'd gotten home that night, looking like he was dead on his feet, I was sitting on his couch, waiting for him.

Tanner's lawyers were more than just good. They were *gooooood*. Within a day of them taking over my divorce, Tammy, along with half the nurses at North Point Pulmonology, had been subpoenaed to testify about Greg's affair. Greg was fuming, but after my attorney filed some fancy request for no contact, he hadn't so much as glanced in my direction. No more flowers or texts. Just blessed radio silence.

It was the first time since I'd found the messages from Tammy that I felt like I could actually breathe again.

Though breathing probably wasn't the best use of my time. But denial had become a way of life.

I was pretending I didn't need to find a less costly place to live.

Pretending I didn't need to find a new job.

Pretending I didn't need to take a good long look in the mirror and figure out who the hell I was.

And I was pretending harder than anything else that Tanner Reese wasn't falling in love with me.

Don't get me wrong. I liked Tanner. *A lot.* He was fun and sexy and sweet. Funny enough, given that the public thought he was a total playboy, he was a little innocent and a lot goofy.

But I was in no place to even entertain the idea of falling in love again.

We could have been perfect together—if I'd met him nine years earlier, when my heart hadn't been on the mend and my ability to trust hadn't been shattered into a million pieces.

But I couldn't turn back time any more than he could heal me.

However, as I was on my back, my hips swiveling, his tongue swirling my nipple, but not one damn thing playing between my legs, none of that mattered.

My thoughts at the moment were very singular.

"Please, I need to feel you," I moaned, tugging on his hand.

I hadn't made out with a man so many times since…well, ever. But Tanner never, ever, never ever ever ever took it any further. It was driving me insane.

Luckily, I hadn't gotten off on his leg like a dog in heat again.

Unluckily, it had taken a massive amount of willpower not to.

His mouth was nothing short of spectacular, and a few days ago, when it had drifted down my neck to my breasts, I'd nearly come unglued. But, despite an embarrassing amount of begging, I'd yet to convince him to have sex with me. I had no clue what he was waiting for. He kept telling me we were taking it slow.

But what could it possibly hurt to fuck me senseless? I swear I'd never been more sexually frustrated in my life.

Tanner, on the other hand, didn't even seem affected. Well, that's not true. He was always hard—beautifully thick, showing from behind whatever pants he was wearing. But he had either the patience of a saint or a blister on his palm because he never once acknowledged any discomfort.

"Slow," he murmured against my nipple.

"Noooo, please no more slow. I'm dying here."

His head popped up, his eyes dancing with humor. "I can't be certain, but I don't think anyone has ever actually died from sexual neglect."

I threw my head back against the pillow. "Oh, goodie. I get to be patient zero."

He crawled up the bed using his elbows, kissing my shoulder before my lips. "You want to dry-hump me again?" he asked, his voice thick with humor.

I cut him a glare that only made his smile grow.

Chuckling, he rolled out of bed, his long cock tenting the front of his low-hung sleep pants. "I promise I'll fuck you soon, you saucy minx."

"Soon as in you're going to grab a condom?"

He shook his head. "I'm going to take a shower."

I threw the covers back. "Okay, I can do shower sex."

He shot me a smirk over his shoulder. "Keep it in your pants, Hartley."

"I'd rather we both got rid of the pants!" I yelled as he shut the bathroom door.

Groaning, and with no other choice, I accepted my new status as born-again virgin and decided to ease my pain with caffeine.

Righting my shirt and then *not* righting my sleep shorts since they hadn't gotten mussed in the first place, I padded barefoot from his bedroom.

I'd spent the night with Tanner several times and had become well versed in the layout of his mini kitchen, but on this particular morning, there was a new addition.

A woman.

I froze mid-step as she turned to face me.

She was older but far from old. Fifty maybe?

Her pretty face lit as soon as she saw me. "Oh, hi there."

"Hi?" I replied.

She got busy with a rag on the counter. "I'm just tidying up in here. I'll be out of your hair in a minute. I try not to clean on the weekends, but Tanner has called me off a lot recently, so I figured I'd come in and play catch-up this morning. Hopefully, Romeo was able to put his dirty underwear in the hamper before you got here."

Ah… The housekeeper.

"Yeah. It was fine." Smiling awkwardly, I walked to the edge of the kitchen, the space too small to comfortably fit us both. "Can I sneak in for a minute to grab some—"

"Coffee?" she finished for me.

"That'd be great."

She went to the Keurig, tipping her chin to the stool on the other side of the bar. "Cream or sugar?"

I followed her direction and settled on the stool. "Both."

She didn't have to walk as much as pivot around the confined space to gather everything. She placed it all in front of me before swinging back around to retrieve my coffee.

"Thanks," I chirped.

"No prob."

She went back to the Mr. Clean routine, and when I was done concocting my perfect cup of joe, I debated if it was ruder to stay or go.

"I'm Rita," I blurted.

"I'm Lynn."

"Nice to meet you."

She glanced up at me. "You too."

Right. Okay. It was definitely ruder to stay. I stood up, the legs of the stool squeaking against the floor.

"So, how long have you and Tanner been seeing each other?"

Shit. I guessed I was staying. I sank back down. "Uh, a few weeks."

Throwing the rag in the sink, she gave me her full attention. "A few weeks? Really?"

For some reason, her surprise wounded me.

I cut my gaze away. "You seem shocked."

"It's just that I haven't seen you before. I figured we'd have run into each other at least once by now. But maybe not, because Tanner hasn't needed me recently."

"Yeah. Weird." I took a sip, thinking the only thing that was weird was this conversation.

"You two serious?"

Now wasn't that the million-dollar question.

I became fascinated with the steam rising out of my mug. "I don't know. We're…spending a lot of time together. Enjoying each other's company."

"Lots of sex, huh?"

My head snapped up, heat filling my cheeks. "Actually, no. Zero sex."

Her eyebrows perked so high that they almost hit her hairline. "Zero? I thought you said you've been dating a couple weeks?"

I rolled my eyes, once again a little wounded by her surprise. "We're taking things slow, okay?" My tone was sharper than I'd intended. "If you must know, I'm in the middle of a pretty nasty divorce, and Tanner's been there for me a lot recently."

She put her elbows to the counter and leaned forward. "How nasty? Jerry Springer or Divorce Court?"

Staring down at the creamy, brown liquid, I sighed, the memory of my damn marriage wounding me this time. "Honestly? Probably closer to Jerry. My ex cheated on me with a nurse at the office we both work at. Got her pregnant and everything. He was acting like a fool trying to get me back, but Tanner was sweet enough to get his legal team involved." I sucked in a deep breath. "So, fingers crossed, if there aren't anymore hiccups, by this time next week, I'll be unemployed, homeless, and broke but free of his bullshit."

When she didn't reply, I hazarded a glance up. The moment her eyes met mine, my back shot straight and my heart lurched into my throat.

Her lips formed a hard slash, and her eyes were a thunderous storm. "You need to leave," she said in a low, malevolent whisper.

"Excuse me?"

She prowled around the bar, her rabid stare locked on me. "Get your clothes, leave, and don't look back. You are not welcome here. Do you understand me? Say you understand me, *Rita*." She said my name like a curse.

I didn't reply because I didn't understand her at all. I didn't know what the utter fuck was happening.

Less than a second later, Tanner gave me my answer as he emerged from the bedroom.

"Hey, Mama. What are you doing here?"

SEVENTEEN

Tanner

MY MOM LOOKED LIKE SHE WAS ABOUT TO SNAP RITA IN half. Usually, I was the only one able to incite that kind of rage from the cool and calm Lynn Reese.

"Is…everything okay?" I asked, tossing my arm around Rita's shoulders, knowing good and damn well *nothing* was okay.

It could be said that I hadn't had the opportunity to tell my mom about Rita yet.

It could also be said that I had been flat-out lying, sending my mom to spas and on shopping excursions to keep her away from my house to avoid this scene right here.

She and my attorney had been quite vocal about me not dating until we got the Shana thing settled. And, at first, I'd agreed.

But then Rita had happened.

"So *this* is why you've been hiding from me?" she asked

without tearing her murderous gaze off Rita.

"Maybe I should go," Rita said, turning on the stool and attempting her escape.

I caught her arm. "Whoa, whoa, whoa. No one's going anywhere. Mom, this is Rita. Rita, this is my mom, Lynn."

My mom laughed without humor. "Little late on that now, aren't you, son?"

"I'm thirty-two. I'm allowed to have a girlfriend without bringing her home to meet the parents first."

"She's married, Tanner. She can't be your girlfriend."

"Oh, wow, this isn't awkward," Rita breathed, rising to her feet. "What if I just go take a shower and give you two a minute?"

Judging by my mom's face, Rita could have taken a month's worth of showers and it wouldn't have been long enough.

I placed a kiss on the top of her head. "Yeah, babe. Sounds good. Put on your sneakers when you're done. I want to show you something out back."

She didn't say another word before trotting away, a full cup of coffee sloshing in her hand.

Mom waited until the bedroom door closed before laying into me. "What the hell are you thinking?"

"First of all, you need to chill out. There's no reason for you to treat her like that."

Cradling her heart, she shuffled around me and then slowly sank to the stool. "Dear God, is it your life's mission to give me a heart attack?"

"I think you're being a tad dramatic."

"And I think you're acting like a damn *fool.* Did you not hear anything Doug said to you when he told you not to start any new relationships? And now you're dating a married woman, who is absolutely using you to fund her divorce and quite possibly her life after her divorce too. Please tell me I did not raise you to be this stupid."

I walked to the coffee maker. "She's not using me for anything. Rita's..." I paused, a smile curling my lips as I searched for the right word to describe her. "Different."

"Shana was different too."

My smile fell, and my gut soured. "Don't do that. Don't even *imply* that Rita is anything like that witch. Night and day, Mom. Night and fucking day."

"Then why have you been sneaking around like you're in high school again?"

"Because of this," I shot back. "Listen to you. You have one conversation with her and you're all up in her face, telling her to leave. I knew this would happen, so I avoided it until I was in a better place and had answers for the seven million questions you're about to ask. I know we're tight and all, but sometimes I need you to mind your own business."

I felt like a dick when she winced.

"That is not fair," she hissed. "I have never meddled in your life. It would be pointless because you're too damn stubborn to listen to me anyway." She put her forearm to the bar and slanted toward me. "But I'm your mother, Tanner. I'm allowed to worry. If that woman had walked out and said you'd taken her out for shrimp and grits and then brought her back here for a night of marathon sex, I'd have offered to cook her breakfast. But she didn't say that. She told me that you two had been dating for weeks. She told me that she was in the middle of a Jerry Springer–style divorce and you were footing the bill. And she told me that, by next week, she'd be unemployed, broke, and homeless. I'm sorry, but after Shana ran you through the mud, I'm not real keen on minding my own business anymore. I am your mother first and your friend last. So, as your mother, I am telling you that woman is no good for you."

My spoon clinked the inside of the mug as I stirred in the half-and-half. "And I'm telling you you're wrong." I propped a hip against the counter and tipped my coffee for a sip. "You remember that fling Porter volunteered us to cater? I met her there. Her douchebag of an ex had his hands on her. I told him to stop and then Rita jumped into my arms like I'd just come back from war." I chuckled. "Okay, wait, that's not helping my case."

"No, it's not," she snapped.

"Okay, how about this? When I'm with Rita, there's not a smooth bone in my body. I ramble with no filter, all the words just come tumbling out because I'm too drunk on her to form coherent sentences."

"That's nice, but—"

"I stand straighter when she's around too. Because, for the first time, I actually care what someone thinks about me. And you know what the best part is? She tells me no. A lot. For weeks, I've been chasing that woman like the sun chases the horizon and she has never once made it easy on me."

"Easy is good, Tanner."

"No, easy is boring, Mom. And I know what you're going to say. It's only been a few weeks, but I promise you, a woman like Rita will never stop making me work for it. And I want that. So fucking bad." I took another sip of coffee because I was getting louder and I needed to buy myself a second to collect my thoughts. When I was sure I wasn't about to burst into song like a fucking cartoon prince, I continued, "Oh, and get this: She laughs at me too. And not because I'm funny. She laughs *at* me."

She curled her lip. "I'm not sure that's a good quality, son."

"It is. Because she gives me shit and argues with me when every other woman just gives me a free pass." I dropped my voice to a whisper. "She sleeps with her hand on my chest, Mom. *My chest*. Please tell me you see the meaning in that."

She looked away. "Jesus, when did you turn into your brother?"

I scoffed. "Now is not the time for insults."

She laughed and gave me back her blue eyes, which matched my own. "So, if this Rita woman hangs the moon, why haven't you slept with her yet?"

I choked on a breath of air. "Shit. How long were you two talking out here?"

"Answer me."

I shrugged. "We're taking it slow."

"That's bullcrap and you know it. You haven't taken anything slow with a woman since you were fourteen and learned you had dimples."

"I just told you how much I like her. Why is it so hard to believe that I'd want to go slow so we don't screw this up?"

"Uh…because you're falling in love with a woman before her divorce is final. That's not slow, Tanner. That's warp speed ahead. But you're not sleeping with her and I want to know why."

"You are entirely too concerned with your son's sex life.

Please speak with your therapist about this."

She rolled her eyes. "I'm still working through you and your brother's teen years in therapy, but I'll be sure to add this to the list."

I took the two steps it required to cross my kitchen and leaned forward on my forearms, mirroring her position and bringing our faces only inches apart. Patting her hand, I smiled and said, "She makes me happy and that's all you need to know. I'll worry about the rest of it, okay?"

A shadow passed over her face. "Have you told her about Shana?"

I smirked because I was about to surprise the shit out of her. "Yep."

Her brows knit together before she verbally punched me in the gut. "Including the baby?"

I sucked in a sharp breath, every molecule burning as they traveled to my lungs. I wanted to lie, but she would have known before the first syllable.

"I knew it!" she exclaimed in a whispered yell.

I shoved off the counter, my neck suddenly itching as the fire in my throat engulfed my entire body. "There's nothing to tell."

"I think when she finds out the woman you broke up with two months ago is currently four months pregnant, she's going to feel a little differently."

I raked a hand through the top of my hair to keep from tearing out of my own skin. "It doesn't matter. It's not my baby."

"We have been through this, Tanner. You and Shana were together for six months and you told me yourself you stopped using condoms three months in. Even if she was out sleeping around, as long as she was sleeping with you too, there's always a chance."

I stared at the bedroom door, knowing that Rita was somewhere on the other side, guilt clawing up the back of my throat. "Why the hell do you keep bringing this up? I have told you a dozen times that it isn't my baby. Let it fucking go."

She stood up fast, stabbing her finger into the countertop. "No. Until that baby is born and a DNA test rules you out as the father, you have to be prepared that it might be yours."

"It's not mine!" I seethed, careful to keep my voice low. Like a caged tiger, I paced the length of that short kitchen so many times that I was dizzying myself with all the turns. But I never took my eyes off that bedroom door. My blood pressure rose with every step, and beads of sweat prickled my forehead. We shouldn't have been having this conversation. It was a non-issue.

But I knew that it wasn't going to be that to Rita. Not after what Greg had done to her.

What the hell was I supposed to do though? I met her the day Tammy told her she was pregnant. What? That same night, on our first date, I was supposed to tell her, "Oh, by the way, my ex is pregnant and she's claiming it's mine and refusing a DNA test until after it's born. But I promise you it's not mine. Though I can't really prove this. Sorry, I know you just met me and all, but I'm going to need you to take my word on this."

No. Fuck that.

I'd wanted Rita from the moment I'd seen her. No fucking way I was drawing that kind of parallel between myself and douchebag Greg.

But that was what she was going to think.

I knew it. And creeping on three weeks later, I still couldn't bring myself to man the fuck up and tell her the truth.

But dammit, the truth *wasn't* the truth.

My mom's face was soft as she stepped in front of me, forcing me to stop. "That's why you're not sleeping with her?"

I craned my head back to stare up at the ceiling. "I don't want her to think I'm anything like him. It's already too similar. But if I sleep with her while lying to her at the same time… I don't know, okay? I just don't know."

She gave my arm a motherly squeeze. "Maybe you should talk to her, then. If she can't handle it, then she's not the right woman for you."

My chest felt like it was caving in as I confessed, "She's the right woman, Mom. I feel it in my bones every time she looks at me. But the timing? It's like fate's cruel joke. She's got so much to deal with over the next few months. Hell, I do too. But I don't want to let her go. If I have to tell her about this bullshit with Shana, she's not going to come back, either. And I wouldn't blame her. Because, right now, I'm doing to her what every other woman does to me. I'm showing her all the pretty stuff in hopes that it will be enough to make her accept the ugly when the time comes."

"Oh, sweetheart," she whispered. "You really like this one, don't you?"

"I do. I really fucking do."

She grabbed both of my shoulders and peered up at me. "Okay, then you just have to make her understand. You aren't like that ex of hers. You're a good man, Tanner. The fact that you're standing here, panicking about it, proves it. It's not like you were out cheating on her. Whatever did or didn't happen with Shana was before you two met. And you and this Rita woman have only been together a few weeks. Who says you need to share all your dirty laundry that soon anyway?"

My shoulders sagged, the weight on my chest becoming heavier. "I did. I pretty much told her exactly that."

She waved me off. "Look, if you feel so strongly about this woman, then you need to find the time to tell her. And soon. The deeper you two get, the more she's going to feel betrayed. It's not going to be easy, honey. But you have to do it. Like, today."

I nodded. She was right. I couldn't stand the constant dread pooling in my gut much longer. It'd been smothering me for too long.

"I think you'd really love her. She's a feisty one." I smiled.

She pulled me in for a hug. "As long as you love her, Tanner, that's all I need."

I leaned away. "Whoa, easy there. I didn't say I love her yet."

My mom smirked. "Yeah, you did. Maybe not those exact words. But you said it all the same."

I grinned. "She's amazing."

"So you keep saying."

"You want to meet her?"

"I already met her and I told her to get out and never come back."

"Okay, so you want to meet her when you aren't the mom version of The Incredible Hulk?"

She sighed. "Since you aren't going to give up without me saying yes. Yes. I'd love to meet her. I'll make you two cream-cheese-stuffed French toast as my apology while I eat my crow."

"Mmm!" I groaned. "You're going to have to raid the fridge downstairs. My grocery lady hasn't been by recently." I winked.

She shot me a scalding glare. "You spent an exorbitant amount of money to send your *grocery lady* to spas around the city because you were too afraid to tell her you had a girlfriend. You could have saved yourself a fortune if you'd fired her instead."

I barked a laugh, and she shook her head, trying to hide her own smile.

She flicked her chin to the bedroom door. "Go on. Tell her it's safe to come out."

I nodded but didn't move. For the briefest second, my mind drifted back to what Rita had said about her parents. I couldn't imagine who I'd be if I'd grown up without my mom and dad the way she had. They had given Porter and me everything they could, including cream-cheese-stuffed French toast while eating crow.

"Thanks, Mom."

She moved around me, heading toward the stove. "Oh, don't thank me yet. I'm about to embarrass the hell out of you."

She would. No doubt about it.

But Rita would laugh. *At* me, of course.

And I would love every single second of it.

EIGHTEEN

Rita

My skin was a suit of wrinkles when Tanner finally knocked on the bathroom door and told me it was safe to come out. I'd have already snuck out the window if his bathroom hadn't been on the second floor. I didn't know that anything could be more embarrassing than getting off while dry-humping my hot celebrity quasi-boyfriend. Though spilling all the Jerry Springer details of my divorce in front of his mom was pretty damn close.

But no matter how long I stood under the two heads of Tanner's shower, scalding water raining down over me, I couldn't wash it away.

He was lounging on the bed like a Greek god, waiting on me when I emerged from the bathroom dressed in a pair of little blue workout shorts, a white fitted tank, and the sneakers he'd told me to put on. I couldn't lie—the shoes were multipurpose. First, for whatever he wanted to show me in the backyard. Secondly, to run from his mom if I needed to make a break for it. Jeesh, Tanner had said I was scary. His mom was terrifying.

Thus, when he told me she was cooking us breakfast and wanted to "re-meet me," I once again stared longingly at the bedroom window, wondering how badly it would hurt if I jumped.

Begrudgingly, I agreed to breakfast, and surprisingly enough, when we walked out of the bedroom arm in arm, his mom was a different person. She had a wide smile and a gentle, teasing demeanor she'd clearly passed to her son. She apologized for snapping at me and then sipped coffee while making us the most unbelievable cream-cheese-stuffed French toast. After tasting her food, I was seriously going to have to step up my game from tuna noodle casserole.

We laughed a lot over breakfast. His mom told me stories from Tanner's youth. Most of them were embarrassing. All of them were hilarious. And Tanner rolled with it, eating with one hand and holding mine with his other. I found out that Tanner paid his mom to clean his house, do his laundry, and shop for his groceries. It was their compromise when he'd insisted that his parents retire early and allow him to take over all of their bills. Well, Tanner said that it was their compromise. Lynn said that her son was helpless in every room of the house outside of the kitchen, so whether he paid her or not, she was still going to be there a few times a week to make sure he didn't drown in dirty laundry. She also said that helping out made her feel like she wasn't freeloading on her son.

Tanner's father didn't share this worry. In a deep exaggerated voice, Tanner made us laugh by impersonating his father.

"I don't give a damn if I am freeloading on my son. That kid freeloaded on me for eighteen years. I'd have a mansion in Maui by now if it weren't for those boys wasting all my money on food and shelter."

I had to admit I was a tad jealous of Tanner's family. They were so dysfunctionally functional, the way a family should be. Love was blazing from their eyes as they talked about Porter and his two kids.

By the time Lynn Reese was ready to leave, all had been forgotten about the way we'd first met. Tanner and I walked her to the door, where she pulled me in for a hard hug and whispered, "Sometimes fate brings you to a place in life for a reason. It's not up to you to figure out what that reason is. It's only up to you to decide what you're going to make of it." It seemed like such a profound comment even if it did confuse me.

With one last smile, she threw a wave in the air and yelled, "See you later, Tootsy!"

"Bye, Mama," Tanner called back, his arm coming down around my shoulders.

I rested my hand on his stomach and kept my gaze on Lynn as she backed out of the driveway. When her car disappeared into the distance, I craned my head back and asked, "Your mother calls you Tootsy?"

"Shut it," he rumbled, but a lip twitch gave him away.

"Come on. I want to show you something." He took my hand and jogged around the side of his house with me in tow.

Tanner had a lot of land for a place that close to the city. Thick trees curtained off areas so that they couldn't be seen from the hammock on his porch, and in all of the time that I'd spent there, we'd yet to go exploring.

We didn't have to go far before a massive playground came into view. The ground was completely covered corner to corner in rubber padding. There were monkey bars, a rope net, rings, lots of hanging ropes, and a huge crescent-shaped ramp at the end. It was far too tall to have been made for Tanner's niece and nephew, but I was confused what else it could be.

"Tada!" he said, waving his hand out like a showcase model.

"What is this?"

He looked at me like I was crazy. "My Ninja Warrior course."

I twisted my lips. "You have your own Ninja Warrior course in your backyard? That seems a bit excessive, even for you. You overcompensating for something, Reese?"

He rolled his eyes and dragged me over to the angled bars. The first set went up, meeting at the peak with a set that went down, shaping it like a roof.

He jumped, catching the first bar, and made quick work of climbing up while saying, "I come out here when I need to think. Porter and I also use it to settle arguments. You were complaining because you missed yoga yesterday, so I thought you might want to give it a go. It's a great workout."

Licking my lips, I became enthralled with the flex of his triceps as his long, lean body swayed on his ascent down the second set.

He dropped to his feet and glanced back at me. "Hop on."

Oh, there was something I wanted to hop on, all right, but it wasn't the bars.

"I've got a better idea. Take your shirt off and demonstrate the rest of it."

He smirked knowingly. "What is with you today? I haven't seen you this horny since—"

"Don't say it!"

He laughed, pausing to rake his teeth over his lip. "I was only going to say a few hours when I had my tongue at your nipple and you were begging me to fuck you."

My breath caught, the memory eliciting a moan. "Why are you so mean to me?"

Shaking his head, he chuckled and moved on, jumping to catch one of the short ropes mounted to a long beam at the top. On the end was a smooth plastic handle hung at the vertical. It looked like it should have slid right through his palm, but with a practiced ease, Tanner held on and swung from one to the next all the way to the end.

I walked down the course, the padded ground giving my steps an added spring. "You're still wearing a shirt!" I called with mock—and a touch of real—annoyance.

"I thought you didn't care about my abs?"

"What? Who told you that crap?"

Smiling, he crouched into a runner's stance while staring down the next obstacle. It was two walls that ran parallel to each other without any kind of grips. They were several feet apart, leaving me curious about how he was going to get through them.

All at once, he sprinted forward, launching himself into space. His left foot landed against the left wall, propelling him to the right before he disappeared inside.

With the sound of his feet echoing off the wood, I hurried to the other side just in time to see him exit—shirtless, like a magician.

"Yesssss," I hissed. Sliding my gaze down his chiseled pecs to his rippled abs, I trotted over to him. "Now, this is what I'm talking about. How about we aim for your pants next?"

His skin was dewy with sweat, and his pulse showed in a vein at his neck.

I circled my arms around his hips and pressed against his front.

His chest heaved from exertion, making him breathy and raw as he said, "You gotta stop, babe. You're killing me. Do you have any idea how bad I want you?"

My nipples tingled as I hoped like hell it was as much as I wanted him. "Enough to finally let me taste that beautiful cock you always keep hidden from me."

Yeah, okay. I was done being patient with the sex thing. I wasn't above torturing him at this point.

His eyes flashed dark. "Jesus, woman."

I pushed up onto my toes, pressing a kiss to his lips, being sure to punctuate it with a sweep of my tongue. "I don't want to go slow anymore, Tanner." Boldly, I reached down and cupped his cock. "Unless you want to go slow inside me."

He tensed, letting out a cursed, "Christ, Rita."

But he didn't move away.

"What do I need to say to convince you?" I purred.

He groaned. "It's not what you need to say. It's what you need to hear."

I quirked an eyebrow. "What?"

Finally, he stepped out of my reach. "We need to talk."

"Noooo. That's the polar opposite of what we need to do. We've done nothing but talk. At the risk of sounding like

Olivia Newton-John, maybe we should let our bodies talk."

His forehead wrinkled. "Is she that chick from *Grease*?"

"It doesn't matter." I followed him forward and teased my hands up his chest. "Come on, honey." I licked my lips. "We're good together. Imagine how *good* we'll be *together*."

He sucked in a sharp breath. Heat and indecision warred on his face, but there was something else there too. I couldn't quite put my finger on it. But it was there, lurking like a dark cloud in the skies of his blue eyes. And like a bolt of lightning, it struck me right in the core of my insecurities.

I rocked back onto my heels. "Is everything okay? You know, with me and you?"

"Yeah!" he replied immediately, looping his arms around my hips. He gave me a warm squeeze. "Absolutely. Why would you ask that?"

"I don't know. You had this look in your eyes, and I got a strange feeling." I shook my head, thinking maybe his constant rejection was messing with my mind. "Just forget I said anything. Sorry."

He dipped down and kissed my neck, murmuring, "You don't need to apologize, babe. But as far as I'm concerned, we're better than good, okay?"

I nodded, feeling sheepish—and relieved. "Right. Maybe we should get back to me forcefully seducing you."

He chuckled and leaned away, the clouds clearing from his eyes.

"Oh, I know. Let's compete for it," I said.

"For what?"

"Sex. You said this is how you and your brother settle arguments. Maybe we could give it a go."

He frowned. "I assure you Porter and I have never run the course to decide if we're going to have sex or not."

"Good. Because…ew." I turned and headed back to the bars. "But you and I can do it. If I win, we have sex. If you win, we can have your boring talk."

"Rita. You're not going to beat me. I've run this course at least a hundred times."

I wasn't. I knew this much. I could probably make it through the bars and the ropes, but I was screwed at the wall-tunnel thingy and the pegboard that came after it. But I was hoping that he'd be as turned on from watching me as I had been from watching him. It wasn't like I had anything to lose. Tanner's foot was still firmly on the sexual brakes. Nothing I was going to say was going to change his mind. But I might be able to *do* something…

"Don't underestimate the power of a determined woman." I tore my shirt over my head and threw it at him. I was wearing a sports bra, but it was the cute, low-impact kind that dipped low in the front.

"Fuck," he groaned, his eyes immediately locking on my breasts like a heat-seeking missile.

"Okay, so the person who gets farthest wins. If we both finish, best time. Sound good?"

His mouth lifted on one side, popping the dimple. "It looks better."

I rolled my eyes. Seriously, why was he making me work so damn hard for this? He obviously wanted me as much as I wanted him.

Whatever. I could do this.

Drawing in a deep breath, I slapped my hand down on

the red button that I hoped was connected to a timer and jumped onto the bar.

I'd been right about the first two obstacles. I cleared them with relative ease. But the walls? Not so much.

"Shit!" I screamed when I landed on my ass, gaining a better appreciation for the rubber matting.

"Ohhhhhh," Tanner drawled, popping his head in between the walls. "That's rough."

"Shut up," I shot back.

When I walked out, he threw my shirt at me. "Put this back on so I can concentrate."

Ducking, I let it sail past my head. "Nah. I'm good."

He toyed with my fingers as we headed back to the beginning, but I slapped his hands away.

When we finally reached the start, he didn't even bother slapping the timer. He took hold of the bar, testing his grip before looking at me. "All right. Here we go. To recap, all I need to win is to get through the tunnel."

I folded my arms across my chest, pressing my boobs up, and replied snottily, "I can hardly wait to have your talk. It sounds so very stimulating. I wonder if I'll be able to walk tomorrow."

He chuckled and swung to the next bar.

"Can I get a clue what this talk is about? Is it possibly a dirty talk?"

"Nope," he said, going up one more.

"Is it a good talk at least?"

He turned to face me mid-swing, hollow fear staring back at me.

"Tanner?" I pressed.

His voice was soft when he finally answered, "No."

Chills exploded across my skin as I watched in horror as the clouds returned in his eyes. "It's about us, isn't it?"

He stilled when he reached the apex of the bars. His dark eyes locked on mine, his face pale and his chest rising and falling with labored breaths that had nothing to do with physical activity.

"Rita," he whispered. And it was sad.

Oh-so fucking sad.

Anxiety mounted inside me. "Answer me."

I had no idea how this had gone from a teasing conversation to me being on the verge of a panic attack. But with every beat of my quickening pulse that he hung there, staring at me, and not saying a single word, my anxiety spiraling higher.

My voice trembled. "Tanner, please. You're scaring me."

In the next heartbeat, his feet hit the ground. It took him four strides to reach me. One arm hooked around my hips, the other going into the back of my hair. He bent, tucking my face into the curve of his neck, and he kissed the side of my face everywhere his mouth could reach, all while murmuring in a sweet and low voice, "Shhh... It's okay. Everything's fine. It's not a big deal."

But it felt like a big deal—even if I didn't have the first clue what it actually was.

My nails dug into his back when he caught my lips.

I was the one panicking, but Tanner tasted like desperation. His tongue searched my mouth while his hands fisted in the back of my hair, the sting at my scalp igniting my body in a conflagration of need.

He was the first to make the move toward the ground,

and I followed eagerly, our kiss never breaking until I was flat on my back. And then it was only so he could shift his attention to my neck.

He continued to chant various versions of, "Everything's fine," as he kissed and sucked his way down my chest. Roughly tearing my bra down, he popped both of my breasts free. I barely felt the spring breeze on my nipple before his hungry mouth sealed over it. He covered my other with his large palm, squeezing almost painfully before following it up with gentle kneads.

"Oh God. Please. Tanner. I want to feel you, baby," I begged, arching off the ground.

And in the miracle of all miracles, he listened.

His hand slid into my shorts, his dexterous fingers circling my clit. "Fuck," he rumbled, sitting up to take my mouth again.

"Yes," I panted, mindlessly grinding into his hand.

The heady combination of his tongue swirling and his fingers playing had a burning need building in my stomach.

I raked my nails down his back as low as I could go, attempting to grab his ass as though I could force him inside me.

He suddenly sat up on his knees, removing his hand. "Fuck. Rita, wait."

"No. No. No. No. No." I followed him, chasing his mouth. "Don't stop. Please."

He kissed me again before palming either side of my face to set me away. "I don't have a condom. We gotta go inside."

No way was I giving him a chance to slow this down.

"I'm clean. I got tested after… Anyway. I also started birth control approximately seven seconds after I came on your leg."

A slow smirk curled his lip, but it was his eyes that showed a blistering vulnerability as they cut over my shoulder, staring off into heartbreaking nothingness.

I paused my frenzy long enough to realize what I was asking of him. Tanner had made it clear that he had quite the track record of women lying to him or using him for their own agenda. Whether it be money, five minutes of fame, or just the thrill taking the great Tanner Reese to bed. He had more than the normal amount of risk associated when having unprotected sex, because I had a sneaking suspicion that not many women would tell him the truth.

"Shit. I probably sound like every woman you've ever been with."

His eyes came back to mine—tragic, heavy, and broken. "No," he whispered. "You sound like Rita." He smiled, but the sadness in his eyes lingered. "It's my favorite sound in the entire world."

"Tanner," I breathed.

But that was all I got out because his mouth came down on mine with a new, invigorated fervor, and in the next second, he pulled my panties and shorts down my legs, pausing at my feet to snatch my shoes off too. He kissed me deep, breaking it only long enough to strip off his own shorts and shoes.

I gasped when the blunt head of his cock met my entrance.

And then it was all Tanner. His searing, blue eyes held mine as he sank into me with a gentle dominance that was almost hypnotizing.

He kissed me dizzy. He held my hand, pinning it over my head. He made me grin against his skin when he rasped a,

"Fuck, why didn't we do this sooner?"

Pure Tanner.

My moans echoed off the trees around us as he rode me hard and steady, his hips rolling and circling, his length stretching and filling me.

I came on a sharp cry that he swallowed as though it were the last drop of oxygen on Earth. And through it all, his body never slowed, never stopped coaxing me through the high or the free fall back down.

I could barely keep my arms around him when I landed back on Earth. But you better believe I kept my eyes open because there was nothing in the world sexier than Tanner Reese on the hunt to find his release.

"Oh fuck, Rita. Oh fuck, baby."

I lost him when he buried his face in my neck shortly followed by the angry jerks of his cock as he emptied inside me.

His entire hard body sagged on top of me. The heavy weight stole my breath, but I didn't dare ask him to move. I rather liked the feel of this beautiful man—inside and out—naked and sated on top of me.

I silently lamented when he pushed up onto his elbows, the playful, blue eyes and teasing smile of the man I loved—

Oh, shit.

Oh, shit.

Oh, fucking shitty shit shit shit.

Oh, God, I was in love with Tanner Reese.

Damn. When had that happened?

He narrowed his eyes. "Why are you looking at me like that?"

Great, the horror must have been visible. "This…is my

after-sex face."

"It's terrible."

I turned my head so I didn't have to look at him as I had a mini meltdown over being in love with him. "Thanks."

He brushed his nose across my cheek. "You're wicked good in bed though, so I'll learn to deal."

"We weren't in bed, and I didn't do anything. All you know is that I can properly hold on while you sex me up on a rubber mat."

He chuckled. "Good to know I did not fuck the smartass out of you."

"Honey, nobody's dick is that big."

His whole body shook as he laughed loudly, the sound curling around me like a warm blanket I never wanted to crawl out from under.

And I loved it.

Probably because I just loved him.

Shit.

He rolled off me and started gathering our clothes. "What do you say we go inside and break in all the places we haven't had sex over the last few weeks, starting with the shower?"

I turned to ogle his unreasonably gorgeous nakedness. "What about your talk? You may have lost the competition, but we should probably still have that chat."

He handed me my shorts and panties, his eyes distant but warm. "It doesn't matter anymore. It actually never mattered at all." He brushed the hair away from my face and kissed my forehead. "And for the record, I didn't lose the competition. I won the girl." He winked, not knowing how right he was.

NINETEEN

Tanner

One week later...

Me: It took eighty-one years for me to get off that damn plane.

Rita: I'm sorry. You really didn't have to fly back and forth to New York in the same day. I could have survived one night without accosting you.

Me: Well, I can't say the same. However, now that you're a hundred years old, I'm concerned with how your tits held up over time.

Rita: You'll be happy to know, after having you legally declared dead, I spent all of your money on plastic surgery. I look as good as the day you left.

Me: I can't possibly think of a better use of my money.

Rita: Don't worry. I saved a little so you can have your wrinkly old-man balls tucked.

Me: And just when I start to think you aren't the perfect woman, you go and surprise me.

Rita: What in the world gave you the idea that I wasn't the perfect woman?

Me: Uh...you had me declared dead after only eighty-one years! I would have waited for you forever.

Rita: And just when I start to think you couldn't get cornier...

Me: Oh, guess what?

Rita: You found a workout video that can turn you into Robb Stark?

Me: Woman! What the hell is wrong with you? Besides. I said, "Guess what." Not, "Be a smartass."

Rita: My bad. Let's try this again.

Me: Guess what?

Rita: What?

Me: I'm not home yet and I need to run by The Porterhouse to pick up something. Want to meet me for dinner?

Rita: And give my attorney a reason to yell at me tomorrow? No, thanks. I'll meet you at your place so we can fuck like the secret lovers we are.

Me: Holy shit! Your mouth is filthy. I like it. Let's eat and then get dessert to-go. I might be able to swipe some of the chocolate syrup we use on the cake.

Rita: Ew. No chocolate syrup. It's not sexy when you wake up at two a.m. looking like you just crawled through the trenches.

Me: Speak for yourself. I'm sexy at all times.

Rita: Except for when you said that.

Me: Fine. Meet me at The Porterhouse and I'll remind

you how sexy I can be.

Rita: Dinner at your restaurant isn't laying low.

Me: Oh, did I forget to mention that I have a surprise for you? It starts with Douchebag Greg… And ends with… Signed the divorce papers today.

Rita: SHUT UP! OH MY GOD!!!!!!! How did they convince him to do that?

Me: I have no idea. But we need to celebrate.

Thirty minutes later, I was standing at the hostess stand at The Porterhouse, greeting gushing customers, when Rita not as much walked through the door as she *pranced* through it. Her huge smile matched my own.

"Excuse me for a second," I told the woman old enough to be my mother who hadn't stopped rubbing my abs since she'd recognized me.

"Hey," Rita breathed when I stopped in front of her. A few hours earlier, that was as far as we could have taken it in public. Now?

"Get over here." I hooked an arm around her back and dramatically yanked her into my arms for a hard, movie-worthy kiss.

She giggled the whole time, and I was positive everyone was watching us.

Whatever. Let 'em stare.

When I finally released her, I gave her a curt nod and greeted, "Miss Hartley."

Her grin stretched. "Well, hello to you too, Mr. Reese."

I toyed with the ends of her hair and very obviously stole a glance down the front of her dress. I still hadn't told her about Shana being pregnant. And it was definitely weighing on me. But I knew the truth, and when the time came, Rita would believe me. End of story. At least that's what I'd convinced myself of while lying in my bed, staring at her the night after we'd had sex for the first time. Not to be confused with all the other nights I'd lain in bed, staring at her over the last week.

Yeah. Fine. I was a little weird. But this woman did it for me—big time.

"You going to stand there and stare at my boobs all night, or are you going to wine and dine me for my celebratory dinner?"

"What if I stare at your boobs *while* I wine and dine you?"

"I would be offended if you didn't."

I proffered my elbow and she linked her arm through mine. Stopping to grab a menu, I stated, "Bethany, we'll be at my table. Can you send someone back?"

She smiled up at me. "Oh, Porter's already back there with his girlfriend. What about table twenty-nine? It's—"

My eyebrows shot up. "Porter's here?"

She nodded.

An idea struck me and I could barely contain my excitement as I looked to Rita. "Does Charlotte know about us yet?"

"No way was I risking that lecture. Plus, she's tight with Greg, being that they're partners and all. I didn't want to put her in an awkward situation if he asked her about us."

"Good," I drawled. "Porter's clueless. My mom has been harassing me to call and tell him about us now that Dr.

Douchebag is treating Travis. But listening to him bitch at me is pretty low on my to-do list. What do you say we kill two birds with one stone and shock the shit out of them?"

Once again, her smile grew to match mine. Seriously, could this woman be any more perfect for me?

"I'll go first and ruffle his feathers. Give me, like, three minutes and then pop over like you just got here."

"You are evil." She pressed up onto her toes and whispered against my lips, "And I love it."

The sound of the word *love* rolling off her tongue made my ears perk. It didn't matter that it wasn't the same love I felt roaring through my veins when I was with her. She loved *it*, not me. But *it* was a start. Everyone had to start somewhere, right?

I kissed her twice more before I finally walked away. Grinning like a fool, I rounded the corner and caught sight of my brother holding Charlotte's hand like the true Reese man he was.

"Well, well, well. What do we have here?" I drawled, stopping at the end of their booth.

"What are you doing here?" Porter asked while shooting me a scowl. "I thought you were out of town still?"

"I just got back. I swung by to pick up a bottle of champagne when Bethany told me you were back here with your *girlfriend*."

"And I'll remind you again, Tanner. Our bar does not double as your personal wine cellar. There's a liquor store two blocks over."

Score! I knew that one would piss him off.

I cut my gaze to Charlotte. She was pretty—simple but

very, very pretty. "You must be the infamous Charlotte Mills."

Her voice was even as she greeted, "And you must be Sloth."

Thoroughly confused, I twisted my lips. "Sloth?"

Her face remained stoic and humorless as she replied, "Yeah. Porter showed me a picture of you. I have to say, though, it must have been an old one, because you haven't aged well." She flipped her gaze to Porter. "I was wrong before. You definitely got the looks in the family."

My mouth fell open. Jesus. And I thought Rita was a ball-buster. Seems both the Reese brothers had a type.

Giving her hand a tight squeeze, Porter crooned, "Is it too soon to be falling in love with you?"

"Yes. Entirely," she said dryly.

Porter seemed entirely unfazed and winked at her. "Okay. I'll wait until tomorrow."

A grin broke across her mouth, taking her from simple to breathtaking. Yeah, Porter had done well with this one.

I blew out a hard exhale, sliding into the booth on Porter's side, practically sitting in his lap until he decided to move over. "Oh, you were kidding."

"Do you mind?" he complained.

"Not particularly," I replied. "So, Charlotte, do you have any idea how much my brother obsesses about you?"

I wasn't altogether sure if this was true or not. But after seeing that smile, I was pretty damn sure he had to obsess about her. Or he was stupid. Which, knowing my brother, could have also been the case.

"Seriously?" Porter grumbled.

She tipped her head to the side and slid her gaze to my

brother, her lips twitching almost imperceptibly. "You obsess about me?"

He shrugged. "No more than you obsess about me."

"I wouldn't be so sure about that," she retorted.

It was at that point that I got downright giddy because I caught sight of Rita out of the corner of my eye.

Showtime!

"She's lying. She's completely obsessed with you," Rita said, sliding beside Charlotte into the booth.

"Uhhh..." Charlotte drawled as she scooted over.

Without missing a beat, I pushed up onto my elbows and leaned across the table, where Rita met me halfway for a quick peck on the lips.

The surprise on their faces was everything I'd hoped it would be. I had no idea how I didn't keel over onto the floor in hysterics.

"Hey, babe," I chirped, reaching out to take Rita's hand.

"Hey. Sorry I'm late. I lost my car keys," Rita replied, completely ignoring the palpable shock like the champ she was.

I stared at her dreamily—only partially an act. "You should have called. I still have your spare. I would have swung by and given it to you."

Porter's slack-jawed shock had me making a mental note to swing by the security office on my way out and see if I could get a copy of this interaction. I was going to blow up a still of his face six feet wide and hang it over my fireplace.

Charlotte found her words first. "Are you two seeing each other?"

Rita's thick, black lashes batted innocently over her green eyes as she spoke out of the side of her mouth. "You aren't the only woman who landed a hot new man. We really need a wine night to catch up."

"I saw you an hour ago!" Charlotte exclaimed. "And literally every day this week. Why do we need a wine night for you to tell me you're dating Sloth?"

Still, utterly confused, I turned to Porter. "She's kidding about the Sloth thing, right? I seriously can't read her."

He hit me hard on the shoulder. "Please, God, tell me you are not sleeping with Rita! Her husband is Travis's doctor!"

Rita scoffed. "I am *not* married."

"Oh, that reminds me," I said. "I talked to my attorney today. He received the signed divorce papers back from Greg."

Porter hit me again. "*Your* attorney is handling *her* divorce?"

Rita pursed her lips and clutched her imaginary pearls. "Thanks, honey. I really appreciate you taking care of that." She then said to Charlotte in a sugary-sweet tone, "Do you guys mind if we do a little switch-a-roo on the seats so I can sit next to my guy?"

"Good idea," I said, lurching out of the booth to let Porter out.

He didn't move a muscle. They just sat there, both of them blinking and staring.

Rita stood and moved in close, pressing her front to my side to give them a front-and-center look at our relationship.

I glanced down at her, fighting the urge to kiss her indecently, only finding success because fucking with my brother was one of my favorite pastimes. I looked back at him and impatiently bulged my eyes. "You gonna get out of there or what?"

"Not until you tell—" He stopped midsentence, something dawning on his face. He immediately slid out of the booth. "Charlotte, can I have a word with you?"

She tore her accusing glare from Rita and asked, "Now?"

"Yes. In private." He smiled tightly, flaring his eyes at her with some kind of obvious urgency.

She blinked for several seconds before sliding out.

"And bring your purse... I need"—He glanced at me as I sat down and pulled Rita in after me—"ChapStick."

"I don't have any ChapStick," Charlotte replied.

"Oh, I do!" Rita exclaimed and then began digging through her bag.

I watched suspiciously as he leaned toward his girlfriend and whispered something to her.

Her whole body jerked as she reached for her purse. "You know what? I think I do have some."

I flashed Rita a questioning glance and she replied with a one-shoulder shrug. What the hell was going on with these two?

"We'll be right back," Porter said, shuffling backward, all but dragging Charlotte with him.

"What was that?" I asked when they disappeared out of sight.

"I don't know, but that was weird. I figured Mom and Pop would still be yelling at us."

"Right? I was really looking forward to Porter losing his shit."

"Oh well. You win some, you lose some." She rested her hand on my thigh and started to peruse the menu. "So, what's good here?"

Smirking, I looked down at her. “Everything. I made the menu.”

She closed the menu and ran the tip of her finger over the black leather exterior. “You made this. By hand? It must have taken you forever.”

I flipped it back open. “No, smartass. Everything on that menu is one of my original recipes.”

“Oh! Show me where the steak with the Asiago cream is.”

“It’s not on there. That’s the Rita Hartley special.”

She beamed up at me, so I stole a kiss.

“But if you want, I can have Raul make it for you.”

She nuzzled her nose with mine. “Nah. It wouldn’t be as good as yours.”

I nipped at her bottom lip. “You’re already getting laid tonight. You don’t need to lay it on that thick.”

She was still giggling when a woman pointedly cleared her throat behind me. I glanced up and found one of the waitresses staring back at me. “Sorry to interrupt. We have a problem.”

I straightened in my seat. “What’s up?”

“There’s a guy at table sixteen who’s sent back his steak three times.”

I immediately rose from my seat. “I thought Raul was in the kitchen tonight?”

She shook her head. “Oh, there’s nothing wrong with his steak. He’s just being rude, and Gus isn’t, well, handling it very well. He got loud with the customer and everyone’s staring.”

“Who the hell is Gus?”

“The new manager. It’s his first night.” She peeked over her shoulder and then lowered her voice. “We’re all kind of hoping it will be his last night too."

"Jesus," I huffed. "Okay, go find Porter about Gus. I'll go see if I can charm—"

"Porter left."

I cupped a hand to my ear. "I'm sorry. Come again."

"He and his girlfriend just took off. Peeled out of the parking lot and everything."

That rat fucking bastard. He knew good and damn well he couldn't leave a new manager alone on his first night. One of us had to be there.

Keywords: *one* of us.

And since I'd shown up on a night when I was supposed to be out of town, that one of us had defaulted to me.

"Uh, Tanner," another one of the waitresses called as she jogged over. "Gus just told the guy to step outside with him. You might want to get over there sooner than later."

Son of a fucking bitch.

I sighed and looked back at Rita. "I'm sorry. My brother's a dick."

She gathered her purse and stood up. "It's okay. Go. I'll meet you at your place later?"

"Shit. We're supposed to be celebrating," I groaned. "I'm sorry."

"Stop apologizing, silly. Go prevent a brawl in your parking lot."

I stared at her longer than I should have considering that the sounds of the argument had started to infiltrate the dining room.

The *I love you* I wanted to say was poised on the tip of my tongue.

We weren't there yet though. Or at least Rita wasn't.

I brought her hand to my lips. "I'll come to your place. It might be late."

She nodded, pressed up onto her toes, and kissed my cheek. "Whenever, baby."

I watched her walk away, then headed toward the lion's den.

All the while texting Andrea to ask for a favor.

TWENTY

Rita

I hated leaving Tanner at the restaurant, but I did it with a smile on my face because, regardless of whether he was with me or not, I was celebrating.

Tanner's attorneys had done the impossible in getting Greg to sign the divorce papers with minimal pushback. Or at least, if there had been pushback from Greg's side, no one had told me. Whoever had coined the phrase "ignorance is bliss" was really onto something.

It probably helped that I hadn't asked for anything in the divorce except for my 401K and my car. My brother had been pissed I didn't go after more. But I didn't want more from Greg. I wanted it to be over so I could move on with the rest of my life. Fighting it out in court with him wouldn't have changed anything. But it would have allowed him to steal more time from me. I'd already given him seven years. That was enough.

At a stoplight on my way back, I sent Sidney a text to let

her know the ink was drying. I didn't bother texting Charlotte. With as fast as she and Porter had dashed out of the restaurant, she was probably on orgasm number three by now. That is if Porter was even a fraction as talented in bed as his brother.

I pulled into my driveway, thinking about how happy I was for her. Charlotte had lived a sad existence. I liked the idea of a Reese man making my best friend laugh again.

My smile died when a dark silhouette I'd have recognized anywhere rose to his full height on my porch.

Fucking Greg.

I slammed the car into park as though the transmission had been the one to invite Greg over and then climbed out. "Why are you here?"

He stuffed a hand into the pocket of his slacks and looked at the ground. "I just need to pick up a few things from the garage."

Bullshit. The only stuff he had in the garage were old high school yearbooks and boxes full of other equally unimportant clutter.

I reached back into my car, slapping the garage door opener. "Have at it." Becoming enthralled with my keys to avoid eye contact, I marched past him.

He caught my arm, gently pulling me to a stop. "Rita, please. Just talk to me. It's done. I signed the papers. I gave you what you wanted. You owe me at least one conversation."

Ice hit my veins as I snatched my arm away. "I gave you everything. What the hell makes you think I owe you anything else?" My hands shook with anger, making it impossible to get my key into the lock.

He stood at my back, so close that his body heat was

suffocating me. "I'm sorry, but you have to make me understand all of this. You gave up on us so fast. I don't see why you wouldn't even try to make us work?"

I spun around to face him. "No, Greg. You don't understand why *you* couldn't *make me* try. That's all this has ever been about. Every single step of our marriage has been about you controlling me."

"Controlling you? Are you kidding me? There's a big difference between taking care of someone and *controlling* them. When we met, you were a mess. You had no car, no money. Your credit was shit. You couldn't even get a lease in your name because you were up to your eyeballs in student loans."

"You just described every twenty-one-year-old kid in America! You act like I was a poor, homeless woman you rescued from a life on the streets. For fuck's sake, I had just graduated with a bachelor's degree from Emory and had been accepted into med school. Med school that I gave up to be with *you*."

He scoffed and raked a hand through the top of his hair. "You didn't give up med school for me. You didn't even get in to med school."

My back shot straight. "What the hell are you talking about? Yes, I did."

He shook his head. "No. You didn't. You got a twenty-six on your MCAT. Even with your GPA, that was nowhere close to what you needed."

I felt like he'd slapped me. "You told me you'd seen people get in with less. You told me I didn't need to retake them."

"It would have been a waste of time. You're not doctor material, Rita. Even if you could have gotten in, you wouldn't have graduated. I didn't want to see you fail anymore."

That verbal punch came so hard that I could barely catch my breath. "You…you didn't want to see me fail anymore? So you told me I got into med school and then proposed, asking me to give it up?"

He reached out and caught the back of my neck. I was in too much shock to push him away.

"You were so fucking stubborn, insisting on doing everything yourself. You barely let me pay for dinner when we first started dating. You were broke and struggling, but you wouldn't let me help. It was embarrassing enough that you insisted on working at the restaurant where all of my friends saw you. Can you imagine how I would have looked if you'd flunked out of med school? Jesus, Rita. Besides, when I asked you to marry me, I didn't hear you arguing about skipping med school. You were relieved."

I wasn't relieved. I was in love. Or so I'd thought.

Tears burned in my eyes, but I refused to free them in front of Greg. "Wow. So you really have been lying to me for our entire marriage."

"No," he said adamantly. "All I ever wanted was to get you out of the ditch your parents all but dumped you in. You were this beautiful, lost woman who needed someone to give her a chance." He bent like he was going to kiss me, so I screwed my eyes shut and turned my head to the side. I felt his cruel lips against my ear as he whispered, "You have never wanted for anything since the day I put my ring on your finger. You work because you want to. You spend my money freely because I want you to have nice things. I don't even say anything about you hanging out with the nurses at work instead of the other doctors' wives like I've encouraged in the past. The only thing I've ever asked of you was to be my wife. And you can't even do that, Rita. I made you the woman you are today and your thanks to me was divorce papers."

The tears were building until I wasn't sure how much longer I could keep them at bay. But, luckily for me, so was my anger.

With my hands at his chest, I gave him a hard shove. "Don't you fucking touch me, you self-righteous prick! I wasn't failing because I didn't get a perfect score on my MCAT. Or because I was broke or working as a waitress. That's life, Greg. You only fail when you stop trying. And you took that from me. You decided I was done. That was not your decision to make. Just like it's not your decision who I hang out with or what I wear or how I cut my fucking hair."

He rolled his eyes. Yes. Rolled them like I was a bratty child throwing a temper tantrum over an ice cream cone rather than a woman enraged over a man stealing almost a third of her life.

"Rita, you didn't have the best female role model growing up. Your idea of dressing up was jeans and a ponytail."

"Don't you dare talk about my mother," I hissed like a rabid animal. "She was shitty and I know it. I don't need you to point it out to me." I sucked in a jagged breath, my entire body vibrating with fury. How was it possible for this man to cut me deeper than he already had? But, right then, I was fileted open. He was right. He'd made me who I was, and I hated myself because of it. "I was broke when we met. I didn't have anything but jeans. I let the girl in the dorm next to me cut my hair once because I didn't have the fifty bucks the lady at the salon wanted, and you know what? That's okay. I'm not fucking perfect, but I spent seven years trying to be that *for you*. Apparently, that was just another failure of mine, because you still went out and slept with another woman."

"She was a mistake."

"You were a mistake!" I roared, my whole body shaking with a punishing combination of anger and adrenaline. "We are *done*. And I mean that in every sense of the word. There is nothing left for us to talk about."

He threw his hands up, allowing them to slap on his thighs when they fell. "And there you go again. Shutting down and quitting on us. You aren't even considering that we could work this out."

I put my fingers to my head and massaged my temple. "Seriously, Greg. What planet do you live on? You just admitted to lying to me and manipulating me for our entire marriage, this being before you cheated on me and impregnated another woman, and you want me to sit down and talk about working it out? You signed the divorce papers."

He took a step toward me and I moved away, my back hitting the door. His palms landed on either side of my head, caging me in.

"I only signed those goddamn papers so you'd drop the boy toy and his team of piranhas. Was that seriously necessary? I looked like a fool with them dragging all of our friends and half of my office in to testify. It was despicable."

My jaw was hard as I snarled, "You need to back up."

He did *not* back up. He got closer. His chest pressed into mine, sending a cold shiver down my spine.

"You never gave a shit about our marriage, did you?" he

spat. "You were so fucking quick to move on when a bigger wallet crossed your path." He leaned down, his mouth coming perilously close to mine. "Say it. Admit it, Rita."

Just over a month ago, he'd innocently kissed me goodbye before going to work. Suspicious and unable to shake the unease in my gut, I'd darted out of bed to check the search history on his iPad.

Everything had changed for me in the next minute.

The betrayal had been paralyzing. The pain, the self-doubt, the mental anguish of knowing I hadn't been enough.

But that was the way it had to be for me to truly throw in the towel on this man. Greg and I had been falling apart for a while. If I was being honest, it had been at least a year since I'd been happy in our marriage. But I wasn't a quitter, regardless of what he thought about me.

The final nail in the coffin was destiny's well-timed announcement about Tammy's pregnancy.

Funny enough, that was the same day I met the whirlwind that was Tanner Reese.

Suddenly, something Lynn had said to me popped into my mind.

"Sometimes fate brings you to a place in life for a reason. It's not up to you to figure out what that reason is, it's only up to you to decide what you're going to make of it."

What I was going to make of this crossroad in my life was still a mystery. But, for the first time since I'd picked up that iPad, I knew without a shadow of a doubt there was a *reason* for it.

After the lies and filth he'd spilled about our past and who I'd been all those years earlier, cheating on me and impregnating another woman was the kindest, most generous thing he'd ever done for me.

Because he'd set me free.

Lifting my chin, I squared my shoulders and leaned into his front until he was forced back a step. "Thank you."

His eyes narrowed. "For what?"

"For showing me what a horrible man looks like. It's really helping me recognize the good ones."

He barked a laugh. "And you think Flanksteak Fabio is a *good* one?"

A smug smile grew on my lips. Tanner would have adored that nickname. Making a mental note to tell him as soon as he got there, I replied, "Oh, I think he's one of the *best*."

He shoved off the door, thankfully giving me space before I was forced to knee him in the groin.

"Rita, you are a shiny, new toy for that man. And when he discovers that you are nothing but rusted-out garbage under that pretty little exterior, he'll be on the next plane back to Hollywood." He shoved a finger in my face and I fought the urge to Mike Tyson the tip of it. "And when that happens, you better not think about crawling back to me. You chose him and we're through."

Jesus, Tanner had been right. Greg was a serious douchebag. He sounded more like the robotic voice on my cell phone than the evil villain he thought himself to be.

Seven years I gave this man. Seven *years*. I was starting to think Tanner's whole flipping-the-switch theory was real. Because my switch for Greg Laughlin was permanently in the off position.

"I'm not sure if you read those divorce papers before you

signed them, Greg, but we're already through. And I wouldn't come crawling back to you if my life depended on it. You have a child to consider now. Maybe you should spend more time worrying about that than a washed-up marriage that was over long before you came between Tammy's legs."

I turned back to the door, my hands no longer shaking, my conscience clear and my head aligned with my heart.

And then Greg proved that he didn't even have to be my husband anymore to break my heart.

"And what about Tanner?" he asked. "You're just going to welcome his bastard child in with open arms? One big happy family? Oh, right. That's okay. Because you're the other woman in that scenario, it's completely acceptable."

I put my chin to my shoulder, chills pebbling my skin and a weight forming in my stomach. "What the hell are you talking about? Tanner doesn't have any kids."

His dull eyes suddenly lit with pure, unadulterated elation, a devious smile tilting his lips. "You don't know?" He scrubbed a hand over his chin. "Damn, I should have led with this."

I didn't want to be interested in anything he had to say. But this was about Tanner, so I turned around. Greg was absolutely a liar, but he was taking entirely too much pride in prepping this verbal weapon for it not to be true.

"It seems your little boyfriend isn't as great as you thought." He leaned toward me. "Or he would have told you about his baby on the way."

That weight in my chest got so heavy that I was barely able to stay on my feet. I swayed back, putting my shoulders to the door. After Greg's betrayal, I didn't have a lot of trust left to put in a person, but I'd never once doubted Tanner.

"What the fuck are you talking about?" I snarled.

Greg only took one step toward me, but there was no mistaking the swagger. "Shana Beckwit? Ring a bell?"

It did. It so did. And, suddenly, I wanted to puke.

Greg continued, his smile wider than ever. "My PI found her while digging into your relationship with that asshole. She was all too willing to give the gory details. Your guy sounds like a real winner. He kicked her to the curb the same day she told him she was pregnant. He's been paying all of her bills, keeping her tucked out of public view like a dirty little secret."

I couldn't breathe or formulate thoughts. It was crazy, but nothing Greg had said to me on that porch had come even close to hurting me like the idea of Tanner lying to me did.

He'd told me about Shana and her stupid book. But why not the baby?

Because the book wasn't true.

Pain, gut-wrenching and bone-breaking *pain*, exploded inside me.

Oh, God. How was this happening again?

After everything I'd told him about Greg and Tammy, he'd kept this from me?

So he could blindside me too?

A silent sob slashed through me.

She was pregnant. Tanner was going to be a dad. I was just supposed to stand by and watch someone else get the family I wanted? Fuck that.

I should have known he was too good to be true. I was just one-named Rita, attempting to play in the big leagues when I'd done nothing but strike out in the minors.

Seven years of my life was a lie. My husband had cheated on me. I hated who I saw when I looked in the mirror. And I'd fallen in love with yet another liar.

I mean, really, if there was ever a time to call it quits in the romance department, this was unquestionably that moment.

I must have looked as shattered as I felt, because Greg opened his arms while continuing to smile and cooed, "Come here, baby."

My chest ached, and my nose stung, tears flooding my vision. I was colder than I'd ever been and it had not one thing to do with the weather. But I would have rather been tied at the stake and lit on fire than accept an ounce of comfort from Greg Laughlin.

"The divorce papers said I have thirty days to vacate the house," I replied, desperately trying to hide the quiver in my voice. "I'll let you know when I'm out. Get your shit from the garage and then forget I exist. Because the moment I walk through this door, that's exactly what I plan to do with you."

And Tanner.

Oh, God, Tanner.

"Rita, come on. We belong together. We both fucked up. I'm willing to forgive you for this whole Tanner thing. Why can't you forgive me for Tammy? Two wrongs. Clean slate."

I bit the inside of my cheek, the pain doing nothing to distract me from the agonizing ache in my chest. I did not have the energy to get into another argument with Greg where I would be forced to point out how absolutely ludicrous his thought process was.

I had no fight left.

I had *nothing* left at all.

But one thing was still true. "I may not know where I do belong in this great big fucked-up world, but I know it's not with you."

He continued arguing behind me.

But I was done.

With everything.

I walked inside, slamming and locking the door, and went straight to my bedroom. After toeing off my heels, I paused to stare at the bed I'd once shared with Greg. Jesus, how was this my life? Divorced from one man. Heartbroken over another. Thirty days from being homeless. Unemployed as soon as I could convince Charlotte to hire someone new.

And broken.

So fucking broken.

I grabbed the blanket off the foot of the bed and dragged it outside. And then, just like the bed, I paused and stared at the hammock. Tanner. I'd had that damn hammock for years, but it was all fucking Tanner now. And with one glance, I lost it—just like I'd lost him.

I didn't want to be inside that house.

I didn't want to be outside that house.

I didn't want to be anywhere anymore.

My knees hit the ground, the tears coming harder.

And I cried and I wept and I mourned.

And then, wrapped in a blanket, I fell asleep on the cold, hard wood on my deck, hoping like hell that, when I woke up, something would make sense again.

TWENTY-ONE

Tanner

"WHAT THE FUCK IS THAT?" I SAID TO ANDREA AS SHE walked into my office at The Porterhouse.

She set a ring box and a stuffed purple monstrosity with gold-sequined wings on my desk. "I think it's a bat."

I picked up the small stuffed animal and turned it in my hand. "Why would you get a bat? I told you to get a fish."

She shrugged. "They didn't have a fish. But they had a bat, and since I'm out running your errands at almost eleven at night, you got a fucking bat."

"A bat makes no sense though. What am I supposed to say? 'And he's a cute rabid animal for you to snuggle with when I'm not around'?"

She gave me a bored glare. "She's a thirty-year-old woman. If she's still snuggling with a stuffed animal when you aren't around, you have bigger problems than it being a bat. Besides, with the stupidity that's in that box, she probably won't even notice the damn thing." She arched an eyebrow. "Are you sure you know what you're doing with this woman, Tanner?"

I snatched up the little velvet box and pried it open. I'd called the jeweler as soon as I'd had former-manager Gus escorted from the premises. He'd designed a few bracelets and such for my mom over the years, but this was the first time I'd ever commissioned him for a ring. It'd cost me a shit-ton of cash to get him to do it on such short notice, but she was worth it. So fucking worth it.

I smiled up at Andrea. "No. I have no idea what I'm doing with this woman. But that's the best part."

"You need to be careful. You haven't known her that long, and after—"

"Don't say her name. Do not even say her name in the same room as this ring. She gets no part of this. None. Do you understand me?"

She rolled her eyes. "Whatever. It's on you, man. You got my dinner?"

"It's in the kitchen. One of the waitresses can grab it for you." I lifted the ring box. "And thanks for picking this up." I jutted my chin toward the bat. "And for that too…I guess."

She smirked, offered me a salute, and then walked out the door.

I rocked back in my chair and picked up my phone.

Me: I'm leaving here in ten. You want me to bring home dessert since I failed on dinner?

Her read receipt never popped up.

I spent the next few minutes making sure everyone was good to close up and gave the kitchen manager my keys to lock up the front too. As I was walking out, I checked my phone one more time. She still hadn't read her texts. I assumed she had fallen asleep.

The drive to her house from the restaurant was entirely too long. I was eager to see her, and as I looked at the ring box on the seat beside me, I was nervous too.

She was going to freak out. Probably laugh in my face. But, like everything with Rita, I was up for the challenge.

When I pulled up at her place, the house was dark, but it was the open garage door that set me on edge. With champagne under my arm, Batty, and the ring in my hands, I hurried up the walkway to her door and knocked.

She never answered.

After several more attempts, including ringing the bell and calling her phone. I started to get worried. She wasn't a hard sleeper. Texts from Sidney or her brother had been enough to rouse her from a post-orgasm coma on the nights she'd stayed with me.

In true stalker form, I decided to go around to the backyard with hopes that she'd fallen asleep on the hammock. But as I climbed the steps to her deck, it was crushingly empty.

When Porter's wife had died, a searing pain unlike anything I'd ever felt had stabbed me in the chest. We'd all been close with Catherine. It was unfathomable that she was gone.

But I'd never, for the rest of my days on Earth, forget the raw, hollow agony carved into my brother's face the first time I saw him after she'd passed.

And the minute my gaze landed on Rita, who was

wrapped in a blanket and lifeless on the ground, I experienced only two paralyzing seconds of what my brother had felt, and it was enough to put me in an early grave.

"Rita!" I roared, the champagne bottle smashing against the wood as I dropped everything and raced toward her.

She shot upright, makeup streaking down her cheeks, fear contorting her beautiful features.

A relief so massive that it made my head spin blasted through my system.

"What? What's going on?" She was the picture of confusion as she scrambled to her feet. Her *bare* feet.

"Don't move!" I shouted, but I was too late. She'd stepped on a broken shard of the champagne bottle.

"Shit!" she screamed, bouncing to her other foot before stepping on another piece. "Shit!" she screamed again.

I got to her in time before she had the chance to change feet again. Hooking her around the waist, I scooped her up off the ground, gave the door a shove, and carried her inside.

"Are you okay?" I asked, taking long steps toward her couch.

She blinked up at me. "What the hell was that?"

"A champagne bottle. Jesus, babe, you scared the shit out of me. Your garage was open and you weren't answering the door. I seriously thought you were dead when I found you." I set her down on the cushion and dropped to a squat in front of her. "Why were you on the ground?"

I watched the light in her green eyes dim into nothingness. It was almost as terrifying as finding her outside.

And then she slayed me with a whisper. "Is Shana really pregnant?"

My entire body got hard, my chest seizing like it had become encased in concrete. What the hell was I going to say? *Yes. No. Let me explain.* Or everyone's favorite response on the topic: *It's not mine.*

In the end, I didn't have to say anything. My face said it all.

"Oh, God. She is," she cried, tears tumbling from her eyes, each one like a razor blade to my soul.

I palmed either side of her face. "Listen to me. Just listen. I can explain. I can explain *everything*."

She batted my hands away. "After everything you knew I was going through with Greg, you never thought to mention that she was *pregnant*?"

"Because it doesn't matter," I implored, desperate for her to believe me.

Abruptly, she stood up, pushing past me. "It matters to me!"

I ground my teeth as bloody footprints smeared on her hardwood. "Rita, sit down and let me look at your feet."

"Fuck my feet. And fuck you too."

With waning patience—at the situation and the fact that there was a *situation* in the first place—I cracked my neck before rising to my full height. "Listen to me. It's not what you think." Jesus, could I be any more cliché? "It's not my baby." Yes. Yes, I could.

She stopped pacing and stared at me. "You sound just like him, you know? Is there some kind of script they hand you when you knock up a woman?"

Lava hit my veins. I was nothing like that fucking douchebag. "That right there is why I never told you. Because I knew you were going to look at me just like you are right now. I'm not your fucking ex. I didn't cheat on you with Shana. I didn't even know women like you existed when I was with her or trust me, I *never* would have been with her."

"Trust you?" she asked on a pained whisper. The blood was pooling around her feet now. Shit. She probably needed stitches.

"Please, just sit down."

Her only move was to plant her hands on her hips. "You want me to *trust* you? We've been together for weeks and you never once thought to mention that you're secretly supporting a woman who is carrying your child?"

The hairs on the back of my neck stood on end. There was only a handful of people who knew I was paying Shana. My attorney had been adamant that it was our best chance at keeping her quiet—at least temporarily. It pissed me off to no end that she was getting a single penny from me. But it pissed me off more to imagine who could have told Rita.

"Who told you that I was supporting her?"

She laughed without humor. "That's the part you're stuck on? Who told *me*? Not the baby she's carrying?"

"No. I'm stuck on the part that I have a restraining order against her because that woman is batshit crazy. And if she's cottoned on to the fact that you're important to me, then I do not put it past her to drive over here and spill a metric fuck-ton of bullshit on you in order to hurt us both."

"So you *don't* support her?"

My jaw ticked as I seethed, "*Who told you*?"

We stared for several seconds, neither of us moving. But, this time, I won.

She rolled her eyes. "Don't worry. It wasn't your precious baby mama. It was Greg. He was here when I got home. Apparently, his PI found her."

Of course it was Greg.

Fucking, fucking Greg.

"That's it. I'm going on a volcano expedition next month," I rumbled. "There's got to be an active one somewhere."

Her eyebrows drew together. "What?"

I waved her off. "What the hell did he want?"

"The usual. To tell me that he sabotaged me from getting into med school so his friends wouldn't laugh at him if—and according to him *when*—I flunked out."

My back shot straight. "What the fuck?"

"That's not even the half of it."

"So give me the other half."

"No," she snapped. "This isn't about Greg. He's a dick. We all know that. This is about *you* having an eerie amount of similarities with him."

"Rita," I warned.

"You had a million chances to tell me, Tanner. A million moments and you wasted them all."

And that's when I lost it. Two long strides carried me to her, where I boomed, "There's nothing to fucking tell! It's not my goddamn baby!"

I shouldn't have touched her when I was that mad, but she had to get off her fucking feet. As gently as I could, I plucked her up, turned, and set her right back down. Then I backed up to give her plenty of space in case I'd scared her.

She didn't look frightened as much as she looked downright murderous. "You need to leave."

I kept my feet in place and bent at the hips to give the illusion of bringing us closer. "Fuck that. We are goddamn adults, Rita. So we are going to have a motherfucking *adult* conversation where you ask questions and I answer them. And while we are doing that, I'm going to take a look at your feet. Because I'm not real excited to talk about my bitch of an ex while you bleed to death right in front of my eyes." I pinned her with a glare, daring her to argue.

She harrumphed. "I can take care of my own feet."

"Probably. But you're going to let me do it so I don't peel out of my own skin while we discuss the dumpster fire that is my life."

She didn't immediately reply, but I could see the gears in her head turning. She was pissed. That much was obvious, but she was hurting too. If she shut down now, there was no telling if I could get back in.

"We're worth a conversation." I tapped over my heart. "You feel it the same way I do. *This* is worth saving."

Her eyes welled with more tears. "I don't think I can do this. If you lie to me..." She trailed off with a shake of her head.

I moved to her, taking her hand in mine before bringing it to my lips. "I'm not going to lie to you. I've been trying to think of a way to bring this up since our first date, but it was just too similar to what you were already dealing with. If you'll hear me out, you'll realize it's not similar in the way you think it is."

"Is..." Her breathing shuttered. "Is this what you were trying to tell me that day we had sex?"

I nodded and kissed her hand again. "I'm not like him. Let me explain. That's all I'm asking."

She cut her gaze off to the side. "I can't deal with her having your baby, Tanner. I just can't. I'll let you explain. But fair warning: I don't think it's going to change the outcome."

"I swear to you it will change everything."

Her greens came back to mine, staring and searching.

And my blues begged and pleaded with everything I had.

Losing her wasn't an option.

"Oh, all right," she finally relented. "There's some bandages and antibiotic ointment under the sink in the bathroom. And grab the white towels. Those are the ones I'm leaving for Greg."

My lips twitched, and she snatched her hand away, pointing an admonishing finger at my mouth.

"Do not even think about smiling right now. I'm pissed and your smile makes me smile, and next thing you know, it'll be a year from now and I'll be rocking your son to sleep. Put that damn thing away."

The only way she was going to be rocking my son to sleep one day was if it was her son too—an idea that usually would have sent me off the deep end, but currently, didn't sound all that bad.

Still, I didn't want her to see my smile. So I did it walking to the bathroom to get Greg's white towels to clean up her bloody feet. Poetic justice if you asked me.

TWENTY-TWO

Rita

I REGRETTED NOT RUSHING OUT THE FRONT DOOR ON TWO gimpy feet, moving to Savannah, and becoming a shrimp boat captain the minute I saw Tanner's smile when he walked away. I was clueless about what he could possibly say to change anything for us.

Even if I could somehow forgive him for not being upfront with me, I wouldn't be able to stay. I wasn't a monster who hated kids or anything. If he'd already had a child, it would have been a completely different story. But I wasn't the type of woman who could stand to be the third wheel while he and Shana started the family I'd always wanted.

All the appointments. The birth. The time they would both want to spend with the baby after it arrived.

I wasn't built for that.

And after everything Greg had put me through, I *really* wasn't built for it.

When Tanner got back, he settled beside me on the couch and patted his lap. Letting him touch me was not my wisest decision, but with the adrenaline ebbing from my body, the wounds on my feet were making their way to my pain receptors.

I rested them one at a time across his thighs.

He groaned, crinkling his nose as he gave them a quick inspection. "Shit. I can't see anything." He pressed a damp towel to my sole, causing a surge of pain to engulf my foot. "Sorry. Sorry. Sorry." He peeked up at me, apology crinkling his forehead.

"I'm okay." At least I was physically. Mentally and emotionally? Not so much. "When did you find out she was pregnant?"

"Two months before I met you," he told my foot.

"And you broke up with her when she told you?"

He nodded. "She said she was pregnant and I walked her to the door, shut it, locked it, and have never spoken to her again."

"That's harsh."

"It wasn't harsh when you kicked Greg out though?"

I winced when he applied pressure to the towel. "Ugh."

"Sorry. Sorry. Sorry," he chanted again. "I'm just trying to get it to stop bleeding so I can see how deep it is."

I blew out a ragged breath. "It was different with Greg. He was cheating on me."

"And Shana was pregnant with a baby that couldn't have possibly been mine. Sooooo…"

"She cheated on you?"

Keeping firm pressure on my feet, he leaned back against

the couch and shrugged. "I can promise you she was no Virgin Mary, but if that baby she's carrying is mine, it was an immaculate conception."

I twisted my lips. "Were you using protection?"

"Nope."

"Then how do you know it's not yours?" I sucked in a sharp breath when a thought struck me. "Can you not have kids?"

He shrugged. "I've never been formally checked or anything, but I'm pretty sure my swimmers are in good shape."

My exhale rushed out; the audible relief was both surprising and embarrassing.

He smirked. "You want babies, Rita?"

I rolled my eyes. "My babies are not the topic at hand right now."

"But you want them. Which is why you wouldn't be able to stay if Shana was having mine." His smirk turned into a smolder.

I nervously tucked my hair behind my ear. "I want a family, Tanner. I won't deny that."

"Me too. Just so you know." Cool and casual, he kicked his feet up onto the coffee table. "We'd make some good-looking kids together."

We would. We so would. But the thought of it only made my chest ache. "And you and Shana?"

"I don't know what our kids would look like, and it doesn't matter because it's never going to happen." He removed the towel long enough to inspect my feet before putting it back.

"How bad is it?" I asked.

"I don't think you'll need stitches."

"You have a medical degree in your back pocket?"

His eyes danced with humor. "Babe, I was a boy who liked to cook in high school. I've gotten into enough fights to know what it looks like to need stitches."

I wanted to laugh. He was funny. But it only made me sadder.

"How do you know it's not your baby?" I whispered.

His smile fell. "Because we weren't having sex."

I blinked at him. Tanner and I had only been sexually active for a short while, but in that time, we'd had *a lot* of sex. On the nights I spent the night with him, he'd spend hours working me over with his hands and mouth before finally giving me his cock. Then he'd wake me up only hours later, slipping inside me from behind. And then, hours after that, he'd wake me up by dragging me on top of him. If neither of us had to work the next day, he'd lazily fuck me in his hammock. And more than once, he'd climbed into the shower with me, circling my clit with his slick fingers as he drove into me hard and fast.

The man was always ready, eager, and willing.

So I found it very hard to believe he'd had a long-term girlfriend he *wasn't* sleeping with. "For how long?"

"The day she told me she was pregnant, it had been over two months."

My head snapped back, shock not just registering on my face but my entire body. "Were you traveling a lot?"

He chuckled. "No. She practically lived with me too. I… wasn't in the mood."

"For two *months*?"

He didn't answer as much as pivot around the question.

"Tampons and shit randomly showed up in my bathroom during that time, so I knew she'd had her period at least once. The doctor confirmed it, saying she was only six weeks along. Shana knows good and damn well that the baby isn't mine. Which is why she's refusing a DNA test until it's born." He shifted uncomfortably. "My camp thought it would be better to shut her up with cash rather than let her drag my name through the dirt while *Simmer* was doing so well in the ratings. Not a single person on my team, including my own mother, believes me that the baby isn't mine. It's fucking disgusting."

I reached out and caught his hand. "Did you tell them you weren't having sex with her?"

He looked away. "I shouldn't have to offer an explanation to anyone about when and where I put my dick. Or in this case where I *didn't* put my dick."

My chest got tight. "But you're telling me?"

He gave me back his eyes, a boyish grin pulling at his lips. "Yeah, because I would really like to continue putting my dick in you. Therefore, it's absolutely your business when and where else I have or haven't put it."

I rolled my eyes. "Such a romantic."

He released his hold on the towel at my feet and took my hand, intertwining our fingers and looking me right in the eyes, sadness and honesty blazing from within. "I would have told you, but I was scared that you'd think I was like Greg. And I know that's no excuse. But I'm crazy about you, Rita. And I panicked that first night when you were hiding in the bathroom. I should have told you then. And I'm sorry you had to hear it from Douchebag Greg. But I swear to you none of this, including Shana's baby, factors into our future."

But he was wrong. So wrong. Because if it wasn't Shana, it was going to be someone else. Every time those clouds entered his eyes, I was going to assume the worst. The jealous girlfriend was only cute for about…never. Eventually, he'd get sick of dealing with the broken pieces of me Greg left behind.

And then I'd lose him.

My stomach pitched as I stared back at him. "Okay."

He blinked. "Okay?"

"Yeah. Okay. I wish you had told me sooner, but I believe you."

He grinned. "That easy?"

I shrugged. "You promised me the truth. And I think that's exactly what you gave me. So, yeah. That easy."

He tipped his head back to look up at the ceiling, breathing, "Thank God, she's sexy and rational."

I giggled, but it was wholly sad. "Hey, why don't you go fill up the bathtub? I think I should probably soak my feet for a few minutes and make sure they're clean before we wrap them up."

"Good idea." He leaned in for a kiss.

I met him halfway for a lip touch, but that was all it was. Two mouths touching, as intimate as a handshake.

At least on my side.

He stood, gently guiding my feet off his lap. Then he made his way to the bathroom.

The minute I heard the water turn on, I jumped off the couch, silently screaming when my feet hit the wood. I tiptoed, wincing with every step to the bathroom.

His head snapped up, his eyes finding mine, just before I slammed the door shut.

"What the hell?" he said.

He twisted the doorknob, but I used my weight to anchor it closed. "I can't do this. I can't do us anymore, Tanner."

"Rita, what the hell are you doing? Open this."

Tanner Reese was my undoing. Call me a coward, but I never would have been able to say this to his face. His beautiful, handsome, smiling face.

But it had to be said. Even if it destroyed me.

"You told me you'd tell me the truth," I croaked.

"I *did* tell you the truth." He gave the door a tug, but I refused to let go.

"No. You gave me *some* of the truth. Greg used to give me some of the truth too. Stuff like: He was going to see a patient at the hospital and he'd be home late. What he neglected to tell me was that he was going to swing by Tammy's on his way home."

"I'm not fucking Greg!" he thundered from the other side of the door. "I wouldn't do that to you."

"But don't you see? You will always be Greg in my head. He ruined me, Tanner. And, eventually, I'll ruin you by making you pay for his mistakes."

There was a thud on the door. "You're not ruined, babe."

My vision began to swim. "I am. I am. I so am. I'm always going to be suspicious. Everything you say. Every time your phone rings. Any time you need to work late. It doesn't matter how innocent it is. I'm going to be Shana one day."

"You are not fucking Shana. Far from it."

"Well, I don't mean exactly her. She sounds horrible. But if I don't take care of myself and get my head together, I can guarantee you that I will be your ex one day."

"Dammit, Rita."

"We're going to push each other's buttons. Me being overbearing. You being aloof."

He gave the doorknob another jiggle. "Get out of the way. I'm coming out."

I didn't move. I just kept crying, and talking, and dying inside. "You want an example? I could tell you didn't tell me the whole truth about Shana tonight. And all I can think about is what you were hiding because I need to brace myself for when it explodes."

"Rita!" he yelled, yanking on the door more roughly.

My feet were killing me, but I held my ground. "And if you want my truth, I never should have been with you."

Everything on his side suddenly fell silent and the doorknob released with a loud click.

My chest was heaving, and my heart was simultaneously pounding and breaking. Everything hurt. And if I just opened that door and let him pull me into his strong arms, I knew he could make it stop. He was Tanner. And I loved him, regardless of whether I should or not.

"I found her book," he announced.

"What?"

"You have to understand. I was at a place in my life where I was miserable. I hated *Simmer*. I hated smiling for the camera. I hated how fucking fake everything felt. Then I met Shana and she felt real. She didn't do all the stuff you do. There was no tuna noodle casserole, and instead of yoga pants, she wore sexy lingerie twenty-four seven. I mean, that's what men want, right? It never felt right with her though. Not like it does with you. There was always just something off about it. But I liked her. And I liked having her around because she made me feel real too. After that, things got better for me. I still hated my job, but at least I had something to look forward to when I was done filming. Then, one night, I was looking for something and I found her book. At that point, most of it was true. Details about our sex life. Details about my daily habits. Details about conversations we'd had where I bashed The Food Channel. It was obvious that it wasn't a journal. She'd been taking notes on our relationship from the very start."

"Tanner," I whispered so softly that I wasn't sure if he could hear me. Doing that kind of thing to any man was messed up on so many levels, but doing it to one as sweet and kind as Tanner was flat-out repulsive.

"You know what I did, Rita? I shut the book, put it back where I found it, went out to my kitchen, and finished making her dinner like nothing had happened. I didn't want to believe that someone I cared about would do that to me. But, most of all, I didn't want to go back to being miserable. So I did the one thing I was with her to escape. I faked it. I went through all the motions for two months, but I couldn't bring myself to have sex with her again. Not even I could fake that. Shit. This sounds so fucking ridiculous. Trust me, I do realize how grossly unattractive and desperate this makes me sound. I won't even tell my mom about this crap."

His words seared through me, burning and twisting as I imagined how he must have felt sleeping in bed at night next to a liar. And then I thought about all the nights I'd done the same thing next to Greg. Maybe I hadn't known about the affair when I'd done it. But I had known I didn't love him.

Tanner's hugs eased my pain like a drug; maybe mine did

the same for him.

Twisting the knob, I gave it a push, but it didn't budge.

"Not yet, Rita."

My heart couldn't take much more. "Honey, please."

"She wasn't happy about me not having sex with her anymore. I don't think she could figure out what was happening, and it made her desperate. I still don't know if she thought she could convince me that the baby was mine or if squeezing money out of me was her plan all along. She wants three million dollars not to publish her piece-of-shit book. That's what her attorney has valued it at." He paused and drew in a long breath. "I'm not doing it. I don't give a fuck what it costs me professionally anymore. But I'm not giving her a single cent more than I already have. She used me and played me for months. I should have seen it coming. She went out of her way to make sure the public knew we were together. She got mad at me once because I didn't introduce her as my girlfriend at an event. Hindsight, I think she just wanted to make sure there were enough people who knew about us to believe her story. I hate her for all of that, Rita. But I hate her more than I ever could have imagined because I think she's going to cost me way more than a few million dollars. I'm terrified she's going to cost me *you*."

I closed my eyes, reality washing over me.

Shana wasn't our problem. Honestly, neither was Greg. Our problem was that neither one of us had any business falling in love with another person when we couldn't even love what we saw in the mirror.

"Why do you keep doing *Simmer* if you hate it so much?"

He laughed sadly. "I don't know. I don't *hate* it…

completely. I love being in front of the camera, but all the acting and none of the cooking… It sucks the passion out of me. And, currently, I'm doing it because I'm supporting a woman who is making my life a living hell. You have no idea how expensive *not* having a baby can be."

"If you're miserable though, why not give yourself a chance to be happy?"

"Pride, I guess. If I quit, I'll look like a failure and, worse, I might actually *be* the failure everyone predicted I would be when I signed on to do the show. You have no idea how much pressure there is to always be bigger and better. A step down might as well be stepping off the map. Trust me, I am not the only chef in the world with a six-pack who knows how to take his shirt off."

Failure. Seven letters that could strike fear in even the strongest of wills. That was not limited to one-named Rita or two-named Tanner Reese. No one was safe from the fear of failure.

I gave the door another push, and this time, it swung open.

He was standing there on the other side, all tall, blond, and mouthwatering. A staggering dichotomy to the insecure man who'd just been pouring his soul out.

"Hey," I whispered.

"Hey," he replied.

"We really have a thing for doors, huh?"

"I love you," he blurted.

I stumbled back, my foot landing wrong, causing pain to explode. I hadn't gotten the first ouch out before he caught me, lifted me, then sank to the floor in the middle of my hallway with me secured in his arms, my ass in his lap.

"I love you," he whispered again. "And I think you love me. Our timing sucks, but I don't want to lose you. This is the first *real* thing I've ever felt with a woman."

"I don't want to lose you, either." I brushed the hair off his forehead, allowing my finger to trail down the curve of his strong jaw. His blond stubble was barely visible, but it prickled against my touch. "And I love you too. But I need some time because I don't love me."

His whole face screwed up tight as he dropped his forehead to mine. "What does that mean? Are we breaking up or just taking a step back? What if we go back to slow again?"

"We suck at slow. I spent the night at your house on our first date."

"So this is it, then? I'm supposed to walk away and forget we ever happened?" He gave me a squeeze. "I can't believe this shit. I finally find the right woman and I'm going to lose her."

"Look at me, Tanner."

His eyes flicked open.

"I need to figure out who I am. And then I need to forgive Greg."

The curl of his lip was so priceless that it almost made me laugh.

"Don't worry. I'll never tell Greg I forgive him. I just need to do it for me. And while I can't speak for you, I think there's a lot of crap you need to figure out also."

He nodded.

I brushed my lips over his. "So maybe we don't look at it like we're breaking up. Maybe we're just shifting our relationship to the back burner to let it simmer while we work on ourselves." I winked, proud that I'd been able to come up with a cooking analogy.

He didn't seem so thrilled. "You know what happens when you let something simmer for too long, Rita? It reduces into nothing. How long are we talking about here?"

My heart sank, and my throat got thick with emotion. "I…I don't…" I didn't get anything else out because he kissed me.

Slow and sorrowful.

Soft and filled with apology.

And still quite possibly the best kiss I'd ever received.

That is until I realized that Tanner Reese was kissing me goodbye.

He broke the connection of our mouths and climbed to his feet with me still held securely in his arms. He carried me to the couch and set me down. "If I don't leave now, I may never find the courage to walk out that door." He put his hands on his hips and swallowed back whatever emotion was trying to escape, and in true Tanner fashion, he covered it with a joke. "It would be awkward as hell if I was still stuck in this house when Greg moves in next month."

I laughed, but it only caused a tear to spill from my eyes.

"Promise me that the minute you've got your shit sorted, you'll come find me. Two weeks, six months, fifteen years—it doesn't matter."

I swiped under my eyes. "It's not going to be fifteen years, Tanner."

He stabbed a hand into the top of his hair. "If it's a day, it's going to feel like fifteen years to me."

"Honey," I breathed.

He cleared his throat. "Listen, do me a favor. Call Sidney and see if she'll come over to help you with your feet. I hate leaving you like this. But I can't stay."

"Okay, I'll call her," I whispered.

He stared at me for a long minute, dread hanging in the air between us. But it was the only way. No matter how much it hurt.

"I love you," he said. "And if you need anything—"

"You will be the very first person I call."

He blew out an exasperated and resigned sigh that said it all.

And then a pain far greater than even the day I'd found out about Greg's affair struck me like a million arrows falling from the sky as I watched Tanner Reese walk out my front door.

TWENTY-THREE

Tanner

MY CHEST FELT LIKE I'D BEEN BEATEN AS I WALKED INTO my empty house that first night. Rita had been right. I had a lot of stuff I needed to work through. I'd been naively hoping she and I could work through our shit together.

It was stupid.

Almost as stupid as falling in love with a woman in the middle of her divorce. But she was *Rita*. Beautiful, kind, generous, smartass extraordinaire. I hadn't stood a chance after meeting that woman.

And it wasn't just her divorce that made our relationship the recipe for disaster. I had issues stacked a mile high that I'd been neglecting for entirely too long.

Could I live with myself if I did another season of *Simmer*?

Why I'd settled for Shana in the first place.

Why I'd pretended for so long with her to keep from being alone.

And the million-dollar question: What I wanted to do for the rest of my life?

I fell asleep in my hammock that night with a highball of Belvedere at my side, a myriad of regrets swirling in my head, and sad, green eyes on the backs of my eyelids.

I didn't feel much better the next morning, but as I stared at a pack of cigarettes, I couldn't bring myself to smoke one. It was a vice that had numbed me through a lot of stressful situations, but it had fixed exactly none of them.

I needed this one to be fixed. Because if and when she came back to me, I needed to be ready.

For the next few days, I went through all the motions: Eat. Sleep. Work. Fuck with Porter. Wash, rinse, and repeat.

But I missed her.

The way she smelled.

The way she felt curled into my side.

The way she smiled at me when our eyes would meet.

Most of all, I just missed talking to her.

I must have typed at least a thousand texts to her. I deleted them all.

She wanted space, and I wanted her to figure out her life in under fifteen years, so dammit, I was going to give it to her.

Simmer was thriving.

The Porterhouse was thriving.

The Tannerhouse was thriving.

TV personality and celebrity chef Tanner Reese was thriving.

Yet I was floundering.

I thought Porter was going to fall out of his chair when I showed up at the restaurant one night after a long day of filming and told him to go home. He blinked at me for several seconds before sprinting past me without a single word spoken. Between the kids and the restaurants, he was burning the candle at both ends. And now that he had a girlfriend, he probably wanted a little more time to use that newfound wick. We really needed to hire someone so he could have more time off.

Or maybe if I freed up, say, fifty hours a week, I could step in and help him more.

That night, after he left, I stood in The Porterhouse kitchen, watching the chefs work. Most people wouldn't understand it, but there was a thrill unlike anything else to be found in a kitchen. Sure, the hours and unforgiving nature of the job were brutal, and by the end of a shift, I was exhausted beyond explanation. But in my chef whites, with sweat beading on my forehead and chaos all around me, the calm I felt combining raw ingredients into a masterpiece with the flick of my wrist was intoxicating. It was easy to become addicted to the hunt and the high of the perfect dish.

Food had always been my passion, yet I'd found myself a career as something of an actor. The money was great, but I didn't need it. I hadn't spoken to my accountant recently, but the restaurants provided Porter with a *very* comfortable income. I was sure they were doing the same for me.

Rita had asked me why I didn't just quit *Simmer* like it was such a simple question.

But it didn't feel simple. It felt like throwing away seven years of my life I'd worked my ass off for.

Seven years.

The exact amount of time Rita had been married to Greg.

And she'd done it. Maybe not by choice, but she'd filed the divorce papers, and survived to see the other side.

I smiled and picked my phone up to text her that our situations were more similar than we'd thought only to put it back down.

For the rest of the week, I went to one of our restaurants to cook every night after I finished filming. God, it was invigorating. And day by day, I started to feel like myself again.

It was almost a wrap on the latest season, and while I did have a press tour lined up, I had a three-month break before I was contractually obligated to *Simmer* again.

I was excited for the time off. But it would only give me more time to think about Rita. She was my brain's favorite subject, my subconscious's favorite obsession, and my heart's greatest torture.

Eight days after I'd walked out of her house, I crawled into my bed, dog tired after a night at The Tannerhouse. I was off the following day, and I had no idea what the hell I was going to do with myself. That's not true. I was going to sit in the hammock from sunup to sundown and stare at the horizon, hoping and praying Rita was somewhere on the other side of it.

I got comfortable on the pile of pillows and blankets, sparing only one longing glance at her side of the bed like the sap I so clearly was, and opened my phone to browse social media before going to sleep.

Her name on my notification screen made my heart stop.

Rita: Oh. My. God.

Rita: Are you insane?

Rita: Tanner? Answer me.

Rita: Call me as soon as possible. I'm freaking out over here like Brad Pitt at the end of *Seven*.

According to the time stamp, the messages had come back to back over three hours earlier. I hadn't checked my phone while I was at the restaurant. It wasn't like I'd expected to get a message from her.

Rita: Are you ignoring me?

Rita: Callllllll me!

Rita: Jesus. Stop pretending you have a life and call me already.

It was a string of shouty, bossy texts, but it made the ache in my chest ease for the first time in over a week. She was reaching out to me. Why, I didn't know, but I didn't care, either.

She answered on the third ring. "I'm glad I hadn't been kidnapped and stuffed in someone's trunk when I sent you those messages."

Her voice. I'd missed it so damn much.

Such. A. Sap.

"I'm glad to hear that too. I don't have the energy for a search and rescue mission tonight."

The line went silent.

"Rita?"

"Before I say anything else, I want you to know that, when you didn't answer my text, I downed a bottle of wine. I cannot be held responsible for anything I say during this conversation. Okay?"

I chuckled. "Fair enough."

"Okay, now that we've got the disclaimer out of the way, I've missed hearing your voice."

I blew out a ragged sigh. "I just thought the same damn thing."

"Have you been drinking too?"

"No. I just got home, actually."

"Home? It's after midnight… Oh. *Shit*. Were you out with someone?"

"Nope. I'm still wallowing over the last woman I lost. You?"

She got quiet again before saying, "I'm sorry. I shouldn't have asked you that. It's none of my business. You're a free man."

It was a rusty knife to the gut. "I'm not a free man, Rita. I'm *your man*. Whether we're ready for it or not doesn't change the fact that I'm in love with you. So you can go ahead and assume that, for the next fifteen years, I won't be *out with someone*."

"What happens at fifteen years and one day?"

"I get sick of waiting and kidnap you and stuff you in my trunk, taking us right back to where this conversation started."

She giggled and it made me smile. Fuck, that felt good.

"Are you as miserable as I am?" she asked.

"I don't know. Does your chest feel like you survived a plane crash only to be hit by a bus?"

"Wow. You are pathetic," she teased. "But you forgot being run over by a train. That seems to be my personal trifecta of misery."

Shit. I had to get off the phone with her. Fast. Because I was less than one minute away from begging her to let me come over.

I'd have given anything to lie in bed, holding her and bullshitting for the rest of the night—and possibly the rest of my life. But no. We were "finding ourselves." Whatever the fuck that meant.

"Listen, I don't mean to be short. But it's late…" *And I miss you so fucking much that it's killing me.* "Did you need something earlier?"

"Oh, right. Yeah. I was outside tonight, packing up my hammock, and found a bat."

I twisted my lips. "Was it dead or alive?"

"It was purple with gold-sequined wings." She paused before finishing. "And it was beside a black velvet ring box."

I smiled and looked down at the bed. I'd been wondering if she'd found that yet. I'd torn out of there so fast our last night together that I hadn't given it a second thought.

I'd assumed she'd find it when she cleaned up the broken glass.

Then I'd felt like a dick for not cleaning up the broken glass.

Then I'd called a company to go clean up the broken glass.

Then I'd decided that sending a six-man industrial cleaning crew to her house wasn't space and hung up.

"Yeah. Sorry about that. It was supposed to be a fish because I know Greg stole yours but I was stuck at work and had Andrea—"

"You want me to give it to Charlotte to give to Porter?"

My chin snapped to the side. "Why would you give it to Porter?"

"I can't keep it, Tanner. I'm not even sure what you were

thinking. But given our current…*situation*, I figured you might want it back."

Pure confusion crinkled my brow. "The bat?"

"No, not the bat. Though I don't understand that at all. But he's cute, so I'll keep him. I'm talking about the ring."

I sighed. "You don't like it?"

"I haven't even looked at it. I only touched it long enough to bring it inside. It's been staring at me all night from across the room. Hence the bottle of wine."

"So open it, crazy."

"Oh, I'm the crazy one? You bought an engagement ring, like, a month after you met me. Seriously, you are the worst slow and casual dater in the world. How many ex-wives do you currently have?"

If I'd been drinking something, that would have been the moment it went spraying across the room. "I didn't buy you an engagement ring!"

"You didn't?" Her voice squeaked at the end.

"Christ, Rita. We haven't even discussed butt stuff yet and you think I'd propose?"

"Okayyyy, we are *never* discussing butt stuff, and it was a freaking black velvet ring box! What was I supposed to think?"

"You weren't supposed to think. You were supposed to open it and look at it."

"Damn. Now, I feel like an idiot. Is it earrings? I considered it was earrings."

I settled deeper into the pillows and smiled. I was supposed to be getting off the phone with her because talking to her was agonizing. However, I was always a glutton for punishment when it came to that woman, so I pressed the

FaceTime button instead.

She accepted right away. “Right, because obviously you need the visual to go with my verbal mortification.”

My heart stopped when she came into view.

She was sitting on her couch, just as beautiful as the day I’d first laid eyes on her. Green eyes. Creamy, white skin. Plump lips.

But her hair—it was brown.

“Holy. Shit,” I breathed.

She sifted her fingers through the top of her hair, shoving it over to one side like I’d seen her do so many times before. “Yeah, I decided to try something different at the salon this time.”

I nodded with wide eyes. “I can see this.”

“What do you think?”

I thought it was hideous. I hated it with a fiery passion, and I wanted my blonde back.

But I fucking loved her, and I knew she was doing this to try to discover who she was outside of Greg. And a step away from him no matter how wrong it may be was a step closer to her coming back to me.

“You are the sexiest woman I have ever seen.”

“Don’t get used to it. I hate it.”

I slapped a hand over my chest and rushed out, “Oh, thank you God.”

A bright white smile split her face. “Judging by that reaction, you’ll also be happy to know that I spent a few hours last night on an app that lets you try different hairstyles. And I hated every single one of them.”

I nodded, not knowing what to say to that but feeling like

I'd won the lottery. She was two steps closer to being back to me.

"What else have you been doing?"

She bit her bottom lip and looked away from the camera. "Oh, nothing really. Just having a staring competition with a ring box which turns out is actually an earring box."

"No. It's definitely a ring box."

Her head snapped back to me.

"Just not an *engagement* ring box. Open it."

The camera jostled as she retrieved it, then settled back on the couch. "I'm nervous."

"Why? If it was anything dangerous, it would have croaked in the last eight days."

Her eyes got wide. "Shit. Was it alive?"

"Open the damn box, Rita."

She chewed on her bottom lip as she popped the top open. A smile climbed up her face. "Oh. My. God." She burst into laughter.

My chest overflowed with happiness as she lifted that tiny toe ring from the box. It was a white-gold band and had a tiny alligator made from emeralds the color of her eyes on top.

"What do you think?"

"Why are you so weird?"

"Did Greg get you diamond earrings?"

Her laughter died. "Tanner."

"What about a tennis bracelet? Pearls? Engraved locket?"

"Oh, honey," she breathed.

"I love you. I wanted to get you something and I figured Greg had already stolen all the good jewelry gifts. So, like I promised you on our first date, I got creative."

Her eyes filled with tears. "I love it. So so *so* much."

I grinned. "Yeah? You gonna wear it?"

She shook her head. "No. Nobody's worn a toe ring since the nineties. But I'm going to have the back soldered closed and put it on a necklace and never take it off."

I stared at her, that hollow ache once again finding me.

And she stared back, unmistakable love shining in her eyes.

It burned like the hottest knife, knowing it was there but knowing I couldn't have her.

"I need you to hurry up," I whispered. "Please, Rita."

She smiled, a tear sliding down her cheek. "I'm trying. I promise. I'm trying."

"Is there anything I can do to help?"

She clutched the ridiculous toe ring to her chest. "Actually, would you mind if I came a couple mornings a week and ran your Ninja Warrior course? I know it's a lot to ask but—"

The idea of seeing her again was like jumper cables to my nervous system. "Of course I don't mind. I'd love to—"

"I won't bother you. I promise. I'll just slip in and slip out. You won't even know I've been there."

My disappointment was staggering. *Dammit. Bother me, woman!*

"I've been trying to go back and take a good look at all of my failures. And, well, I fell on my ass pretty hard that day."

"You also got the best orgasm of your entire life a few minutes later. So I'm not sure I'd consider that a failure."

"The best orgasm of my entire life, huh?" She twisted her lips to the side.

A laugh sprang from my throat, but I really just wanted to

kiss that expression off her sexy little mouth—and then keep her forever.

But telling her that wasn't going to get her back any faster.

"Whatever you need, Rita. If you feel like stopping by the house, I'll make you breakfast."

"You're sweet, honey. But I think I need to do this on my own."

Fuck.

"Okay. Then…I guess…"

"I'll see ya when I see ya?"

Shoot me. "Yeah. Sure. I'll see ya when I see ya."

"Thanks for the toe ring."

I love you. I miss you. Come over. "You're welcome."

"Bye, Tanner."

"Bye, Rita."

TWENTY-FOUR

Tanner

EVERY MORNING FOR THE NEXT SIX WEEKS, I TOOK STALKING Rita Hartley to a new level as I stood at the window of my guestroom, sipping coffee and secretly cheering her on. We'd only spoken once after that night she'd found her toe ring, but every morning around six, she was on my Ninja Warrior course. She'd sold her BMW SUV, which honestly surprised me because it was the only thing she'd wanted in her divorce. Now, she drove a little red Jetta that was so perfect for her it made me smile every time she pulled up.

I wasn't positive why she was spending so much time on that course, but her determination was inspiring. She fell more times than I could count, but she always got up, tried again, and usually fell again too.

She cried the day she made it through the wall tunnel. On her knees, violent sobs shaking her shoulders, and it wrecked me to helplessly watch her breakdown.

But she'd asked for space.

A few days after that, I lost her behind the trees. The suspense was killing me. I'd hired at least ten different tree services to cut them down but canceled them all.

She wanted to do this alone. I wasn't happy about it, but there wasn't much I was happy about during those weeks.

The judge denied our last attempt at preventing Shana from publishing the book.

Simmering Love—yes, that was the damn title—was set for a summer release, just two weeks after Shana's child was due. I assumed after the DNA test came back she'd need another source of income besides my wallet. But make no mistake, she was still very much making a living at my expense.

Surprisingly enough, when I finally faced the kick in the balls head on and went to the president of The Food Channel, he didn't seem too concerned about Shana's book. I believe his exact words were, "Do you think there's a man in this building who hasn't snorted coke off a hooker's tits?"

I was standing there, so there was at least one.

He didn't fire me. Or even give me shit. He simply gave me the card to the network's PR firm and told me to have them put their heads together with my team to spin this in a positive light.

I wasn't sure how that was possible. But I still had a job when I walked out of his office. A job I hated and dreamed about quitting on a daily basis, but a job nonetheless.

I continued spending several nights a week in the kitchen at one of the restaurants. Getting back to the basics was amazing for my mental health. I did my best thinking over a frying pan. Which was good because, even outside of Rita, there was a whole hell of a lot of shit I needed to think about.

Porter's life once again imploded, and to top it off, his son's health was declining so rapidly that it had my whole family paralyzed with fear.

My mom cried all the time. My dad was losing his mind, pacing and cursing at all hours of the night. And for the first time in my entire life, I was the one to pick up the pieces of my family.

At the end of those six weeks, things were far from over for the Reese family. But the sun was starting to show on the horizon, leaving me nothing but more time to think about the one who had gotten away. Well, almost gotten away.

She was currently drenched in sweat and walking toward her car in my driveway.

It was a Saturday. She didn't have to work, and neither did I. We could have spent the whole day together chatting and catching up. Friends. We could be friends, right?

I was sick and tired of watching her walk away every day, knowing she was so close and still unreachable. My hands ached to hold her, but I'd have happily settled for a conversation.

Finally, on a warm morning early in June, I broke.

"Rita!" I shouted, jogging through my front door.

She stopped with her back toward me but didn't turn around when she yelled, "Yeah?"

"Can I talk to you for a minute?"

Her shoulders did a slow rise toward her ears before dropping back down. "About what?"

"Um, about the fact that I'm about to cook breakfast for two and I'm only one person."

Her hair, which was thankfully blond again, swished when she shook her head. "Not today, Tanner."

"Tomorrow?"

She shook her head again. "Not tomorrow, either."

"Okay, so what about the next day, then? Really, I'm free for the entire month. Just pick a date. Any date."

Suddenly, she spun around to face me. Her eyes were red rimmed, but she was wholly pissed off. "No dates, Tanner! And at this rate, maybe never again."

My back shot straight. "What do you mean never again? It hasn't been fifteen years yet. And if it has, you need to get your sweaty ass in the trunk of my car."

She shook her head. "We should both probably go ahead and accept that this is over. I can't do it anymore."

"Do what?" I snapped, walking toward her.

"This!" she yelled, her voice echoing off the brick driveway.

I stopped short of reaching her, my stomach twisting into a knot. "What are you talking about?"

She chewed on her bottom lip. "I can't get up the warped wall."

It made me an asshole, but I smiled. "You got all the way to the end?"

"Yeah, like two weeks ago, and I can't get up the fucking warped wall." She sucked in a shaky breath and then burst into tears. "And I don't want to be a doctor. And I like high heels and dresses. And I love yoga and even Pilates too. I like getting monthly facials and pedicures, even if they are expensive, and I should probably be saving for retirement. And, and, and…do you have any fucking idea how many calories are in bacon?"

"Uhhh," I drawled, buying a second to find the string that

would tie all of that randomness together. I came up empty-handed. "Come here, Rita."

"No." She threw her arms out to the sides. "I'm still the same person. It's been almost two months and nothing has changed."

"Good!" I replied, closing the distance between us. I pulled her in for a hug, which might have done more for me than it did for her. "I never wanted you to change."

Her arms remained at her sides. "I'm tired, Tanner. I'm so damn tired."

"So come inside and lay down with me. We'll take a nap."

She stepped out of my hold. And then two more steps back until she was out of my reach altogether. "No, because I'm going to leave as soon as we wake up. Do you understand that? Maybe I'll leave for another two months. Maybe it really will be fifteen years. I have no idea how long this is going to take me. But you deserve better than that. And I'm not sure I can ever *be* better than that."

The hair on the back of my neck stood on end. "What's happening right now? I mean, seriously, what the fuck is happening right now? I just wanted to see if you'd have breakfast with me. That's all."

"I see you watching me," she whispered like it was a secret. "When I get here. When I'm running the course. And you stand there even when you can't see me through the trees, because you're still there when I give up for the day."

"Okay?" I shrugged. "I like seeing you. I said you could use my course, but I never said I wasn't going to stalk you. Price of admission."

She started to smile, but her face crumbled. "You have to

let me go, Tanner. I don't even know if the woman you fell in love with is real. You're a good guy who doesn't deserve to be sitting on anyone's back burner. Especially not mine."

I blinked. Once. Twice. Three times. Tears were pouring down her face. but for the life of me, I couldn't figure out why. "Relax. This isn't a big deal, Rita. I just wanted to see you. I miss you, okay? Sue me. I've been doing a lot of thinking and I wanted to tell you about it. God forbid maybe run a few ideas past you and get your opinion. But now you're talking about back burners and bacon? And I'm really getting the feeling that you're working up the courage to walk away for good."

Her breathing shuddered, and she looked down at her feet. "We have to stop."

"We already did stop," I snapped, the panic that she was slipping through my fingers making my voice rougher than I'd intended. "This *is* stopped, and *you* decided that. You don't get to take the stop away from me too. We will continue this current stop until *I'm* done. And I'm not fucking done with you, Rita. I haven't even gotten started. I said I would give you time. So take some fucking time." I couldn't breathe, but I couldn't stand there any longer, either. I turned on a toe and marched away.

I told her I'd wait. She didn't get to decide for how long. We were good together. We were *right*. We just needed some time, and she was going to take that fucking time whether she wanted to or not. And then she was going to come back to me.

Because she was mine.

And, damn it, I was hers.

I went back inside, beelining straight to my hammock. It was a mistake because I couldn't keep the memories of her hand on my chest that first night together out of my head.

To top off the shittiest of shitty days, I got an email from my attorney later that afternoon that turned me into a vortex of anger. It was the table of contents of Shana's new book.

I broke my phone.

I broke my laptop.

Then I nearly broke my hand putting a hole in wall.

I couldn't hold on to the one woman I wanted to keep.

And I couldn't get rid of one who wouldn't let go.

I spent the rest of the day on the phone with my attorney.

And then I continued to be pissed off, so I watched five episodes of *Game of Thrones* I'd already seen but assumed Rita hadn't because watching TV without her was the only immature passive aggressive way I could think to hurt her without actually hurting her. It backfired because it only made me miss her more.

When I finally calmed down enough to entertain the idea of sleep, I shot her a text.

Me: I'm sorry I was watching you. And for everything else too.

Me: Except for how many calories are in bacon, because trust me, if I could control that, it would have been zero years ago.

Her read receipt popped up, but she didn't respond.

Nor did she show up the next morning.

TWENTY-FIVE

Rita

Three days later...

USING MY TOE, I PUSHED OFF THE WOODEN RAILING ON MY tiny balcony. The sun was going down, and while the view of a lagoon at my new apartment paled in comparison to the lake at my old house, I still loved it.

Because it was all mine.

Some people—cough, Sidney—thought I should have been out letting the wind blow through my hair on the adventure of a lifetime to fall in love with myself again. But let's be honest, that crap only worked in the movies. In real life you can't just get on a plane and go backpacking through Europe on some mission of self-discovery. The way my life was going, if I wanted to find the real Rita Hartley, all I had to do was look in the shoe department at Saks.

What? I was a single woman with no children. Shoes

were my babies.

Besides, I had a new job that would most likely frown upon me taking a month off after being there for a week. Dr. Blighton was nice but not that nice. I still had no idea what I wanted to do with my life, and it was frustrating me to no end. I'd bought an MCAT study guide, read two pages, and promptly put it away. Two pages and I was positive that ship had sailed. So, due to the need to eat and pay rent, I took another office manager position while I was figuring it out.

I nabbed my glass of wine and a piece of Asiago from the cheese-board-for-one and went back to staring. It was shockingly similar to what I had done only a few months earlier when Greg had to work late. But, this time, I did it sans the wedding ring, so everything tasted that much better.

I hadn't been back to Tanner's since our fight on his driveway. I couldn't stand knowing that I was hurting him, and every day, as I selfishly went to his house to run his course, that was exactly what I was doing.

At first, I'd wanted to finish that course to prove to myself that I wasn't a failure. I was woman, hear me roar and all that jazz. But every day, every fall, and every bruise, it became more and more personal to me. Those obstacles were symbolic of my life and every failure Greg assumed I would make. Conquering it became my obsession.

But that damn warped wall. I just couldn't get up it. I ran as hard as I could. Jumped as high as I could. It didn't matter. I always went sliding back down. I hoped if I could just get to the top, I'd feel like a different woman. And then I could look in the mirror and see someone other than Greg's failure of a wife.

God knew nothing else had changed about me in the last two months. Secretly, I think that pissed me off more than the warped wall.

The pressure I felt knowing that Tanner was waiting on me was suffocating. Guilt consumed me each time I caught sight of him standing in that window—watching and waiting for me. I never should have told him that we were going to simmer for a while. He had taken it literally, watched pot and all.

So, in what I was learning was true Rita fashion, I quit. On him. On the wall. On me.

Proving once and for all that Greg had been right about me.

I took a sip of my wine, gave the hammock another push, and ignored the tear rolling down my cheek. My doorbell rang just as nightfall snuffed out the sun.

Only a few people knew where I lived, and I'd talked to Sidney less than thirty minutes earlier. She was already in a nightgown and chilling on the couch with Kent.

There was only one other person it could be.

"Your timing only serves as further proof that you are a vampire," I greeted.

Charlotte's expression was unreadable. "As a testament to my love, I almost burst into flames twice on the way over here."

I smiled and shoved the door wide in invitation. She accepted and walked in.

"Nice place," she said.

And it was. Again, my house with Greg was nicer, but this one was mine. So I loved it that much more.

"I barely recognize you without scrubs on," I teased, settling on the couch.

She sat on the other end. "Ah…yeah. I've…taken a little time off recently."

I leaned over and gave her hand a squeeze. Her life had been nothing short of a Lifetime movie recently. I'd tried to be as supportive and involved as I could, but Charlotte wasn't the social type. Leaving her alone was more often than not the best course of action.

"How ya holding up?" I asked.

The corner of her mouth lifted in a very unlike Charlotte Mills half grin. "Really well, actually. Really. *Well.*"

She pulled her hand away, and I reclined back against the couch.

"So, what has you risking your life for a visit tonight?"

"Tanner."

I froze.

She swayed her head from side to side. "Well, that's not totally true. Porter's worried about his brother. Seems old Sloth is going off the deep end. He paid some woman three million dollars not to publish a book about him."

My back shot ramrod straight. "He paid off Shana? Why? I thought—"

She shrugged. "The fact that he has three million dollars sitting in the bank is making me reconsider calling him Sloth. Christmas will be here before you know it." She was joking, but not even a hint of humor crossed her face. "What's going on with you two?"

I cut my gaze away. "Nothing."

"Right. Let me rephrase. *Why* isn't anything going on

with you two?"

I forced a smile through the pain. "It's complicated."

She quirked an eyebrow. "I'm the queen of complicated, Rita. Lay it on me."

I laughed. She wasn't wrong. "I'm just out of a divorce. I can't get into another relationship."

"That would have been a great thought to have *before* you got into a new relationship. Not a few months *after* you fell in love with him."

I swung my head her way. "Who said I fell in love with him?"

"Tanner. Though his mom thinks he was your rebound. You've got a total mama's boy on your hands."

"You know, in theory, best friends dating brothers sounded really fun. I'm seeing now that it will have its downfalls."

"Spill it, Rita."

I groaned. "He wasn't my rebound. I *do* love him. But we can't be together until I figure out who the hell I am, and I have no idea how long that's going to take. But Tanner… The man is stubborn as hell. He told me he'd wait fifteen years, and I really and truly think he meant it. I can't do that to him." I closed my eyes. "Don't get me wrong. I really *want* to do that to him because the idea of him being with another woman…" I trailed off, shaking my head. "But he deserves better."

"Better than you? Not possible."

My eyes flashed open. Charlotte was not the friend who wasted words on pep talks. If it wasn't an absolute fact, it wasn't worth her breath.

"Wow," I breathed. "I think that might be the nicest thing you've ever said to me."

"Then I'm shit for a friend and you need to promote Sidney unless I can turn it all around today. Agreed?"

"Sure." I sucked my lips between my teeth and bit down to stifle my laugh.

"Rita, I need you to listen to me. And, like, *really* listen to me." She leaned in close, her brown eyes locked on my greens. "You're better than Greg Laughlin."

I scoffed. "I know that. But Tanner…"

"You're better than Greg," she repeated.

I rolled my eyes. "Fine. But we were talking about Tanner."

"Rita, listen to me. Greg. You're better than him. You always have been. You always will be."

I glared at her, frustration mounting. "Do you hear the words that are coming out of my mouth right now? I'm not talking about Greg."

"*You* are *better* than *Greg*."

"But what if I'm not!" It just came out. My hand flew to my mouth as if I could catch the words in thin air and shove them back into the dirty little place in my subconscious where they originated.

I didn't really think that, did I?

Charlotte clapped her hands and shot to her feet. "I knew it! That son of a bitch got in your head."

But Greg had gotten into so much more than just my head.

"Did you know I didn't get into med school?"

She blinked, then shook her head.

"Yeah. Apparently, you need more than a twenty-six on your MCAT. Greg assured me I didn't, so I never took them a second time."

She winced.

"He told me it was embarrassing enough that I worked as a waitress, he didn't want more of it by watching me flunk out of med school."

"God, he is a prick."

"I think he was right though."

She tilted her head to the side. "I *know* he was wrong."

I drew my knees up to my chest. "I don't want to be a doctor, Charlotte. I don't think I ever did. It wasn't my dream like it was yours or even his. It was just something that I thought would make me enough money to escape who I was. He asked me to marry him and follow him to his residency and I said yes before the question had fully escaped his lips. I don't know what that says about me. That I just gave up so easily."

My voice shook, but like a dam had been broken inside me, the words wouldn't stop coming. "I kept my hair short for him. I wore clothes I thought he would like. I did yoga and Pilates to keep in shape for him. It was all for him. I'm disgusted at myself for letting him do that to me. It's like he sculpted me into this little doll that fit his needs and I hate her and I don't know how to shed all of that and find the real Rita Hartley. Greg is with me wherever I go, and I don't want Rita Laughlin to be with Tanner Reese because I don't want Greg to ruin us too."

She stared back at me, stoic as ever. "Why haven't you cut and dyed your hair?"

"I did! And it looked like crap, so I dyed it back."

She nodded. "Last time I saw you, you were wearing new heels."

"There was a sale."

She nodded again. "You still going to yoga?"

"I can't eat cheese and wine if I don't."

Then I entered the Twilight Zone, because a huge Porter Reese smile stretched across *her* mouth like there was some kind of Freaky Friday mix-up at the lab.

"I have a theory." She sat on the edge of the couch, her knees turned toward me, bringing her closer than Charlotte had ever been by choice. "I'm about to blow your mind, so I really need you to be ready."

I stared. My mind was already blown from the fact that she was so close to me, so I couldn't imagine what she was going to say.

"What if"—her voice got low as she swayed closer, downright playful—"Rita Hartley spent the last seven years pretending to be Rita Laughlin?" Her eyebrows shot up and she quickly leaned away like I really was about to explode.

"What?"

She rolled her eyes.

Jesus. Who was this woman with humor *and* facial expressions?

"Come on, Rita. Think about it. You're *you.* You like all of that stuff because *you* like it. Sure, Greg may have exposed you to some of that stuff. But you don't like it because he did."

I shook my head. "I don't know if that's true."

"If Greg told you during the peak of your marriage that you weren't allowed to eat your precious cheese anymore, what would you have said?"

"I'd have told him to shut his damn mouth with that sacrilege."

"Exactly! And what if he told you he liked you better as a redhead?"

I sighed. "See, I probably would have tried it."

"And when you hated it?"

"I'd have gone back to blond."

"Right! Because *you* didn't like it. Tell me something that Greg loved. Like, what was his favorite food?"

I blinked at her. Then blinked at her.

Then I blinked at her so many times that it was as though she'd become a character in a flipbook. My chest got tight, and my nose started to burn.

"Shrimp and grits," I finally whispered. "He loved them. And I hated them so much."

"So you didn't eat them."

I shook my head, not able to trust my voice. I'd never eaten grits. Not even when chef Kevin Story had offered them to me on my first date with Tanner. And sure as hell not just because Greg liked them.

Oh. My. God. Maybe she was right. *Dear Lord, please let her be right.*

"Rita, you married an asshole because you loved him. And you decided not to fight for medical school because it wasn't *your* passion. Then you fell out of love with him and did the best you could to make an unhappy marriage work until he cheated on you. In case you missed it, Greg is an *asshole*. Of course he's trying to take credit for the incredible woman you are. But that's nothing more than his delusions of grandeur. He didn't make you who you are today. So you've shed the only thing you needed to shed from that toxic relationship—*him*." She grinned with pride.

I stared up at her in pure shock. "When did you learn how to smile?"

She pointed to her mouth. "Since…Porter."

"I can see this," I smarted, but my mind was still swirling.

Maybe all of my soul searching had been worthless effort. What if I couldn't escape who I was—because there was nothing to escape?

God, Charlotte was good at this. It was like a hidden superpower.

"You've really been holding out on me all these years." Chewing on my thumbnail, I stood up and started to pace. "Keep talking. What about Tanner?"

"What about him?"

I stopped and looked at her. "Do you think it's too soon for us to be together?"

"Yes. Absolutely."

My shoulders fell.

"But it's not my relationship, Rita. What do you think?"

I *thought* I missed him.

I *thought* I wanted to be with him.

I *thought* I loved him more than I'd ever even considered loving Greg.

"I'm scared," I admitted. "Tanner's different. He…"

"Makes the world stop?"

Touching my lips, I croaked, "Oh my God, that's the corniest and most accurate thing I've ever heard you say."

She laughed. "Does he make you happy?"

"So so so happy."

"*Then let him keep doing that.* Happiness is hard. I understand the concept of loving yourself before you can love someone else. It's important. But having regrets isn't the same as hating yourself. This world is a dark and unforgiving place. If Tanner is your light, you have to stop being afraid and hold on to it. You deserve to be happy. And Greg has fucked with your head enough, but I bet you anything that Tanner would be willing to wade into that mess if it means he gets you."

"He would. He so would."

"Then there is your answer."

I sucked in a ragged breath. "What if he doesn't want me back?"

"Three million dollars is a lot of money to spend on a woman you don't want a future with."

I stumbled back a step. "What?"

She smirked. "Chapter thirty-two in that woman's book was entitled 'Rita and the Fish.' Apparently, Greg wasn't the only one watching you two."

My mouth fell open. "What. The. Hell? That bitch was the one who stole my fish?"

"Yep. But don't worry. Tanner negotiated its release as part of the deal. She was also required to move back to California, submit to the DNA test before the birth of the baby, and agree to never contact him or you again."

"Holy. Shit."

"Call him, okay? Don't move in with him. Don't marry him. Don't get pregnant with his child. Just take it slow and *call him*."

"We suck at slow."

She laughed and pulled me in for a hug that shocked me more than anything else she'd said. Yeah. Porter was *definitely* Charlotte's light.

She released me and headed to the door, calling, "Slow-ish will be fine. By the way, he's working at The Porterhouse tonight if you wanted to go see him."

"He's working there? Like, cooking?"

"Yep. Porter says he's been there a lot recently." She drummed her fingers on the doorjamb. "So, do I get to keep my number-one best friend position or what?"

I dug the alligator toe ring I'd had put on a necklace out of my shirt and brought it to my lips. "Yeah, and I decided to give you tenure too. So your job is secure for the foreseeable future."

She grinned and then she was gone, leaving me standing in my living room, wondering if I had enough peas to make this right.

TWENTY-SIX

Tanner

I WAS GOING TO DIE. PURE EXHAUSTION WAS LIKE A DRUG, and as I drove home from the restaurant at a little past one in the morning, I was overdosing. When I cut the engine and hit the button to close my garage behind me, I didn't immediately move. It seemed like entirely too much work to get out of the car, go inside, take a shower, and collapse into bed.

Maybe just a quick nap in the car would do the trick. I lolled my head back and allowed my lids to fall closed, my mind slowing to a halt almost immediately.

Somewhere between a second and a decade later, I was roused back to consciousness by the ding of my phone. I prayed that it wasn't a problem locking up the restaurant because Porter would kill me if I left it open all night, but there was less than a zero percent chance I'd be able to make it back.

My body jolted, a surge of energy blasting through my veins, when I saw her name on the screen.

Rita: Are you going to sit in the car all night?

My head popped up and I looked to the door, but it was closed, no sign of Rita anywhere. My lips curled into a smile.

Me: I thought stalking was my job.

My stomach was in knots for the next two minutes as that text bubble played on the screen letting me know she was typing.

Rita: It was. Until I realized that, while our timing sucked, we did not. And I'm willing to exclusively wear your favorite yoga pants, including dry-humping you in them if that's still your thing, and to make a million tuna noodle casseroles, with peas of course, and then get old and fat on your couch, holding your hand because I love you with every part of me, including parts that I hate and you will probably hate one day too. But if you're willing to have me, I'm willing to make your life totally miserable.

I couldn't breathe. It was as if all of the air in not only that car but the entire state of Georgia had vanished.

I read it three times, gave my nuts a painful tug to make sure I wasn't actually asleep, then read it again.

And again.

And, fuck me, I read it *again*.

My thumbs hovered over the phone, but I had no idea how to reply.

Rita: P.S. I'm on the Ninja Warrior course if you'd like to start the misery tonight.

I was out of my car and racing around the side of my house in the very next beat.

God. I was such a damn sap. I didn't give the first fuck.

There were spotlights surrounding the course. Porter had insisted we have them installed after the great midnight napkin debate. I'd never been so thankful in my life.

Her face was bright, shyly smiling back at me.

My future was suddenly brighter.

She was standing at the end, wearing my favorite yoga pants and a matching tank top, her hand nervously toying with a necklace that I hoped like hell was my alligator.

I glanced down at myself, feeling superiorly inadequate for the first time in possibly my entire life. My T-shirt was covered by no less than a hundred stains that had seeped through my chef's jacket.

She was beautiful, and I looked—and probably smelled—like I hadn't showered in a week.

"Any chance you can help me with something?" she yelled.

Anything as long as it means you're staying. "Sure."

"For the past few months, I've been trying to finish this damn Ninja Warrior course. But no matter how hard I try, I can't get past the final obstacle."

"It's because you're the size of a toddler."

She glared and the pressure that had been mounting in my chest since the day I'd walked out of her house finally rushed from my body.

"Don't look at me like that," I said, strolling toward her. "That glare is why I fell in love."

"Really? Not my ass?"

I swayed my head from side to side. "And your ass too."

She smiled, but her chin quivered the closer I got. "I thought I had to do it on my own, Tanner. I thought that—"

"You were right. We needed some space."

"We did?" she whispered.

Stopping in front of her, I snaked a single finger out to hook one of hers. "I paid Shana off."

"I heard. Charlotte told me. Including the fish, which I'm not going to lie… The idea of her going into my house is a tad scary."

"I agree. And I am so sorry about that. My life was a clusterfuck. I had no business dragging you into that until I got my shit sorted."

"She stole my fish, but your attorneys handled my divorce. I'm pretty sure *I* dragged you into far worse."

I kissed the palm of her hand before intertwining our fingers. "Your attorneys were cheaper though."

She bit her bottom lip. "Yeah. Sorry about that. I wish I'd known. Trust me. Whatever she was going to publish about me was not three-million-dollars juicy."

"Right? The skeletons in your closet can't be that scandalous. You wouldn't even discuss butt stuff with me."

She slapped my chest. "So why'd you pay her, then?"

"The same reason you gave Greg the house and refused

alimony. I got to the point where I didn't care about the money or the principle of it anymore. I just wanted her gone so that I could move on with my life."

"Three million dollars though? That's highway robbery."

"The relief I feel is worth billions."

She looked down at her toes. "Out of curiosity. Do you…have billions?"

I smirked. "Nope. But what I do have is a stubborn pain-in-the-ass woman who has offered to make my life miserable. And I love her so fucking much that I'm dumb enough to volunteer for the job."

Her head came up, surprise etched in her features. "Yeah?"

"We've got time, Rita. I'm not a patient man, and I'm not going to lie: I want a life with you. One day, I'm going to put a ring on your finger. And not long after that, I want to start filling bedrooms with green-eyed babies. But I want time with you first. I want to travel and—"

"Don't say backpack through Europe."

"Psh. You roughing it? I'm signing up for misery, not hell."

She giggled and it hit me deep in a place that was only for Rita.

"Just because I fell in love with you in a matter of days rather than years doesn't mean I suck at slow." I tugged her into my arms. "I want to get to know you, especially these pieces of you that you hate, because I guarantee I'm going to love them so hard."

"I'm crazy," she whispered.

I dipped for a lip touch. "We all are, and if you're up for

the challenge, so am I."

Her face got soft. "You're a sweet guy, Tanner."

"I know."

She beamed up at me. "Good to see some things never change."

Unable to stop myself, I kissed her smiling mouth.

"Just to be clear," I mumbled against her lips. "We still get to have sex in slow mode, right?"

"So so so much sex," she whispered, her hand snaking down to my ass. I had no choice but to allow mine to follow suit.

I swallowed her moan as I pressed her against my thickening cock. "Let's go in. I need a shower, and your new job description requires you to wash my back."

She backed out of my hold. "No, wait. I need you to help me up the warped wall first."

"Now?" I adjusted my erection.

"Now, Tanner."

I let out a sigh and started toward the base of the curved ramp. "This was the misery you were talking about, huh?"

"Get used to it."

Oh, I absolutely would.

She backed up several feet and got low. "Ready?"

I shrugged. "As I'll ever be."

She ran at a full sprint. Her foot landed on the bottom of the wood, her short legs taking three steps before she jumped, missing the ledge at the top by a mile. She came sliding back down. "What the hell! You were supposed to help!"

I laughed. "What do you want me to do? Throw you up

to the top?"

"If that's what it takes. Yes."

Chuckling, I shook my head. "You need to lean back instead of forward. You're trying to climb the wall. All you need to do is run up it. Watch." With my exhaustion long since forgotten, I got a running start. Two steps up, I jumped, catching the lip. "See?" I dropped, sliding down rather than pulling myself up to the platform.

"I'll bust my ass if I lean back."

"You'll never be able to scale that thing though. You need to run up it."

"It's really high though."

"Fourteen feet to be exact."

She glared.

I fell in love again.

"Look, it's mental. You can't be afraid of falling back down or you'll never reach the top. You have to go after it with a hundred percent confidence."

"Holy shit." She stared up at it. "This wall really is symbolic of my life."

I grinned. "Then I better get to the top." I backed up, sprinted up, and this time climbed all the way to the platform.

"Tanner, wait—"

But it was too late. There was a blanket laid out near the back, two candles, wine glasses, and a white casserole dish in the middle.

The sap part of me stirred with emotion. "You made me a romantic dinner?"

She peered up at me. "It's tuna noodle casserole. Which

I'm not sure if you actually like or not, but at this point, it's kinda our *thing*. So you're going to have to choke it down for the rest of your life."

I didn't like it. Not even a little bit.

But I loved her.

So I could deal with the rest.

I nodded a million times.

"Move. I'm going to try it again. I used the stairs to set that up and it pissed me off, being up there without earning it. So we may be out here for a while."

I'd have spent the rest of my life on that platform, waiting for her. And as I watched her fail repeatedly for over twenty minutes, I feared that was exactly what I was going to have to do.

"Yes!" I boomed when her hands finally caught the top of the wall.

"Oh my God!" she yelled, dangling in the air. "I got it! I got it!" She paused. "Shit, now what?" Panic edged her voice. "Oh, God, I can't pull myself up, I'm going to fall. Shit. Tanner, I'm going to fall."

I chuckled. "And this is why I was waiting at the top of the wall that symbolizes your life." Grabbing both of her wrists, I dragged her to safety.

She was flat out on her back, panting and covered in sweat. Her hair was stuck to her face, her makeup smeared to hell and back. But she was mine. All fucking mine.

I sank down, pulling her into my side. "So, you want to get married or what?"

She slapped my chest. "God, how is it possible for you to be this bad at slow?"

"Okay, okay. Fine. So, what's your stance on butt stuff?"

She burst into laughter, filling me in unimaginable ways, because I knew, slow or not, that her laugh was going to become the soundtrack of my life.

And I'd never been so ready to press play.

EPILOGUE

Rita

Five years later...

"UNTIL NEXT TIME, KEEP ON SIMMERING." TANNER threw the towel over his shoulder and winked at the camera.

"And cut!" Andrea called. "Nice job, everyone."

My husband's grin fell, and his eyes came straight to me. "How ya holding up?"

I blew out a controlled breath and continued to pace a path through the downstairs of our house. I lifted my phone to face him, displaying the contraction timer. "Fifteen minutes, but they're getting closer."

He swallowed hard and forced a smile. He hated seeing me in pain, but when you were forty-one weeks pregnant, there was nothing but pain.

Turns out, Tanner was really freaking good at slow. We'd

dated for eighteen months before he dropped to a knee. When he did finally propose, it was sweet and simple and not at all over the top.

Just kidding. It was pure Tanner Reese shenanigans.

He'd invited all of our friends and family over for a barbeque. It was quite the party, what with all of my one-named friends gaping at all of his two-named friends while trying to be discreet. They failed miserably. That was where simple and sweet ended.

The real shenanigans began with a guy from Florida he'd hired to bring in three alligators and walk them around on leashes. It was the craziest thing I'd ever seen. But that wasn't even the most ridiculous thing Tanner did that day. He'd hired one of those skywriters that usually spelled out romantic phrases in the clouds. Only it didn't write *Marry Me*. Oh, no. That would have been too cliché for Tanner. Instead, it wrote *Winter is coming.*

I giggled—until honest to God, half of the cast of *Game of Thrones* came marching out of the wood line in full costume, some of them even riding horses. When they finished their march, Jon Snow—*Jon freaking Snow*—handed Tanner the ring box. It didn't surprise me in the least that Robb Stark was notably missing. So, finally, surrounded by our friends, family, three alligators, and the cast of our favorite television show, Tanner asked me to be his wife.

I said yes. Until he pointed out my name would be Rita Reese. Then I said no, because…Rita Reese? *Really?* He laughed, slid a monster of a rock on my finger, and then kissed me breathless.

When he was done, I said yes again.

We got married one year after that in a sweet and simple backyard ceremony.

Just kidding. It was pure Rita Hartley—soon-to-be Reese—shenanigans.

His pond and the surrounding areas were transformed into a majestic forest. Crystals hung from the trees, twinkling white lights were wrapped around the trunks, and blooming blue hydrangeas supplied a pop of color. There were no chairs or sides of the aisle, just dozens of white hammocks the guests swayed in as we exchanged our vows. When we were officially pronounced man and wife, the party moved to three giant tents adorned with more flowers, more crystals, and even more lights. I'd seen Tanner smile a lot over the years, but never as much as he had that night as we'd danced until the wee hours of the morning, matching bands on our ring fingers.

Another contraction hit me hard, stilling me mid-step. Tanner jogged over, and with his hands on my hips, he helped me balance. He breathed with me, whispering words of encouragement when my uterus finally released its death grip on me.

"We got time for one more reshoot?" Andrea asked.

"No," Tanner snapped.

"Honey, finish up. I don't want you to have to work tomorrow if she gets here tonight."

His body turned to stone. "Did you say *she*?"

Fuck.

I'd made it over twenty weeks without slipping up on the sex of our baby. He hadn't wanted to know. I couldn't not know. So he'd stepped out of the room while the ultrasound tech had given me the news. I'd cried, and Tanner had spent the afternoon talking himself in circles, trying to figure out if the tears were good because I was getting the daughter I wanted or bad because I was getting a boy that I also wanted, but not quite as much.

I went back to walking with hopes of evicting his daughter. "I didn't say anything. I don't know what you're talking about."

"Ho. Lee. Shit. We're having a girl. Oh my God, I'm going to have a daughter."

"Wow," Andrea smarted. "Congrats. I can't think of a man less equipped to deal with raising a daughter than you."

"Right?" Tanner replied.

"No, not right," I called. "You'll be great with a girl. You didn't think you'd be good with a son before Jackson."

"I'm still not sure I'm good with him. He cries when you leave the room."

"It's because I have boobs. I've seen you cry a few tears for the same reason."

"This is true," Tanner mumbled.

It took a few years of me working at the doctor's office to figure out what I wanted to do with my life. Funny enough, it had been right in front of me the whole time. Every year when I'd been working for Greg, I'd spent nine months busting my tail to plan and execute the Spring Fling. We'd made thousands of dollars to donate to charity, all while giving back to our patients. And I'd loved every second of it. Yes, it was stressful, but it was also incredibly rewarding. The problem was: Charity was only lucrative to the soul, and having a healthy sense of self-worth didn't pay the bills. It drove Tanner crazy that I continued to work after we'd gotten married, but I'd learned from my mistakes with Greg. I needed my own identity, so I wasn't quitting until I was good and ready.

Good and ready came in the form of two little pink lines.

Jackson Thomas Reese was by far the greatest thing I would ever do with my life, and soon, his sister would join those ranks if ever she made her grand entrance.

That little boy owned Tanner and me from the minute we saw the flutter of his heart on an ultrasound. He was born with blond hair, and, now, at fifteen months old, his eyes hadn't decided if they wanted to be green or blue. I thought he looked like Tanner. Tanner thought he looked like me. Neither of us cared because he was perfect in every way.

It was while I was pregnant that I'd started a non-profit business that helped charities organize fundraising events. It gave me something to keep busy, but even better than that, it gave me a sense of pride. I was making a difference in the community.

Having my own business had allowed me to take an extended maternity leave after Jackson was born, and desperate not to miss a minute, Tanner took a few months off as well. Apparently, he *really* sucked at taking it slow in the baby making department, because I was pregnant again before Jackson turned six months old.

"It's one scene," Andrea argued. "You had sauce on your shirt."

"People drip sauce on their shirt when cooking," Tanner argued.

"Yes, but the great Tanner Reese doesn't. So grab a clean one and let's finish this."

His worried, blue eyes came to mine. "You think I have time?"

I looked at my phone, the timer creeping on five minutes. "If you hurry, you won't even miss the next contraction."

Shortly after we'd gotten back together, Tanner had gone to The Food Channel with plans on walking away from *Simmer*. It didn't quite work out that way. What he ended up walking out with was a multimillion-dollar raise for a quarter of the episodes, a clause stating that he no longer had to take his shirt off, and a smile on his face. Despite getting almost exactly what he'd wanted, he was nervous the ratings would tank without his abs. But that was crazy. People didn't watch Tanner because he had a six-pack—I mean, I did occasionally while he was taking a shower. They watched because Tanner was an excellent chef who was charming and funny. And six episodes later, the ratings had proven that people liked watching him even fully clothed.

It was all about balance with Tanner, and with fewer episodes to film of *Simmer,* he was able to find his Zen cooking at the restaurants two nights a week. He was always exponentially happier after a night in the kitchen, regardless that he was a zombie the next day.

"Okay, I'll hurry," he said, walking away.

He hadn't made it two steps away when someone dropped a baby off the Empire State Building and directly into my pelvis. I screamed, doubling over as amniotic fluid ran down my legs.

"Rita!" Tanner called as he caught me.

I'd been through the whole labor-and-delivery process once already, so the pain shouldn't have surprised me. But this… This was enough to close the baby factory forever.

"I…I, uh." I dug my fingernails into his forearm. "I'm… either dying or in labor. We should probably go to the hospital either way."

Over the years together, I'd fallen more and more in love with Tanner. Our marriage was far from perfect. We fought. We made up. We had staring contests that he always lost. He couldn't hit the laundry hamper if he was standing inside of it. And, yeah, not only had we found each other's buttons, we pushed them on the regular.

But through it all, we laughed.

And smiled.

And we loved each other—utterly and completely.

In the beginning, I'd been so focused on the fact that we'd met at the wrong time.

I should have just been grateful that fate had chosen for us to meet at all.

McKenzie Caroline Reese was born on a sweltering summer night, screaming at the top of her lungs, and giving me a whole new reason to breathe.

As the nurses cleaned her up, the most beautiful, incredible, and wonderful man, who I was lucky enough to call my husband, stood over her bassinet with tears in his eyes, *holding her hand.*

THE END

OTHER BOOKS

The Retrieval Duet

Retrieval

Transfer

Guardian Protection Series

Singe

Thrive

The Fall Up Series

The Fall Up

The Spiral Down

The Darkest Sunrise Duet

The Darkest Sunrise

The Brightest Sunset

The Truth Duet

The Truth About Lies

The Trust About Us

The Wrecked and Ruined Series

Changing Course

Stolen Course

Broken Course

Among the Echoes

On the Ropes

Fighting Silence

Fighting Shadows

Fighting Solutude

ABOUT THE AUTHOR

Born and raised in Savannah, Georgia, Aly Martinez is a stay-at-home mom to four crazy kids under the age of five, including a set of twins. Currently living in South Carolina, she passes what little free time she has reading anything and everything she can get her hands on, preferably with a glass of wine at her side.

After some encouragement from her friends, Aly decided to add "Author" to her ever-growing list of job titles. So grab a glass of Chardonnay, or a bottle if you're hanging out with Aly, and join her aboard the crazy train she calls life.

Facebook: www.facebook.com/AuthorAlyMartinez

Twitter: twitter.com/AlyMartinezAuth

Goodreads: www.goodreads.com/AlyMartinez